I0564221

For Aiza and the next generation of fantasy writers, who have the courage to follow the path where it leads and never stopped believing in magic.

An
INHERITANCE
of FAERIES

Ravencroft Hall
Book #1

KAT ROSS

An Inheritance of Faeries

Copyright © 2026 by Kat Ross

All rights reserved. No part of this book may be reproduced in any form or by any electronic or mechanical means, including information storage and retrieval systems, without written permission from the author, except for the use of brief quotations in a book review.

This story is a work of fiction. References to real people, events, establishments, organizations, or locales are intended only to provide a sense of authenticity and are used fictitiously. All other characters, and all incidents and dialogue are drawn from the author's imagination and are not to be construed as real.

AI Use Restriction: Without limiting the author's exclusive copyright, any use of this publication to train, develop, or improve generative artificial intelligence (AI) technologies, machine learning systems, or large language models is expressly prohibited. The author reserves all rights to license use of this work for such purposes.

ISBN-13: 978-1-957358-23-9 (ebook)
ISBN-13: 978-1-957358-24-6 (paperback)

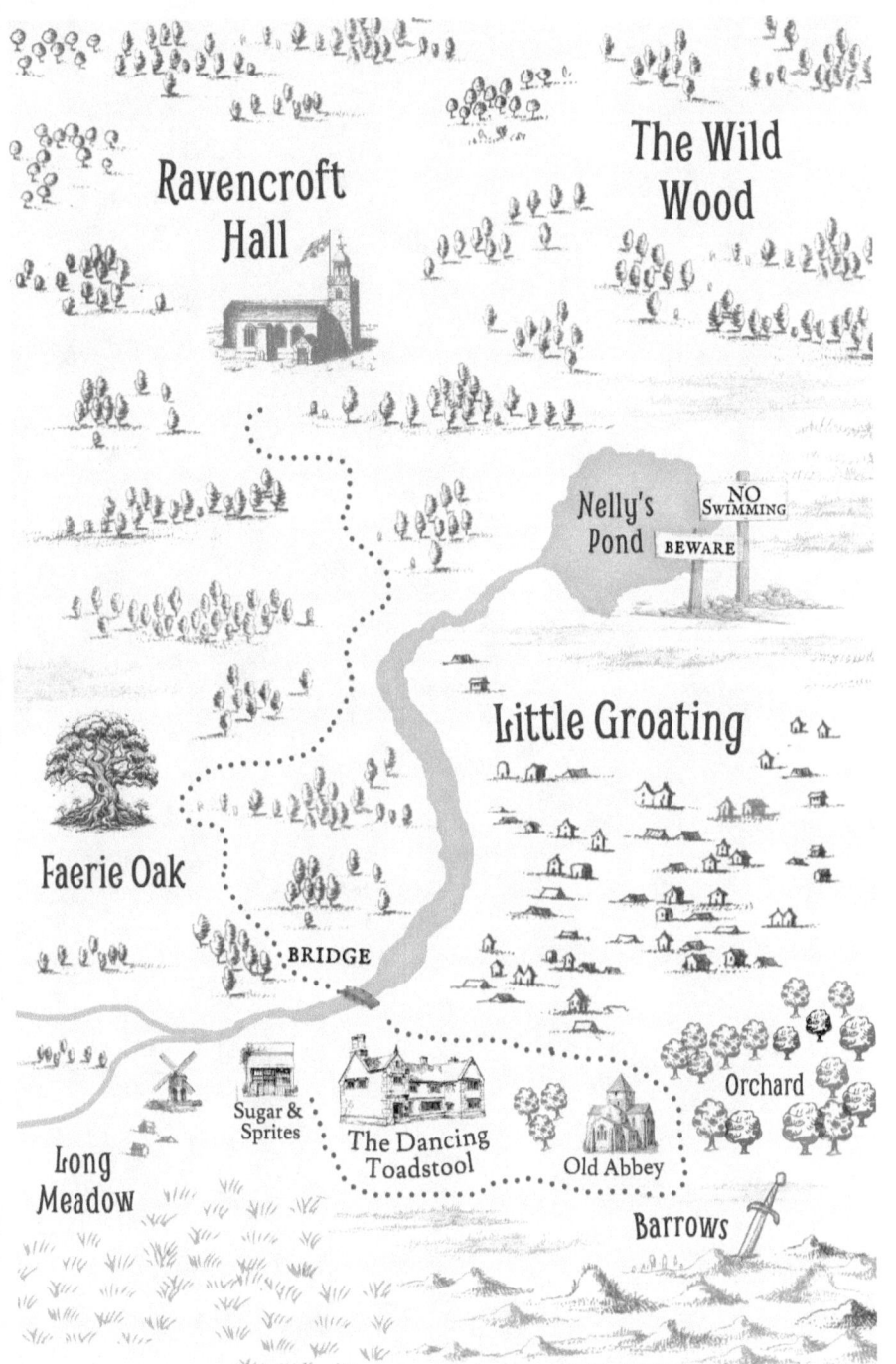

Ravencroft Hall

The Wild Wood

Nelly's Pond

NO SWIMMING

BEWARE

Little Groating

Faerie Oak

BRIDGE

Sugar & Sprites

The Dancing Toadstool

Old Abbey

Orchard

Long Meadow

Barrows

Kitty's Walking Tour

1

THE RELUCTANT HEIR

There inevitably comes a moment as you step between the gargoyles and spy Ravencroft Hall at the end of its beech-lined drive when your palms go all clammy and your throat locks up.

The part of your brain that stops you from doing stupid things rouses itself and starts shrieking, *Turn back now, you fool, or forever regret it!*

At this point, about one in ten visitors will drop their brochures and flee. The rest stop dead, silently trembling. An unlucky few pee their pants (not just children, mind you, but grown men). It's nothing to be ashamed of. The nameless dread afflicts everyone, even me, and I've crossed the boundary hundreds of times.

It was the last tour of the day, about two o'clock, and the sun was still high, gilding the windows of the manor house. I unglued my tongue from the roof of my mouth and donned a confident smile.

"Just keep walking, that's it," I said, shooing the bewil-

1

dered tour group along the road. "What you're experiencing is an old spell to ward off trespassers, it can't hurt you."

I'd warned them before—several times—but these admonitions never sank in.

A thickset man with a walrus mustache gave a croak of protest. I took out my thermos and filled a tin cup with tea. "Drink this, sir, it does wonders."

It was a special brew of catmint and Earl Grey with loads of sugar. Though his hand trembled, the colour quickly returned to his pasty face. I passed around tea to the rest of the group and did a head count, feeling relieved. Eleven, all apparently still sane. No runners and no accidents.

That first step past the gargoyles was the worst; then the effects began to fade. Still, it was my habit to distract my clients with chatter.

"You'll notice that there are no gates at the entrance of the Ravencroft estate," I said. "Can anyone guess why?"

A teenaged girl self-consciously covered her braces with one hand as she spoke. "Faeries detest iron?"

"That's right! And the Ravencroft power stems from an ancient bargain with a faerie court. Iron is forbidden on the estate, so the Ravencrofts cast a spell to keep people from wandering about instead." I winked at her. "But we won't let that stop us, will we?"

I turned to the manor house, which had two brick wings jutting out from a central axis. "The Hall dates back to 1490. It's a magnificent example of Tudor architecture—"

"Tell us about the evil wizards who lived there!"

That was the girl's brother, who had a striped rugby shirt and troll-like tuft of ginger hair. His name-tag said Archie.

"Ah yes," I said. "Let's cut to the good stuff, shall we? Well, the Ravencroft family is a minor offshoot of the Lancasters. It was their magic that helped Henry VII defeat the Yorks at

Bosworth Field and gain the throne. They ruled here ever after, until Ransom and Desdemona Ravencroft joined a cabal of dark wizards seeking to overthrow the queen. Happily, the scheme was revealed and they were exiled from Britain."

I collected the tin cups, stowed them in my pack, and got everyone moving up the gravel drive, phone cameras out and clicking away. "That was twenty years ago. The house has sat empty since."

"Kin we go inside?" asked a man with thick glasses and an even thicker Scottish burr.

"I wish! But I'm afraid the house is off-limits."

Archie scowled. "Why?"

"Because there are spells inside that would kill us all in an instant," I said, which might be true. "But I'll tell you about the dungeons and the secret library. And we'll take a scenic path through the grounds that will bring us quite near a faerie tree. Did everyone bring sweets?"

The group held up bags of humbugs and pear drops from the gift shop.

"Excellent." I drew a deep breath. The sun was in and out of pillowy clouds, and a warm breeze rippled the meadow grasses. "It's perfect weather for faeries. I have a feeling we'll spot some today."

There were always dryads at the orchard tending the apple trees. It's the reason we had the best cider in the county. They knew me well and usually allowed a glimpse of themselves.

"Can we go into the Wild Wood?" Archie asked.

I hesitated, pretending to consider his request. People want to feel like they're getting a unique experience for their five quid. If it's against the rules, that's even better.

"I don't usually go into the Wild Wood, it's terribly

dangerous," I said with reluctance. "But maybe this once. Not too far, though."

He pumped a victory fist as his sister covered a metallic grin. Their parents shared a look of alarm.

Since the unfortunate incident with that Swedish family, I kept my tour groups to the outer fringes of the Wild Wood. It surrounded the estate and the nearby village of Little Groating, where I lived with my Nan. The forest stretched for miles in every direction. There were no roads—not *mortal* roads, save for a few narrow lanes. The motorways all went around it, never through. Nan said it was the Raven-crofts' magic that "protected us from modern stupidity."

The Wild Wood was lovely in every season. Green in spring, gold in summer, copper in autumn, and silver in winter. The leaves never fell, just changed colour. I'd met a fae prince there when I was a child, and you never forget such a thing. It gave me a lifelong fascination with the Fair Folk.

I still walked in the Wild Wood alone sometimes, through the deep glens where the trees grew tall and straight like ships' masts, but I didn't bring tour groups anymore. In my defense, I will note that the Andersens were found eventu-ally, not *too* worse for wear.

"If you'll have a look at your map," I said, "you'll see that we're coming up on Nelly's Pond." I pointed to the left. "It's about half a mile that way."

Everyone but Archie dutifully examined their brochure, which had my hand-drawn map on the back. Archie was studying Ravencroft Hall with a speculative gleam in his eye, and I resolved to keep a close watch over him. He seemed the sort who was all too capable of sneaking off and causing mischief.

"The Nelly Longarms in the pond has lived there since the time of King Arthur, maybe even longer," I said. "She's a water hag, similar to a grindylow." I shuffled nearer to Archie, who looked over at me. I held his gaze as I said, "She's known for dragging children into the water, especially ones who don't do as they're told."

"I thought that was just a myth," someone at the back of the group called out.

"Not at all," I replied, still looking at Archie, who stared back defiantly. "Now let's go have a look at the front of the house, I'll tell you more of the history. And you can get some good pictures there."

The prospect of mugging for selfies in front of the home of notorious dark wizards got the group moving with new enthusiasm. We were about halfway up the drive when a muffled scream cut the air. It came from the direction of Ravencroft Hall.

The first rule in faerie tours is that one must project an aura of calm cheerfulness at all times. I smiled. "Don't worry, I'm sure it's noth—"

My reassurances were cut off by another scream, long and lingering. Everyone fell silent, their attention riveted on the house. I wondered if it was a banshee, but that seemed unlikely. They were Irish for one thing, and I'd never heard of one in these parts.

"Wait here," I told them, and turned to hurry up the road. The voice sounded human, though one could never be certain.

A topiary maze shielded the front entrance from view, the hedges grown tall and wild over years of neglect. I rounded the corner and saw a blue automobile parked at a rakish slant before the doors. At the same instant, they were violently flung open and a man came rushing down the front steps. He windmilled his arms about like he was fending off a swarm of wasps. When he drew closer, I saw that his hair was infested with pixies. They were tugging at the thick black locks and chittering with glee.

I smothered a laugh. Served him right for breaking into the house. He wore a casual city suit and I guessed he was writing a story on the twentieth anniversary of the Ravencroft scandal. I was only seven at the time, but I remembered the reporters descending on Little Groating when it first happened, asking questions about Ransom and Desdemona. They had a son, too, though no one knew what had happened to him. Then the years passed, the house sat empty, and the reporters stopped coming.

He shouldn't have forced his way inside, but it must have taken quite a bit of nerve to pass the gargoyles alone. I decided to take pity on him.

"Stop swatting at them," I advised. "Just stand still for a moment."

He shot me a baleful look but obeyed. I fished in my pocket and found some candies. The kindly village doctor was always passing them out, but he was half-blind so sometimes you got mints, and sometimes you got mothballs. I sniffed to make sure, then held out my open palm.

Six pairs of beady eyes fixed on me. Their pointy ears cocked. One started to drool.

Pixies can't resist sugar. They dove for the peppermints, spindly fingers outstretched, then spirited the candies back into the house. The front door slammed behind them.

I lowered my voice. "Look, I won't report you, but you ought to leave. There's probably all sorts of nasty traps in there."

"I'm grateful for the aid, but who *are* you?" the man asked in an exasperated tone, raking a hand through his hair in a vain attempt to smooth it down.

He was close to my own age, maybe a year or two older. Quite tall and with a level gaze that showed no sign of embarrassment—or remorse at being caught. Of course, I was trespassing too, but not *inside*.

"Kitty Boot," I said, extending a hand, which he shook once, firmly.

"Richard Ravencroft." He peered past my shoulder at the tour group, who stood down the drive watching us with interest. "And who are they?"

Oh no. I studied him with a sinking heart. How did I not see it immediately? His nose was hooked like a bird of prey, his brow high and proud, his eyes black as obsidian. In short, the very picture of a Ravencroft. As he was too young to be Ransom, I assumed he must be the son. And dark wizards were not known for their gentle natures.

My mouth went dry with dread, though this time it wasn't nameless. It was standing right in front of me, waiting for an answer.

"Ahhh. Lord Ravencroft." I turned to stare idiotically at my clients. Not a single plausible lie came to mind, so I was forced to tell the truth. "Er, sorry, it's a walking tour," I mumbled, a guilty flush rising to my cheeks.

"A walking tour," he repeated. The friendliness faded from his face like a cloud blotting out the sun. I couldn't blame him. He assumed we were here to gawk, which was more or less accurate.

I rushed to fill the silence before he smote me with dark magic. "Yes, I lead them twice daily on the weekends. People come from all over to see the faeries. Most take the train to Southlea Cross, it's about thirty minutes from the village.

Not all of them make it here, about half get lost and wander in circles until they end up back at Southlea."

I barked a too-bright laugh. "Which is a very quaint little place, I'm sure they enjoy it. But my Nan says the magic only lets some of them through so we aren't overrun. Of course, you managed to drive right up to the front door! That makes sense. I suppose the magic knows you."

My head cocked at a weird angle, all on its own. "Do the gargoyles terrify you like the rest of us? I've always wondered."

At this juncture, I managed to shut my mouth and pause for air.

To my vast relief, Richard Ravencroft seemed bemused. "No, Miss Boot, the gargoyles don't trouble me."

"Right." I glanced at the group, which had grown bored and started to take pictures again. "Well, I ought to be getting back."

He regarded the house. "I'd planned to stay here while I settle some business matters, but . . ." The windows eyed us broodily, and I felt certain I saw shadows flitting behind the glass. "I've changed my mind. Is there still an inn down at the village?"

I nodded. "The Dancing Toadstool. You won't find a better breakfast anywhere. Fresh-baked current scones every morning!"

Did I really just say that? Oh, God. Dark wizards don't care about scones!

He muttered something inaudible. "Thank you, Miss Boot. Now I'm afraid I must ask you and your tour group to leave. I'm sorry, it's just . . ."

"Hideously awkward," I finished. "Of course. That is, *yes.* Good afternoon, Lord Ravencroft."

"Good afternoon, Miss Boot." He squared his shoulders

and strode back into the Hall. I watched him go, heart racing. Richard Ravencroft was back! I was bursting to tell Nan straight away—once I finished the tour. We still had a few stops to make . . .

I did a quick head count and felt my stomach lurch. *Where was Archie?*

2

A SWIRL OF BLACK BUBBLES

I scanned the drive, the overgrown topiary, the tall meadow grass that fringed the Wild Wood. No sign of our ginger Houdini.

Then I heard it. The distant, echoing thunk of rocks hitting water—which narrowed the search considerably.

"Nelly's Pond," I muttered. "Of course he's gone to the bloody pond."

Archie's parents wore frozen expressions I recognised from years of wrangling tourists: a blend of embarrassment, panic, and the hollow certainty they were about to become the next cautionary tale in the gift shop.

His mother, whose name-tag said Sara, stared at me with wild eyes. "He wouldn't. Not after you told us the legend of the water hag."

"You'd be amazed what children will do," I replied, "especially if they're expressly warned not to."

Archie's father was already jogging down the drive, shouting his son's name with the desperation of a man who'd promised his wife a fun, magical, risk-free day out. The rest of the group followed, the other parents clearly relieved that it wasn't *their* child.

I took off sprinting down the hill east of the Hall. The shortest way to Nelly's Pond—there was no actual path for obvious reasons—wound through a marshy hollow that never quite dried out, even at the height of summer. My boots sank with every step, and the air grew thick with the smell of standing water.

The steady, rhythmic splash of something being thrown —again and again—into the pond grew louder.

I crested the last hummock and caught my breath. Archie crouched at the water's edge, shirt untucked and wellies caked in mud, lobbing pebbles at the surface. He turned at the sound of our approach, wearing the look of smug satisfaction perfected by twelve-year-old boys the world over.

"See? There's nothing in there," he called. "You made it all up!"

"Archie, come here this instant!" his mother shrieked, as though volume might penetrate the fortress of his idiocy.

I hurried down to the pond, holding out a hand in what I hoped was a calm and authoritative manner. "Step away from the edge, please."

Archie rolled his eyes and threw one last stone—a flat skimmer, which zipped across the water with a satisfying succession of plips.

That's when I saw the ripples. Not the concentric rings formed by his barrage of pebbles, but a low, purposeful wake that cut through the duckweed, heading for Archie like a shark's fin. Something big and dark glided under the water, breaking the scum with a slick curve of greenish flesh.

I sloshed through the mud and grabbed the boy by his striped rugby shirt, yanking him backward just as an appendage burst from the pond and slithered up the bank. The arm—grey-green, rubbery, and about as long as a garden hose —groped around for a few seconds, then withdrew in a sulky manner, leaving only a swirl of black bubbles on the surface.

Archie stared at me, then at the water, then at his parents, and started to cry. "It tried to get me," he wailed.

His mother swept him up, sobbing and scolding in equal measure. Archie's father knelt by the bank, poking at the muck with a stick as if hoping to find some evidence it had all been a trick of the light. The rest of the group stood a safe distance away, regarding me with new respect.

I brushed the mud from my leggings, a futile endeavor that only got my hands dirty. "I told you she was real."

"Is it even safe to be here?" demanded the man with the walrus mustache.

"Perfectly safe, now that Nelly's had her fun," I lied. "But I think we've had enough excitement for one afternoon."

The tour group took this with minimal grumbling, though I caught the Scottish gentleman mutter something under his breath about "English hospitality." We retraced our steps out of the bog and across the small wooden bridge to the village, Archie's mother clutching his arm in a viselike grip.

By the time we reached the High Street, dark clouds had rolled in. The first fat raindrops splattered the cobbles as I shepherded everyone to the Dancing Toadstool, whose mullioned windows glowed yellow and inviting.

Nan and I lived at the inn, which was owned by Sanaja Deen, the mother of my best friend Layla. Besides leading walking tours, I helped out with the breakfast service. The Deens were like my second family—more like my first, really, since I had no siblings and my parents were almost never home.

I shed my macintosh, shook out my damp hair, and was halfway through unlacing my boots when I heard Nan's grey parrot declare, in a voice of doomsday relish, "You are a wolf and apostle of Satan!"

Sir Francis Drake had once been owned by staunch Lutherans, or so Nan claimed, and he'd picked up their polemical worldview.

"What did that bird say?" asked Walrus Mustache.

"Never mind," I replied brightly. "Let's get you settled with a nice hot beverage."

I directed the group to a long table by the window, fetched a round of cider, and doled out blankets from the basket by the hearth. Barbarossa, the inn's cat who was named for a famous admiral of the Ottoman navy, prowled up and circled the table twice before deciding they were no threat to his regime.

Archie, now sheepish, was plied with shortbread. The rest of the group took turns telling the story of the arm from the pond, each time the limb growing longer, greener, and more festooned with aquatic horrors.

I wandered over to Nan, who sat throned in her red velvet smoking jacket by the fireplace like the villain in a seaside detective novel. She was knitting a small orange scarf for Quince, the resident brownie. Some stories claim you shouldn't give brownies clothes or they'll leave, but that's rubbish. Quince had served the Dancing Toadstool for generations and took great pride in his appearance. He loved gifts of clothing—the gaudier, the better.

Nan was ninety-two and still sharp, but her knees got achy with stairs so she'd taken a ground floor room at the inn. Most days, you could find her spinning tales by the fire with Dr. Singer, her needles clacking away.

"I see you survived the wilds of Ravencroft," Nan remarked. "Any casualties?"

"Not a one," I said, which was happily true. I dropped into an armchair and lowered my voice to a stage whisper. "But I have other news. Guess who's back?"

Nan's needles paused. Sir Francis Drake, sensing drama, rotated his head and fixed me with an intent glare. "The Antichrist!" he screamed.

Nan shushed him and leaned forward. "Who?" she whispered with a gleam in her eye. The woman did love gossip.

"Richard Ravencroft," I hissed, making sure no one at the other tables was listening—though the news would spread soon enough. "Ransom and Desdemona's son. I met him at the Hall. He was being mauled by pixies and I saved his bacon."

Nan gave a short, delighted cackle.

"The boy is back?" said Dr. Singer, lifting his bushy white brows.

"Not exactly a boy anymore," I corrected. "He's about my age, I'd guess. Tall, dark hair, that Ravencroft nose. He'd just come out of the Hall, shouting his lungs out."

Nan set her knitting in her lap. "Well, well." Her blue eyes narrowed thoughtfully. "And what sort was he?"

"Sort?"

"Ravencrofts come in all sorts, Kitty. Some benevolent, others cruel as winter frost." She picked up the tiny scarf again, needles clicking with renewed vigor. "Richard's grandfather, old Lord Edgar, would give bread to hungry children with one hand and hex their fathers with the other if they were late with the rent."

Dr. Singer nodded. "I remember Edgar. Terrifying man. Had a laugh that could curdle milk."

"What were Richard's parents like?" I asked. "I mean,

before the whole—" I waggled my hand in the direction of "attempted coup and subsequent national disgrace."

"The father—Ransom—now there was a complicated soul," Nan said. "Hot-tempered and ambitious, but always generous toward the villagers. I was shocked when they were arrested. The mother, though . . ." She pursed her lips. "A bit of a mystery. Beautiful, of course. She's French and Spanish, from the Questel wizard line."

I settled deeper into my chair, sensing a story brewing. Nan's memories stretched back further than anyone else in the village, and her tales were better than any history book.

"They used to throw parties that would last for days," Nan said, her eyes misting with memory. "Coaches coming and going at all hours, lights blazing from every window of the Hall. Wizards from across Britain and the continent would visit. Once I saw a man gallop past the inn on a horse made of shadow—just darkness with two green flames for eyes."

"You never told me that part before," I said, fascinated.

Nan shrugged. "I haven't thought of it in years." Her eyes focused on me again. "What else did the young lord tell you?"

I reviewed our brief encounter. "Not much. He was planning to stay at the Hall, but the pixies changed his mind. He asked about a room at the inn."

Nan smiled, a mischievous glint in her eye. "A Ravencroft under our roof. Now that's something I never thought I'd see."

Dr. Singer cleared his throat. "I treated Richard once. Must have been . . . oh, before the scandal certainly. He was seven or eight. Scarlet fever."

"Was he very ill?" I asked.

"Quite, but strong. Recovered quicker than most. His parents doted on him." Dr. Singer adjusted his round spectacles, which were as thick as jam jars. "Ransom barely left the boy's side—read to him for hours. The mother was more reserved, but she brought in specialists from London and even a healer from somewhere in the Alps. Expense was no object where their son was concerned."

"And what was he like? Richard, I mean."

The doctor's round, bearded face softened. "Polite lad. Well-mannered even when feverish, which tells you something about a person's character. I remember he asked if scarlet fever would let him breathe fire since it made him 'all red like a dragon.'"

I smiled at the image. "Hard to picture him as a child. He seemed . . ." Unhappy was the word that came to mind, but I didn't know the first thing about Richard Ravencroft. "Stern."

"Twenty years in exile will do that to a person," Nan said with a note of sympathy. "Even if he wasn't the one exiled, being left behind can be just as hard."

"Do you think he's here to meet with the high fae?" I asked.

Every wizard family in Britain and Europe had ancient pacts with fae courts. The bargains were the source of their magic, that much was common knowledge.

But the courts of the high fae were very different from the lesser orders of faeries that lived in and around Little Groating. Dangerous and powerful. The thought sent a thrill through me.

Nan's knitting needles stilled again. "It must be why he's here—to claim his inheritance from the Court of Silver Shadows. Magic is in his blood."

"Well, I for one am glad he's back," Dr. Singer declared, patting his pockets until he found one of his lavender mothballs. He offered it to me with a trembling hand. I took it with a murmur of delight and slipped it into my pocket when he wasn't looking. "Ravencroft Hall needs a master. It's not right, the way it's been sitting empty all these years."

Nan nodded in agreement. "The land needs its lord. The faeries need their wizard." She pointed a knitting needle at me. "Mark my words, Kitty, things will change now. For better or worse remains to be seen."

"He behaved decently," I said. "Not what I expected from the son of dark wizards. Though he wasn't exactly pleased to find me leading tours on his property."

"Can you blame him?" Nan snorted. "Poor man comes home after twenty years to find tourists tramping all over his lawn."

I felt my cheeks heat. "I'll apologise properly when I see him again."

"Which might be sooner than you think, if he's looking for a room," Dr. Singer said, glancing toward the door.

I stood up, realizing Mrs. Deen should be told that we might have a very important guest. "I'll go warn the kitchen."

"Do that," Nan said. She set her knitting aside and took out her pipe, lighting it with a taper from the fire. "And Kitty? Have a care. Some Ravencrofts are kind, some are mercenary, but they're all slippery as the eels in Nelly's pond. The trouble is you can't tell which is which until it's too late."

Sir Francis Drake chose this moment to screech "Capitalist pigs!" and then, for reasons known only to himself, "Soup's on!"

"That's a new one," I remarked. "I thought he was owned by Lutherans?"

"Oh yes, he was," Nan replied, her lips twitching, "but they sold him to some anarchists after that."

I stared at her for a long moment. "I think you teach him these things for your own amusement."

Nan had also claimed at various times that Sir Francis

Drake was owned by pirates and a pair of notorious poisoners from Berlin.

"Nonsense," she replied, blowing smoke rings at the ceiling.

I stood up, trying not to laugh. "I'm going next door to tell Layla and Briar the news."

As I turned to go, I caught Dr. Singer leaning toward Nan, whispering something that made her laugh riotously. The two of them had spent almost every day together since their beloved spouses died—which was going on ten years for Nan and eight years for Jacob Singer. He was infatuated with her, everyone could see that.

I smiled. Whatever complications Richard Ravencroft's return might bring, at least some things would never change.

3

ABSOLUTELY NO
FAERIES HERE

Sugar & Sprites occupied the inn's former carriage house. Layla and Briar had converted it into a bakery and gift shop three years ago, selling everything from cupcakes to souvenirs—all faerie-related since that's what Little Groating was famous for.

The second floor was a cosy one-bedroom flat, but during the day they were always in the shop—Briar conjuring up mouth-watering sweets in the rear kitchen and Layla dealing with customers or, when business was slow, poring over books behind the counter.

The shop had an extensive collection of faerie lore: tomes on swan maidens and Sleeping Beauties of the Brambles, godmothers and May queens and the shape-shifting Tempestarii who dwell in airy cloud castles.

Shall we tell you stories of succubi and broom riders, Ladies of Winter and the Wild Hunt? Moon-faced Lorialets and the luminous Encantada? There are as many kinds of fae as stars in the sky, and Layla knew them all. She was a true scholar, introverted and a touch morbid, her dry humour a perfect complement to Briar's outgoing, cheerful nature.

The bell tinkled as I walked in, but my oldest and dearest friend didn't look up, so absorbed was she in the thick leather-bound volume propped before her. This was typical of Layla, who had the enviable ability to shut out the world and focus intently on whatever she was doing.

She perched on a stool, glossy chestnut wisps escaping her waist-length braid. She wore jeans and a tight pink t-shirt that said *Run Along, Foolish Mortal*. Her glasses had slipped down her nose, and she pushed them up absently with one finger as she turned a page.

"If you're looking for the last cinnamon roll, Briar just packed it up," she said, eyes still scanning the text.

"Can you *smell* me?" I asked. "Or have you grown eyes in strange places?"

Layla finally looked up, blinking owlishly. "I wish."

"Actually," I said, strolling up the counter, "I've got some hot gossip."

That got her attention. She closed the book—*Unseelie Courts of the Hebrides*. "Did Dr. Singer finally pop the question to Nan? I bet ten quid he gathers his courage before Christmas."

"Sorry, guess again." I waggled my eyebrows.

"God, you're annoying. Out with it!" Layla exclaimed, poking me with a plastic wand from a jar on the counter.

I leaned forward. "Try a dark wizard returning after twenty years of exile."

Layla's big brown eyes widened further. "The Ravencrofts are back? How is that possible? I thought they'd been banished for life."

"Ransom and Desdemona were, yes. But their son turned up this afternoon. Now where's your bubbly half?"

As if summoned, Briar emerged from the back room toting a cloth-covered basket, her fiery red curls bouncing with each step. Flour dusted her apron and a smudge of chocolate marked her freckled cheek.

"Richard Ravencroft is back," Layla announced. "Kitty found him."

"I didn't find him, exactly," I said. "More like *he* found *me* giving a tour on his property. It wasn't my finest moment." I sniffed the basket. "What are you doing with that?"

"Back off," Layla admonished. "I've started taking the day's leftovers to Madame de Berry's house. Her boarders have them with tea."

Madame de Berry was a flamboyant, kindly woman with loads of money from her five ex-husbands who took in the village elders once they got too frail to live alone. Layla often spent her spare time visiting since, like me, she loved the old stories.

"Never mind that," Briar added impatiently. "Tell us everything."

I recounted the story, not leaving out a single detail from the pixies in Richard's hair to his irritated demeanor. By the time I finished, both women were cackling with laughter.

"And he's staying with Mum?" Layla asked. "Wow."

"Maybe," I said. "He asked about the inn, but I don't know if he'll actually turn up."

"Do you think he plans to move back?" Briar asked. "I mean, permanently. Will he reopen the Hall?"

I shrugged. "No idea. He seemed put off by the pixies, though."

"Wouldn't you be?" Layla's tone was dry. "Prankish little things. They once stole all my bookmarks and replaced them with oak leaves."

"I remember that," Briar said. She turned to me. "So what's he *like?*"

I considered this. "Oh, you know those aristocratic types. He wore an expensive dark suit that made him look a funeral director—"

At that moment, the shop door swung open and a gust of rain swept in. We all turned, frozen like a tableau of startled woodland creatures, as a tall figure stepped over the threshold, ducking slightly to avoid hitting his head on the low doorframe.

Richard looked just as surprised to see me as I was to see him. He cleared his throat. "Pardon me. I'm looking for the . . . Dancing Toadstool, was it?"

Layla recovered first, beaming one of her rare grins at him. "It's just next door, Lord Ravencroft." She pointed. "The big stone building with the green shutters."

"Thank you." He paused, then added, "Miss Boot. We meet again."

I tried on a smile that felt more like a grimace. "Indeed! What a coincidence."

"Briar Godwin," said Briar, striding forward to extend a hand with her usual confidence.

Richard shook it warmly. "You're American."

Briar nodded. "From Vermont. I took a backpacking trip through England five years ago, stopped here and never left." She glanced at Layla. "That's my wife, Layla Deen. Her mother owns the inn."

"A pleasure to meet you both," Richard said. "Might I ask . . . a silly question perhaps, but . . . "

"There are no silly questions around here," Briar said amiably. "Fire away."

Richard gave her a wan smile. "Are there faeries at the inn? I would much prefer a room with no magical creatures, if that's possible." He glanced at the ceiling beams as if expecting pixies to descend at any moment.

I was about to confess that the inn had a brownie when Layla cut me off. "There are absolutely no faeries at the Dancing Toadstool," she said solemnly. "You have my word."

Richard looked relieved. I shot her a warning look, which she ignored.

"I'll show you the way," I offered, "since I'm heading back there anyway."

He hesitated. "I hate to be any trouble. If it's right next door—"

"Oh, it's no trouble at all!" I said, heading for the street before he could say no.

Richard gave Briar and Layla an absent wave and followed me out. "May I leave my car there?" he asked, looking up and down the street. "I don't want a ticket, but I don't see any signage."

He'd parked it askew outside Sugar & Sprites, one wheel on the kerb, and I wondered how long he'd had his driving licence.

I eyed him quizzically. "Of course you can. You're the lord of the Hall."

He blinked. "Very good. I won't worry about it then."

He took a suitcase out of the boot and headed for the front door of the inn. I hurried to keep up with his long strides. "Will you be staying long, Lord Ravencroft?"

He glanced at me. "Just Richard is fine. And by the gods, I hope not."

The last was said with such feeling that I dropped the matter, though I did feel a twinge of disappointment.

"The Dancing Toadstool is as old as Ravencroft Hall," I said, falling into tour guide mode. "It used to be a guesthouse for the ruined abbey down by the orchard. I suppose you never visited before?"

"My parents wouldn't allow me to come down to the village," he said shortly.

Richard visibly steeled himself as he opened the door. Thankfully, my tour group had already left for Swanlea Cross, leaving a handful of regulars nursing pints and gossip. Nan was in the midst of recounting one of her adventures to Dr. Singer, who listened intently even though he must know all her stories by heart: snowy head slightly bowed and hands folded over his walking stick as though bracing for a squall.

Conversation ground to a halt at Richard's appearance. The room went tomb-quiet except for Sir Francis Drake, who chose that precise moment to belt out, "What do you do with a drunken sailor?" at top volume. I bit my lip to keep from laughing as Nan jabbed irritably at the bird with the stem of her pipe, her eyes never leaving our visitor.

Richard's gaze swept the room, faltering when he spotted the parrot on Dr. Singer's shoulder. He cleared his throat. Before he could say anything, Sanaja Deen glided forward, her emerald sari catching the firelight. She was in her mid-fifties, dark hair threaded with grey and pulled into a bun, with the same large dark eyes as her daughter. A smile warmed her face.

"Welcome to the Dancing Toadstool," she said, her British accent lilting with a faint Sri Lankan cadence. "You must be Lord Ravencroft." She gestured toward an empty table by the window. "Please, sit. You look as though you've had quite a journey."

Everyone was doing that peculiar dance of pretending not to stare while stealing glances from behind mugs, books, or in Dr. Singer's case, a bobbing Sir Francis Drake.

"That's kind of you," Richard replied stiffly, "but I would prefer to go straight to my room."

"Of course." Mrs. Deen caught my eye. "Kitty told us to expect you. It's all ready. Will you be coming down for supper?"

"I've had a tiring day," he said. "Perhaps you can leave it on a tray by the door?"

Mrs. Deen beamed at him with motherly affection. "Of course. Any food allergies?"

Richard shook his head. He took out his mobile phone and stared at it. I knew what he was thinking. *No bars.*

"Er, is there a wi-fi password?" Richard asked.

It was probably the thousandth time Mrs. Deen had fielded that question. "I'm afraid not," she said. "There's no signal in the village."

He blinked. "None at all?"

"None at all," she said gently. "You'll have to drive to Southlea Cross if you want internet. Now, come right this way, let's get you settled."

Richard gave me a dazed nod and followed her up the stairs, leaving us all to wonder just what he was up to.

THE INN WAS NEVER ENTIRELY QUIET, NOT EVEN IN THE DEAD of night. It creaked and stirred as if dreaming, and every so often the wind would howl down the chimneys and rattle the windows with the force of an angry bill collector.

I lay in bed waiting for the moment when every guest would be deep in slumber and Quince began his nightly duties. It was the best time to have a chat with our resident brownie without risk of discovery, and I had questions that needed answering.

The return of Richard Ravencroft had sent my mind spinning all evening. Nan's words about the family—some kind, some monsters—kept replaying in my head. If anyone might have the inside scoop on the heir, it would be the Fair Folk who'd lived alongside his family for centuries.

When the grandfather clock in the second-floor hall chimed three, I slipped from beneath my quilt, wincing as my bare feet met the cold floorboards. I pulled on a pair of wool socks and wrapped myself in a flannel dressing gown over my pyjamas. My bedroom was tucked up under the eaves of the inn, a cosy garret with slanted ceilings. Tonight it felt too small to contain the speculation swirling around my mind.

I grabbed a candlestick from my bedside table and lit it with a match, cupping my hand around the flame as I eased my door open. We had electricity but we kept the old ways, too, since that's what the Fair Folk preferred. I knew every treacherous board in the staircase and avoided them without thinking—third from the top, the middle of the seventh, and nearly the entire bottom half.

The common room was dark, lit only by the dying embers in the hearth. Sir Francis Drake drowsed on his roost, head tucked beneath one wing. Barbarossa, the ancient black cat who had strutted into the inn one rainy morning and claimed us, lay nose-under-tail on the flagstones by the hearth. He cracked an eye to assess whether I was worth the effort of acknowledging. Apparently, I wasn't; he stretched, yawned, and went back to sleep.

I made my way to the kitchen and paused in the doorway. Quince worked nights when the house was asleep, whirring through the rooms with a manic energy that would have shamed even the most fanatical housekeeper. Tonight he was standing atop a soup tureen, wielding a polishing rag with both hands. He wore a waistcoat fashioned from a potholder and the new orange scarf Nan had made for him, looped in jaunty fashion around his neck.

"Good evening, Master Quince," I said softly.

Brownies are jumpy creatures; the last time I'd startled him he'd vanished for three days and left the inn in a state of total disorder. Quince gave a theatrical jerk anyway, then relaxed and doffed his cap. He was small and wiry, about knee-height, with skin like boot leather. He had a nest of wiry hair and his eyes were dark as hazelnuts, gleaming with a quick, clever shine.

"Hello, Kitty," he piped. "Couldn't sleep, eh?"

"Too much excitement." I set the candle down by the sink. "We have a Ravencroft for the first time in twenty years. It's thrown all of us off."

Quince's thin lips twitched. It wasn't a smile—he rarely smiled—but it came close. "Was there something you needed?"

I sat on one of the kitchen stools. "Just information, if you're willing to share it."

Quince paused in his polishing. "Information is dear, even for friends."

I'd come prepared to haggle. From the pocket of my dressing gown I produced a silver thimble, one Nan had picked up on her travels in Morocco. It was engraved with tiny stars and moons. Quince's eyes lit up.

"I suppose that's a fair trade," he said grudgingly, though I knew how much he coveted thimbles. Nan was always complaining that he filched them from her sewing basket. "What do you wish to know?"

"Richard Ravencroft is staying with us tonight."

Quince sniffed. "So I've heard."

"What do you know about him?" I asked, sliding the thimble across the table.

Quince's fingers twitched, but he didn't reach for it yet. "The young lord? Nothing. He was a boy when they took his parents away. I've no dealings with Ravencroft Hall. The inn is my home and that's that."

I nodded. "Of course, and it will always be your home. But surely you must have heard *something*. The Fair Folk talk amongst themselves."

Quince stiffened. "I am not some common gossip, indulging in hearsay and idle chatter."

"Of course not," I said quickly, knowing it would be fatal to offend him. "I only thought you might know something about the Hall. It's been empty for so long, and now the heir returns. What he decides will affect us all, dear Quince."

He harrumphed and held the thimble up to the candle-light, admiring the craftsmanship. "Ravencroft Hall has *not* been empty," he said after a moment.

A chill crept up my spine. "You mean the pixies?"

Quince studied the thimble, then tucked it into the tiny pocket of his waistcoat. "When the wizards left, other things moved in. Things that should have remained in the Wild Wood." His dark eyes glinted. "Worse than pixies, Miss Kitty."

"Are they still there now?" I asked. "If so, we must warn Richard—"

"From what I understand, they have gone," Quince said, turning away.

He never lied, but he rarely told the whole truth either.

"What about Richard?" I pressed. "Is he like his parents?"

Quince began to polish the silver. "The young lord has

been away for twenty years. Who's to say what he's become? Magic changes people, but so does its absence."

I leaned forward, frustrated by his evasiveness. "You must have some idea. Is he dangerous? Nan says some Ravencrofts can be trusted, but others are slippery." I frowned. "Or maybe she said they're all slippery."

"Your Nan is a wise woman." Quince set down a butter knife. "But I am not in the business of judging wizards. You'd do better to ask Nettle about such matters."

I blinked. "Who's Nettle?"

The moment the name left my mouth, Quince's demeanor changed. He cast a suspicious glance around the room, as if afraid we might be overheard. "I've said too much," he muttered. "Forget I mentioned it."

"But who is—"

Quince scurried over to the saucer of cream Mrs. Deen had left for him and gulped it down. "No more talk. I'm off duty." He grabbed his cleaning rag and dove behind the sugar canister, leaving a faint whiff of cinnamon in his wake.

I sighed. Brownies were like that. A riddle in a waistcoat and loyal only to a point. I wanted to press him, but Quince could be temperamental and I didn't fancy waking up to find all my shoes missing.

"But thank you for the thimble," his disembodied voice called softly. "It's very fine."

"You're welcome," I replied. "And thank you for . . . whatever it is you've told me."

I picked up my candle and trudged back to the staircase, churning with new questions. *Nettle.* The name meant nothing to me, but clearly it meant something to Quince. Another faerie? One connected to Ravencroft Hall?

I was so deep in thought that I nearly walked straight into a door that suddenly opened in the upstairs hallway. I jumped back with a yelp, my candle flame dancing wildly. Richard stood in the doorway wearing a blue dressing gown, his hair fetchingly rumpled.

"Miss Boot?" he said with a look of confusion. "Is everything all right? I heard voices downstairs."

My heart skipped several beats. How long had he been awake?

"Oh, you know how it is . . ." I stammered, trying to look as if wandering about at four in the morning was normal behavior. "I just went down for some hot milk. I often have trouble sleeping, milord."

"Please, just call me Richard." He frowned. "But I distinctly heard you talking to someone."

"Ah." I swallowed hard. Layla had expressly promised Richard we didn't have faeries. "I was talking to myself. Old habit, I'm afraid."

Richard tilted his head. "In two different voices?"

I felt heat rush to my cheeks. "Yes, well, it feels more like a proper conversation that way, doesn't it? One voice asks the questions, the other answers. Much more satisfying than just monologuing. Less mad, I think."

"Less mad," he repeated slowly. "To have conversations with yourself. In different voices."

When he put it that way, it did sound unhinged. I squared my shoulders and doubled down. "It's quite therapeutic, actually. You should try it sometime."

Richard studied me for a long moment, and I had the distinct impression he was trying not to laugh. "That makes perfect sense, Miss Boot."

There was a tiny curve at the corner of his mouth that told me he didn't believe a word but was polite enough to pretend. I couldn't help but smirk back at him, relieved at not being caught in a direct lie.

"Call me Kitty," I said. "If I must call you Richard."

He raised an eyebrow.

"Since we've met each other in our nightclothes, I think we've bypassed formalities," I added with a grin.

For a moment, I feared I'd overstepped, but then he gave me a small, elegant bow. "Very well, Kitty. Though I make no promises about remembering this exchange in the morning. I find I'm not at my sharpest at four a.m.."

"That's quite all right. I suspect neither of us is." I took a step back, covering a yawn. "I should let you get back to sleep."

"Yes." He hesitated, then added, "Good night, then, Kitty."

"Good night, Richard."

He closed his door. As I made my way upstairs to my room, I couldn't help but wonder what sort of Ravencroft he would turn out to be. Richard had been perfectly polite thus far, but monsters didn't always show their teeth right away, did they?

And what about this mysterious Nettle that Quince refused to discuss?

I closed my bedroom door behind me, blew out my candle, and climbed back into bed. The sheets were cold, but my mind still buzzed with questions. I drifted off to sleep thinking of dark, guarded eyes and a name that had made a brownie tremble.

Nettle. Who—or what—were you, and what did you know about Richard Ravencroft?

4

BARGAINS & BLOODLINES

Morning at the Dancing Toadstool was my favourite time of day. The common room smelled of buttered toast and coffee, and a fire in the hearth kept the autumn chill at bay.

On the weekdays when I wasn't leading tours, I'd take a long ramble after the breakfast service was over, down through the grassy Barrows where rumour said ancient kings were buried in the hills.

The only drawback was a regular customer named Silas Grimes, a tenant of my parents who was renting Lothian Cottage. Grimes painted watercolours; he'd turned up a couple of years ago and had a sour, grumpy disposition. Needless to say, he was not well liked.

This morning, Silas Grimes sat at his usual table, face buried in a newspaper as he ate his eggs and kippers, though he kept glancing at the stairs leading to the second floor.

Word had clearly spread that the Ravencroft heir had taken a room with us, and the common room was far more crowded than was normal for a Monday morning. When at last Richard made an appearance, there was a brief hush before the villagers pretended to go back to their conversations.

Richard looked around, then took a solitary table by the window. I poured a mug of coffee, squared my shoulders, and marched over. "Good morning," I said breezily, setting the mug down. "Breakfast is on the sideboard. Do you care for sugar and cream?"

He wore the same dark suit from the day before. He'd shaved and combed his hair, but the dark half-moons under his eyes hinted at a restless night.

"Black is fine, thank you," he replied in a distant tone.

I'd hoped he might be a little warmer since our predawn encounter in the hall, but he seemed preoccupied. So I summoned my courage and decided to ask him point-blank what we were all wondering. I figured we had a right to know.

"Do you plan to stay at Ravencroft Hall once the, ah, pixie infestation is dealt with?"

Something flickered in his eyes. "No, Miss Boot. I'm selling it."

I nearly knocked over his mug. *Selling it?*

"Yes. My parents are in exile, and I have no desire to assume the burden of a large country estate. Once I conclude a personal matter, the Hall will be on the market."

"But it's been in your family for centuries," I protested. "You can't just—"

"I can," he said, gently but firmly, "and I will. The place is a mausoleum. I have no fondness for it, nor for the memories it holds."

I stared at him, stunned. "Who would even buy it?"

"Several parties are interested," he replied. "Don't worry,

I'm sure the new owners will be well-liked. Perhaps they'll even permit you to continue your walking tours."

That stung, though I suspected it was meant as a kindness. "Right," I said bitterly. "Because what Little Groating needs is a wizard estate without any wizards in it."

Richard busied himself smoothing out creases in the tablecloth, an obvious ruse to avoid my gaze. "I *am* sorry, but I have a life in London that I intend to return to as quickly as possible."

Dr. Singer spoke up. "Young man, some inheritances aren't so easily shed. The old families and the land have connections."

"And you are . . .?"

"Jacob Singer," the old doctor supplied. "I'm the village physician."

"Ah. Well, Dr. Singer, I happen to be a medical doctor, too. As such, I deal in science, not superstition and folklore. I'm here to sell a property, nothing more."

I couldn't help myself. "But the faerie roads, the Wild Wood—the village depends on the protection of the Raven-croft magic." The words tumbled out in a rush. "If you sell the Hall to someone who doesn't understand—"

"Miss Boot," Richard said, turning those obsidian eyes on me, "I'm sorry, but my mind is made up." He drained his coffee and stood abruptly. "Good day to you all."

Richard left before I could devise a suitably cutting rejoinder, coat slung over one arm and keys jangling in his hand. I watched from the window as he strode to his dinged-up Mini and drove away in a spray of gravel.

I swallowed my fury and stomped over to Nan, who sat in her usual spot by the fire, darning a sock and looking for all the world as if she hadn't heard a thing.

"Well," she remarked mildly, stabbing her needle through

the heel, "*that* was instructional. Did you really think bullying him would get you anywhere, Kitty dear?"

I flopped into the chair next to her, feeling like I'd just been ejected from a moving train. "I suppose you guessed he was planning to sell the Hall."

"No, but I can't say I'm shocked," Nan replied. "He's a modern man, and modern men have no use for faeries and family curses."

I let my head fall back, staring at the smoke-stained beams overhead. "Can he even *do* that? I thought wizards were tied to their ancestral land. Blood and soil, and all that."

Nan grunted. "They are, but the world changes. Magic fades. People forget. These days, I suppose you can sell anything if you hire the right solicitor."

"But what will happen to the . . . to the magic?"

That scared me the most. We were an oasis of the mysterious, peculiar, and downright impossible in the midst of a mundane world. It wasn't just the lack of internet or even reliable landline service. Little Groating and the Ravencroft Estate were virtually unchanged from the old days. This was an enchanted place in every sense of the word—and now we might lose it all.

Nan set aside her darning. "Well, as you know, every wizard family has a contract with a faerie court. It's a matter of protection and power. The wizards preserve the land, and in turn they are granted the use of magical spells."

A silence fell over the room, broken only by the crackle of logs in the fireplace and Sir Francis Drake's dark mutterings about "scurvy knaves."

"So what happens if he does sell it?" I wondered.

"Then the magic will go with him." She turned to me with a determined gleam in her eye. "I think we need to show Lord Ravencroft exactly what he's so eager to abandon, don't you? But be careful, Kitty. Wizard business is always dangerous."

AFTER THE LUNCH SERVICE, I LEFT THE INN BY THE GARDEN gate and followed a footpath that curled past the church's graveyard and into the Wild Wood. The rain had let up, but the sky hung low and sullen, the light flat as a pressed flower.

The Wood was restless: birds flitted in and out of the branches, and something—not squirrels—made the dry leaves rustle even when the air was still. I walked fast, hands stuffed into my pockets, eager to burn off the anxious energy left by Richard's announcement.

The Wild Wood had always been my refuge. I knew every path and mossy log, every glade where the sunlight broke through like gold coins scattered by a careless thief. But today the place felt as taut as a held breath.

It was the home of my oldest faerie friend, Nyx—one of the very few besides Quince who knew my true name. Her oak lived stood at the center of a glen, ancient and sprawling, its trunk split by lightning and healed over a dozen times. In summer, the tree was so thick with gold leaves it looked like a crown for a sleeping giant. But now the branches were nearly bare, and the ground beneath was a patchwork of yellow and russet leaves rotting where they fell.

Never had I seen the oak in such a state. Dread pooled in my stomach as I stopped at the edge of the clearing. "Nyx?" I called. "It's me, Kitty."

There was a silence, broken only by the distant cry of a rook. Then the dryad stepped from the oak's shadow. A head shorter than me and willowy, skin brown as bark. She was barefoot and wore a tunic of moss.

Nyx smiled, but there was sadness in it. "The air is full of questions lately. And none of them are friendly."

I crossed the clearing, careful to avoid the roots of her beloved oak. Nyx held still as a deer, watching me with the patience of a creature who measured time in centuries.

"Richard Ravencroft is back," I said. "He plans to sell the Hall."

Nyx nodded. "The wind told me."

"I'm worried about what it means, Nyx. For everyone."

She considered this. "The old magic was already fading. The Ravencrofts are the last anchor in this part of the world. Without them, the doors will close. The Wild Wood will shrink to a memory, and I must follow the spirit of my tree."

A lump rose in my throat. "You mean you'll leave?"

Nyx shrugged. "When the mortal world does not want us, we will go. But I will miss you."

"Don't talk like that," I said, surprising myself with the sharpness of it. "There has to be something we can do. Can't you enchant him? Or—"

She shook her head. "He is not a wizard in his heart. He carries the blood but not the will to renew the bond."

The news hit me hard. Even when his parents were banished, I'd always assumed the line would continue. That a Ravencroft would return someday—even a distant cousin. If the last one broke the pact . . .

"You said the doors will close. What exactly does that mean?"

Nyx sat upon the lowest branch, her legs swinging. "In the days of the ancient kings, there were many portals to the Otherworld. The bargains kept the worst of us out and the best of us in." Her smile was brittle. "The end is always dangerous, Kitty. But I suspect it will be quiet. A forgetting, not a war."

I wrapped my arms around myself, cold and weary. "I don't want to forget."

"Then fight for us," Nyx said, raising a small fist. "There is still time. The Hall is not yet sold."

"Why would Richard listen to me? He's made it clear that his mind can't be changed."

Her laughter was like summer rain. "I have known you all your life. You are clever and stubborn. If anyone can do it, you can."

I didn't believe her, but I nodded anyway.

Nyx hopped down from her branch and stepped into the shadow of the oak. "You will not see me for a while," she said. "There is little to do now but wait."

An instant later, the clearing was empty save for drifts of golden leaves.

Yet I stayed for a while, thinking about bargains and bloodlines, about what it meant to belong to a place that was vanishing by the day. But I wasn't ready to let go, not yet.

I *had* to change Richard's mind.

5

FENWICK

W alking home from Nyx's oak, my thoughts drifted to the day I first fell under the spell of the Wild Wood.

I was seven years old and still living with Nan at Lothian Cottage. My parents were away more often than not—painting popes and rubbing elbows with continental nobility —so I spent more time at the Dancing Toadstool than my own home, soaking up the warmth and bustle and endless bowls of rice pudding.

Layla's father had disappeared two years before. Mr. Deen went into the wood one spring morning to hunt mushrooms and never came out. The woods kept him, and that was that.

Everyone in the village came together to support poor Mrs. Deen. Even as the months passed, she clung to the hope that he was still alive and might return someday. They had emigrated from Sri Lanka when they were both twenty. Sanaja's father didn't approve of Arush because his family was poor, so the young couple eloped.

Sanaja's mother, who had a soft heart and wanted her own daughter to marry for love, secretly gave them Sanaja's dowry money to start a new life together. They took a plane to England but decided that London was too crowded. They wanted to live somewhere quiet, like the village they both came from, so they hopped on a train and began traveling around the countryside. As fate would have it, their journey led them to Southlea Cross, and then Little Groating, where they stumbled over the Dancing Toadstool.

The inn was up for sale and they bought it with Sanaja's dowry money. Sanaja always said that the inn chose them and not the other way around, because several other people who had wanted to buy it before them suffered improbable setbacks, but when the Deens tried to buy it, all the paperwork went smoothly.

I learned most of this after Mr. Deen disappeared. I remembered him as a gentle man with a ready laugh, but his face soon grew fuzzy like a half-remembered dream.

Layla had two brothers, twins, who went off to boarding school after it happened. As for my best friend, she grew even quieter. She'd always loved books, and she immersed herself in faerie lore, bent on learning all she could about the ways of the dark fae. She told me they must have ensorcelled him, but fae were notoriously capricious, and they might be bored of him by now.

We hatched a plan to make a trade with the fae, but then Layla fell sick with a fever. Her birthday was coming up, and I decided that it would be a fine gift to bring her father back myself.

Of course, the Wild Wood was forbidden to me. But it never took much coaxing to get Nan talking about the fae.

She'd said, "The Wild Wood keeps what it likes," and I said, "What if you try to take something back?" Nan pursed her lips. "I suppose you'd have to be very cunning. And very polite."

I nodded seriously, as if I were either of those things.

The morning of the rescue, I left a note under Nan's teacup—"Gone to pick apples, back for lunch"—and stuffed my backpack with cheese and watercress sandwiches, a half-eaten chocolate bar, and a thermos of fresh milk, plus an assortment of thimbles for bargaining. I wore my favourite ratty trainers and red coat with brass buttons, feeling invincible. After all, I knew Quince the brownie and he was friendly enough.

The Wild Wood began just beyond the last cottage east of Nelly's Pond (which I gave a wide berth to; I wasn't *entirely* stupid). Its outer fringe looked airy and inviting. Through stands of beech with red-gold leaves, I glimpsed the hint of a path.

Part of me—the same part that shouts a warning when I pass the Ravencroft gargoyles—woke up then. *This is the gravest folly, Kitty Boot,* it said. *You'll go in and you won't come out again, just like Mr. Deen.*

I almost turned back. But then I pictured Layla's face when she saw her father walk up to the inn, me leading him by the hand. In this fantasy, he was still carrying the basket of mushrooms in the other, as if no time had passed at all.

I drew a steadying breath and took the path.

I hadn't gone more than twenty steps before I looked back and saw that the civilised world behind me had vanished. It was as though I'd been instantly transported to the heart of the wood. The sunlight turned green and watery, and everything smelled of moss. In front of me lay a perfect circle of red-capped mushrooms the size of dinner plates.

I halted at the edge, remembering Nan's warning: never step into a faerie ring unless you want to dance forever.

There were other rules, too. Never accept food or drink, and above all, never tell a faerie your true name.

I picked my way around the mushrooms, along a twisting green road sunk deep into the earth like a dry riverbed. The trees—oak and ash-—grew closer together, and the ground sloped down into a hollow choked with brambles. The air grew colder, and I felt the prickly sensation of being watched.

I turned slowly, scanning the undergrowth. Nothing moved. Even the birds had gone silent. I told myself it was just nerves, but then I heard it—a giggle, high and sharp, coming from somewhere just out of sight.

The fine hairs sprung up on the nape of my neck. I made to run away and that's when I got snagged. A bramble caught my sleeve and wouldn't let go. I tugged and twisted, but it only made things worse—the thorns bit into my arm, and my red coat was caught fast.

Mocking laughter came again, closer this time. It sounded like three or four voices at once, all jeering in harmony.

I froze, my quick, panicked breaths steaming in the icy air. I felt quite certain that the bad faeries who'd taken Mr. Deen were coming for me next.

A shape stepped into the clearing.

He was tall and pale, his hair black as a raven's wing. He wore a cloak of dark blue silk, caught at his throat with a silver clasp. He looked at me and said something in a melodic language I didn't recognise—but the edge of anger was unmistakable. I was so scared that I gave a tremendous yank. Thorns raked my wrist, but I managed to break free and rabbit across the clearing, away from this terrifying apparition.

"Please don't go!"

The entreaty was uttered in English this time. His voice held such loneliness that I stopped running. I think he put a bit of magical command in it too, though the memory is muddled now.

I held still as he walked up to me, slow and cautious like one might approach a skittish animal. He was just a boy—or *appeared* like one. The clearing had fallen silent, the watchers gone, and my fear drained away as I understood that he had driven them off. That his anger was directed at the bad faeries, not at me.

"Are you a prince?" I asked, because that was the only thing that made sense.

He considered this. "I am called . . . Fenwick." He studied me like I was some magnificent curiosity. "What's your name?"

I nearly told him, such was my relief at being rescued, but I remembered myself at the last second.

"Rosemary," I said. That was Nan's name, and the first one that came to mind.

He bowed to me. "I am delighted to meet you, Rosemary. How did you wander so deep into the wood? It's dangerous here for mortals."

He was right, though I was tired of people telling me that. I lifted my chin. "I came looking for my friend's father. He was gathering mushrooms and disappeared. Have you seen him?"

Fenwick gazed down at me seriously. "I'm sorry, I haven't. Do you want me to show you the way out? You'll be safe with me."

Suddenly, I didn't want to go home. Later, I wondered if he didn't put an enchantment on me, but I don't think he had. I was just reluctant to end my adventure so soon.

He seemed to sense my hesitance and asked if I wanted to

see his favourite places first. It would be rude to refuse, and the Fair Folk were easily offended. Fenwick's face brightened at my eager nod, and I knew I'd guessed right. My faerie prince *was* lonely.

We spent the rest of the afternoon climbing trees and picking berries and cooling our bare feet in silver streams. I'd lost my trainers somewhere, though I couldn't recall taking them off. Around lunchtime, Fenwick brought me to a hill where the sun broke through in fat, buttery beams and the grass was like a fluffy quilt. We lay back, eating watercress sandwiches, and made a game of seeing pictures in the clouds.

Fenwick was nothing like the boys in the village who were scornful of girls. He had courtly manners and was pleasant to look at, too, sharp-featured like a fox.

Sylvan fae watched us from the shadows: sprites, dryads, even a pair of brown, pop-eyed brownies who bowed to Fenwick with great formality. I could tell he was important.

When I asked again if he knew where Mr. Deen was (because even good fae could be tricksome and didn't always tell the full truth), he grew sombre. "Sometimes the Wood gives things back, but only if they wish to return."

That seemed unfair. "You mean Mr. Deen doesn't want to go home? I don't think that's right. He must miss his family."

I thought of Layla, reading lore books late into the night under her covers, and Mrs. Deen, whose eyes were still red and puffy around Christmas and birthdays.

"Then I shall keep an eye out for him," Fenwick promised.

The shadows were growing long and I realised that I'd better get back home before Nan got worried. Fenwick led me along one of the sunken faerie roads for what seemed merely a minute or two, and pointed through the trees. I saw the dark glass of Nelly's pond in the distance and a smudge of smoke from Lothian Cottage.

He stopped at the edge of the wood and regarded me for a long moment. Then he bent down, took my small hand in his, and kissed it, the lightest brush of his lips, which were quite warm.

"I hope you'll come back, Rosemary," he said.

I solemnly promised that I would. He gave a bittersweet smile and vanished into the wood. When I turned back to Nelly's pond, lanterns bobbed like drunken fireflies all across the fields and I knew I was in trouble.

I ran down the hillside, muddy, scraped, and missing a brass button, shouting "It's me!" at the search party. I expected Nan to be furious, but when she saw me, she burst into tears and crushed me into an embrace so tight I thought my ribs would crack.

I was strictly forbidden from entering the Wild Wood ever again, but of course the lure of seeing Fenwick proved too strong. Once Nan's watch over me slipped, I went back—many times—and called his name from the edge.

He never answered, and I never did meet him again, though as I grew older I walked farther and farther on the faerie roads, hoping that I might. I saw Folk aplenty, but the bad ones left me alone. Maybe they remembered that I was under Fenwick's protection.

Layla says—half-joking—that my faerie prince ruined me for mortal men, but I don't think of it that way. He opened my eyes to a world that ran parallel to the everyday, just out of sight. Once you've glimpsed it, nothing else compares.

That was why I started the walking tours, so I could share it with others. Nothing beats the look on a person's face when they first see a faerie. Some laugh and some cry, but they all go home forever changed.

It was why I spent moonlit evenings ambling through the Barrows. Why I had no interest in the young men of the village, though a few had tried to court me.

It was why, even now, I walked in the Wild Wood and took the long way home whenever life felt too small. There were worse things than being ruined by a faerie prince. And there were far worse things than believing, at least a little bit, in magic.

6

THE SHORT MATCH

I called an emergency council just before closing time at Sugar & Sprites. Not all of the core cabal could be mustered—Mrs. Deen was tied up at the inn with an industrial-scale lentil delivery—but Layla, Briar, Nan, and Dr. Singer turned up.

We commandeered a table facing the rear garden and Briar laid out a plate of ginger cookies. The rain had swept the last customers home, leaving us free to plot.

Briar poured coffee and passed around the still-warm cookies. "So," she said, "how doomed are we, exactly?"

"That depends," said Nan, "on whether the new Ravencroft is as stubborn as the old ones."

Dr. Singer looked at me over his spectacles. "You met him, Kitty. Is he open to persuasion?"

I shrugged. "He's polite, but he won't be easy to budge."

Layla, who had come armed with a notebook, started a new page with a decisive flourish. "We need a name. I propose we call ourselves the Committee to Save Little Groating."

"COMSLIG," Briar said. "It does have a ring to it."

"Can we say COMSLUG instead?" I ventured. "It's catchier."

"But there's no U in Little Groating," Layla pointed out, chewing the end of her braid. "And how is a slug catchier?"

"What do you have against slugs?" Nan demanded.

"Let's just call ourselves the Committee," Briar said before an argument broke out. "Raise your hands if you approve."

We all raised our hands.

"At least that's done," said Layla, crossing it off in her notebook. "Now, for the first order of business—Richard Ravencroft. He needs to be reminded what's at stake. All the things that would vanish if the Hall is sold. The local magic, the faeries, the—" She paused, tapping her pen. "—sense of continuity."

"I'm not sure you can put a price on that," said Briar, "but I like where your head's at."

"Let's make a list of ideas," Nan agreed. "It will help us focus."

I was secretly pleased; there's nothing so comforting as a list in a crisis.

We started scribbling down any mad thing that came to mind. Briar proposed a fundraiser to buy the Hall ourselves, but it must be worth millions and no one in the village had that kind of money, not even Madame de Berry.

Layla wondered if we could persuade Quince to cast a spell on Richard, but that too seemed like a long shot—and morally questionable. Nan suggested slashing the tires of his automobile, which was the most practical idea but yielded only a temporary solution.

Once the first, slender round of ideas was exhausted, we settled into a collective funk, staring at the diminishing pile of cookies.

Nan finally broke the silence. "I say we try to get to know the man. Find out what motivates him."

Layla nodded. "He's staying at the inn, so we have access. Kitty, you're the obvious choice. You already have a rapport."

"A rapport?" I snorted. "He practically slammed the door in my face this morning."

Dr. Singer gave a little cough. "Perhaps we could invite him to supper in the private dining room?"

I had my doubts but deferred to the collective wisdom.

The only flaw in the plan was that, for the next three days, Richard was a ghost. He would rise at the crack of dawn, help himself to coffee from the sideboard, and then go rattling off up the hill in his Mini, only to return quite late, grim-faced and in a foul humour. Any attempts to speak to him were curtly rebuffed.

It went on like this until Friday evening. We were gathered before the hearth at the Dancing Toadstool, nursing hot toddies with a generous dollop of whiskey.

"If he won't talk to us here," Briar announced, "we must go to him. We can't let him leave without hearing us out."

"Are we storming the manor?" asked Nan, with a piratical glint in her eye.

"Keelhaul that filthy toff," shrieked Sir Francis Drake. "Smash the system, comrades!"

"Not *storming*," said Briar, ignoring the outburst, "just popping in for a neighborly visit. With baked goods."

There was no argument: in rural England, one does not refuse a visit with baked goods. We drew lots to see who would go, and naturally I got the broken matchstick.

The following day, Briar packed a basket of fragrant sweet buns. Dr. Singer wished me luck and pressed a lavender mothball into my palm. "For courage," he said with a kindly smile.

It was drizzling by the time I crossed the bridge and reached the long drive to Ravencroft Hall. The gargoyles glared down at me from their stone columns at the gate, yet upon crossing the threshold I felt only a lukewarm malaise, the sort that precedes a mild case of the sniffles.

This bothered me, so I took a brief detour to examine Nyx's oak. More golden leaves lay drifted at the roots, and the bare branches looked brittle as old bones. It struck me with fresh urgency how much was at stake. Ravencroft Hall wasn't just a house. It was the anchor for everything strange and wonderful in this corner of the world.

I squared my shoulders and marched up the drive. If Richard was determined to abandon his birthright, he'd have to give me a satisfactory explanation. And if that failed, I'd throw the sweet buns at him.

I RAPPED ON THE KNOCKER, WHICH WAS SHAPED LIKE A SNAKE eating its own tail, and waited, rain sliding down the back of my neck. No answer came, but Richard's Mini was parked at a careless slant in the circular drive.

I banged again, louder this time, and waited. Still nothing. If he was home and ignoring me, that was one thing, but the house was monstrously large and it was possible he didn't hear me, so I went around to the side entrance.

The servants' door was unlocked, the kitchen in ruins. Smashed crockery littered the floor, flour dusted every surface, and the smell of curdled milk hung in the air. The sight made me clutch the basket tighter.

"Hello?" I called. "It's Kitty Boot. I've brought buns!"

My voice echoed back in the cavernous kitchen. I thought

about leaving, but the possibility that Richard might be tied up by pixies and jabbed with an oyster fork persuaded me to continue on.

I advanced carefully, nudging aside a broken plate with my boot. The rest of the house, as glimpsed through the swinging door, was even less inviting. The entry hall's flagstone floor was cracked like an old tooth, and the walls were lined with suits of armor, each holding a weapon that looked disturbingly well-oiled.

Along the grand staircase, a dozen oil portraits glared down. They had the same dark eyes, the same beaky noses, the same attitude of aristocratic superiority. One of the Ravencroft ancestors—a woman in a blood-red dress—seemed to watch me as I crossed the foyer.

I hesitated at the bottom of the stairs, debating whether to risk the upper floors. On the one hand, I didn't fancy getting murdered by a ghost or a deranged house-elf. On the other, if Richard really was in trouble, I'd never forgive myself for abandoning him to the mercy of whatever haunted these walls.

The second-floor library was worse. Books had been pulled from the shelves and scattered across the rug, which was stained with something that looked like old ink but could just as easily be dried blood. A reading chair had been upended, its legs savaged by what appeared to be tiny, sharp teeth.

I had a sudden, strong sense of being watched by invisible eyes.

"Nettle?" I ventured, recalling the name given to me by Quince.

A malevolent laugh was the only response. It came from everywhere and nowhere.

I edged past a grandfather clock whose pendulum had

stopped at midnight and peered down the dim corridor, which seemed to stretch as long as the village High Street. It was clear to me now why he was bent on selling the place, and why he looked so grim when he returned to the inn every night.

I ate two buns to bolster my courage, then searched the rest of the second floor. It was mostly bedrooms, along with a rear staircase and a nursery. Some of the rooms were untouched, while others had been ransacked, drawers open, carpets heaved aside. I felt the unseen faerie shadowing me, though it did nothing.

I was about to head back down to search the first floor when I heard a faint sound above me—a shuffling, then a dull thump.

The attic.

"Richard?" I called.

There was another thump. I hurried up the narrow stairs to a landing, still clutching my basket of now-cold buns. A muffled voice came from behind a large wardrobe.

I set the basket down and wedged my shoulder against the side. With a loud scrape, the wardrobe slid aside, revealing a door. I pulled it open and found Richard, who looked sheepish.

"You've made a habit of rescuing me," he said.

"It's turning into a full-time job," I replied. "I suppose that faerie locked you up?"

"You've met it?" he asked anxiously.

"Sort of." I picked up the basket. "Would you like to get some fresh air and have a bun?"

Gratitude flooded his face. "Yes," he said with quiet feeling, "I would."

We escaped the Hall without further incident and stood under the dripping eaves. Richard accepted a bun and wolfed it down in two bites as if he'd not eaten a proper meal for days. There was something so vulnerable about it that I felt my resentment dissolve, replaced by sympathy.

"This place is a handful, isn't it?" I said, breaking the silence.

He gave a low, tired laugh. "You have no idea." He took another bun, chewing thoughtfully this time. "I know the villagers are unhappy that I mean to sell," he said, not quite looking at me. "But I have . . . other business to conclude first." He paused, as though weighing the wisdom of confiding in the local tour guide.

I waited without saying anything.

Richard took a breath. "There is a family heirloom some-where in this house. I can't leave without it."

"A magical heirloom?"

He nodded. "My parents hid it before the scandal. They said I would need it someday. I don't want it, but it's unspeakably dangerous and I can't just . . ." His mouth twisted. "They didn't tell me where they put it. Now I'm here, and the house is . . ."

"Not exactly welcoming you back with open arms," I finished.

So he couldn't leave until he found this magical heirloom. My spirits lifted. It would buy us some time, at least.

"I've been searching," Richard continued, "but there are so many rooms. And my efforts are undermined at every turn by that damned faerie!" Angry spots of colour bloomed in his cheeks, and his dark eyes flashed. "The problem is I can't *see* the creature. Only its handiwork."

I shrugged. "The Folk like to play games. But you're a wizard. Can't you banish a rogue faerie?"

He scowled. "That would require magical training, which I don't possess. My parents were exiled when I was ten. I spent my formative years as the ward of the Earl of Pembroke. Boarding schools in Scotland, then Oxford. The only incantations I know are the Latin names of bacteria." Adding defiantly, "And I prefer it that way."

Well, that explained a great deal. My passionate entreaty —*"If you leave, the Wild Wood withers. The faerie roads close. The magic fades"*—died on my tongue. He would care nothing for any of those things.

"Perhaps if you tidy up, you'll find what you're looking for," I suggested.

"I already have," he replied tightly, "several times, but every night it all resets. Everything is thrown back into chaos by the next morning. Sometimes it's even worse than when I started."

I ate a bun. "Classic sabotage. Certain fae species abhor order."

He raised an eyebrow. "You have experience with this sort of thing."

"I know a little," I said. "Would you like help?"

He blinked, surprised. "You'd do that?"

Yes, why on earth was I helping him? This was exactly the sort of snarl we'd hoped for. Yet he looked so pathetic standing there, gaunt and weary, that I relented.

"I can't find your heirloom," I said, "but at least I can tell you what sort of faerie is tormenting you. Layla's the real expert. She can give you advice once we know the particulars."

It would probably be bad advice, but I didn't tell Richard that.

He laughed, a real one, and for the first time I saw how attractive he was. Not handsome in the traditional sense, but there was an almost boyish mischief lurking beneath that stark facade.

"You're a good person, Kitty Boot," he said.

I shrugged, embarrassed. "Let's get started before the faerie regroups."

WE WENT BACK INTO THE KITCHEN. IT HAD NOT IMPROVED IN our absence. The air still reeked of sour milk, and the detritus of a ruined pantry lay everywhere. Richard started gathering shards of crockery. I rummaged around until I found a broom, keeping a wary eye on the corners. An unnerving tension hung in the air, the kind that precedes a thunderstorm or a family argument.

"So you've never actually seen the faerie?" I asked, whisking the broom at a drift of flour that had somehow made it to the top of the larder.

"No," Richard replied, "but I can hear it sometimes. It laughs at me." He shivered. "A nasty laugh."

We worked side by side, stacking plates and righting chairs. The sense of being watched grew with every minute. At one point, as I bent to pick up a shattered teacup, a bag of powdered sugar sailed through the air and exploded in my face.

There was a moment of silence as the cloud settled. I sneezed twice, dusted myself off, and glared at the kitchen door, which now hung ajar.

"This one's got a mean streak," I muttered, as Richard offered me a handkerchief.

We attacked the mess once more, but our efforts were soon undone. The dustbin tipped itself over. The broom bristles shot out like quills from a porcupine and embedded themselves in a cabinet. At one point, Richard was locked inside the pantry for a full ten minutes while I fended off a rain of walnut shells from the upper shelves.

"You're being hazed," I said as he finally escaped, black hair festooned with cobwebs.

He groaned. "At least at boarding school the bullies were predictable."

I mulled over our options. "It's a boggart, I'm fairly sure. They're brownies that have gone feral. Usually it happens if the house is abandoned for too long. They get offended and turn vicious."

He gave me a baleful look. "So I'm to blame, in other words."

I shrugged. "Has the Hall ever sat empty before? Of Ravencrofts, I mean?"

He thought and shook his head. "Not to my knowledge. And we've lived here for five centuries."

I liked the sound of that "we." It might mean he was softening.

"Well, there you have it," I said. "You'll have to win the boggart over."

He groaned theatrically.

"But in the meantime," I said, "I have a quick fix so it doesn't drive you mad." I rummaged through the pantry until I found a box of salt. Unlike everything else, it was untouched. "Boggarts don't like salt," I explained. "If we salt the windows and doorways, that'll show it who's boss."

Richard looked heartened. Together we circled the kitchen, drawing thick white lines along the windowsills and doors. As we did, the temperature dropped, and the laughter stopped.

When we finished, I looked at Richard. "Now we wait."

It didn't take long. A violent rattling erupted from the scullery, the door slamming back and forth though no wind could have moved it. I stood my ground, arms crossed, and Richard watched me with wary admiration.

"You can show yourself," I called, using my sternest voice.

For a moment, nothing happened. Then a shape flickered into being—an outline of a small, wiry creature, its eyes like black glass, teeth bared in a rictus of fury. It hissed, then vanished.

"Boggart," I confirmed. "A textbook case."

Richard exhaled. "It's gone?"

"For now."

He sagged against the counter, relief written all over him. "Thank you."

I smiled. "Don't thank me yet. You still have to find your heirloom."

He grinned and squeezed my hand. Just briefly, but it sent a jolt through my entire arm.

"Thank you for all your kindness, Kitty," he said. "I've had enough for today. Would you like a ride back to the inn?"

7

YOU VULGAR BOOR

I hadn't ridden in a car since my parents left for the last time and Madame de Berry drove them to the train station at Southlea Cross in her ancient Volvo. They were heading to London and then New York to show their paintings in a prestigious gallery, and I'd tagged along to see them off.

My parents are both warm, energetic types. They hugged me and promised to be back in a few weeks. Which turned into a few months, and then two and a half years.

Anyway, I'd never gotten my licence so I wasn't qualified to judge Richard's driving, though I will say that he gripped the steering wheel with the grim resolve of a man about to perform open-heart surgery in a canoe.

He didn't speak at first, just adjusted the rearview mirror and started the engine. I set the empty basket on my lap— we'd demolished the sweet buns—and buckled in. The rain had slackened but a strong wind rose, swaying the beeches that lined the drive.

"May I ask you something?" Richard ventured as he

steered around a crouching beast that might have been a lion; the topiary was so overgrown, it was hard to tell anymore.

"Be my guest," I replied.

He sped down the drive and passed the leering gargoyles so fast I felt hardly a blip of unease. "How did you end up giving walking tours?"

Ravencroft Hall receded in the side mirror, a dark smudge crouched on its hilltop. I cleared my throat. "I *am* sorry about that—"

"Don't be, it's fine. I'm just curious. Do you have an interest in local history?"

I thought of Fenwick, my fae prince, but that wasn't a tale I shared with strangers—especially ones who disliked the Fair Folk.

"I never planned on it," I replied. "But a few years ago, people from Southlea Cross began wandering over, looking for faeries. I liked talking to them, so I'd take them to places where I knew the fae lived, and sometimes they'd show themselves."

"Aren't they famously shy?" Richard asked.

"Some are. Others enjoy being seen by mortals. And they know me."

He nodded encouragingly.

"At first, it was just for fun," I continued. "But more visitors kept coming, from farther away. Briar was one of the first Americans. She booked a weekend at the inn, met Layla, and refused to leave when her visa ran out. They married a year later and opened Sugar & Sprites when we all turned twenty."

"That's the bakery?" he asked.

"And souvenir shop, and bookshop, and de facto town square. Layla runs the front, Briar bakes in the back. Anyway, people started offering me tips. Eventually, Layla talked me into charging for a tour. Five quid a head. Approximately ninety minutes, and it includes cookies and hot tea."

The car rattled over the narrow wooden bridge to the village.

"Why didn't tourists come before?" he wondered. "If Little Groating is famous for faeries?"

I glanced at his hawkish profile. "To be honest, it was partly the media coverage."

"My parents," he said grimly.

He clearly didn't like being reminded of the scandal. But I saw a chance to work my secret mission into the conversation.

"Yes, but my Nan thinks that's not the real reason. It only got really busy about ten years after your parents left. She thinks the magic that hid us from the world started to fade since there were no Ravencroft wizards at the Hall. So while I do enjoy the extra income, it makes me worried, too."

Richard was silent for a minute or two.

"Have you ever left Little Groating?" he asked casually.

I sighed at the deflection. "Once, when I was thirteen. My parents took me to London for a weekend. They'd just been discovered and were showing their work at a pub in Clerkenwell."

"They're artists?"

I nodded. "They started off painting the Fair Folk. My mother had a special talent for capturing the essence of the fae. Once they got famous, they switched to abstract portraits."

"Did you like it?"

I frowned. "The paintings?"

Richard smiled. "London."

"Truthfully? It was exciting, but the crowds were a bit

much. I prefer it here," I added firmly. "What do you like best about London?"

"It's anonymous," he replied. "No one knows you, and no one cares who you are."

"That sounds lonely. What if you're sick? Who will bring you soup?"

"I have friends," he said, a bit defensively.

"Sorry, of course you do, I didn't mean . . ." We passed a hedgerow and I leaned across him to point. "Oh, that's the spot where the French ambassador's boy had his shoes stolen by pixies. It made the *Telegraph*."

Richard braked hard, then accelerated, thrusting me first against the steering wheel and then his broad chest. He smelled nice, like wool and shaving soap.

"Er, sorry, Kitty." He slowed again to peer at the hedgerow. "You're not joking."

I shook my head. "The poor boy had to go home in borrowed slippers."

Richard gave a short laugh. We zipped down the last hill toward the village, its windows glowing like cat's eyes in the dusk, and jolted to a stop outside Sugar & Sprites, one wheel lodged on the kerb and the other threatening to demolish a decorative flowerbed. Richard turned off the engine, but made no move to get out.

"I'm out of my depth," he admitted. "The house, the boggart, the—" He waved a hand, encompassing the general weirdness of my world. "I could use your help, Kitty. Just for the short time I'm here. I can pay you, of course."

He said it with a kind of hopeful dread, as if expecting me to laugh in his face. My heart beat a little faster. "You want to hire me? As a . . . faerie consultant?"

He nodded, a faint flush creeping into his cheeks. "If you're going to keep rescuing me, you ought to be compensated for it." When I hesitated, he added, "And it'll make up for the lost income from your walking tours."

I pretended to consider, then stuck out my hand. "Deal."

He grinned and shook it, his grip strong and warm. "Can you start tomorrow?"

"After breakfast," I agreed. "I have to speak with Mrs. Deen. I help at the inn, but it shouldn't be a problem."

"Excellent." Richard hopped out and came around to open my door with a gentlemanly flourish. He seemed in much better spirits not having to face the boggart alone.

THE KITCHEN OF THE DANCING TOADSTOOL WAS THE BEATING heart of the inn—a warm, spice-scented sanctuary. I found Mrs. Deen standing at the enormous old stove, steam rising in lazy curls toward the ceiling beams as she stirred a cauldron-sized pot of dhal curry.

Layla and Briar were chopping carrots and potatoes while a loudly purring Barbarossa wound between their legs. The cat always fawned over Layla, and she bent to give him a scratch behind the ears.

"Where's Nan and Dr. Singer?" I asked.

"He's got a cough," Briar explained. "Nan's with him, playing gin rummy, I think."

Jacob Singer lived just down the High Street, and his cottage was about as far as Nan went on her own these days.

"I'll bring them both supper when it's ready," Briar said. "Now dish, Kitty. What happened with Richard?"

Layla handed me a peeler and I set to work on a pile of potatoes. "I have a new job title," I announced in haughty tones. "Faerie consultant to the heir of Ravencroft Hall."

There was a beat of silence. Then Briar made a noise somewhere between a whoop and a cackle.

"I knew it would work!" she cried, brandishing the paring knife. "The Committee's plan is working!"

"What plan?" asked Mrs. Deen over her shoulder.

"The plan to stop the annihilation of all we hold dear," Layla replied, pushing her glasses up her nose. "We sent Kitty to win Richard's trust, and now she has."

I shot her a warning look, but Mrs. Deen just beamed at me. "I'm sure you can convince him to keep the estate. Maybe even get him to reinstate the village Christmas party."

Briar leaned forward. "What's the pay? Is it per faerie, or just hourly?"

"I don't know. I don't care about the money." I sighed. "There's a nasty boggart up there that's not helping our cause."

Layla winced. "Do you know its name?"

I shook my head. "I thought it might be Nettle, but when I said the name aloud, it had no effect."

"Well, you'll need to find out," she said. "And appease it somehow. Boggarts won't stop until the offense has been forgiven."

Mrs. Deen handed me a spoonful of dhal to taste. It was scorching hot and delicious.

Layla looked at me over the rim of her glasses. "And Richard, what's he like?"

I considered. "He's stubborn, but not cruel. I don't think he had a very happy childhood. He was sent away when he was ten to be the ward of some non-magical earl. Then boarding schools in Scotland. You can hear the soft burr in his voice. He must have been there for years."

"Poor boy," Mrs. Deen muttered. "Imagine being packed off to live with strangers. Losing one's home and family. I wonder why his parents didn't just take him along to Romania?"

"Leverage," Layla said. "I was reading old news articles about the scandal this morning. As long as Ransom and Desdemona's only son is in Britain, they won't dare to stir up trouble. Leaving Richard behind was part of the banishment deal."

There was a brief silence. Sir Francis Drake, who had been lurking in the shadows, seized the opportunity to bellow, "Pretty little vial, pretty little death!" and then, "Where's the rum?"

As I think I mentioned before, the list of his previous owners included a pair of notorious purveyors of poison from Berlin. But Sir Francis often mixed up the things he'd learned from the anarchist pirates—and the Lutherans, of course.

Layla made a kissy noise and held out her hand. Sir Francis hopped aboard, bobbing his head. "You vulgar boor, blockhead, and lout," she recited, quoting from Martin Luther's tirade against Duke Henry of Brunswick.

"You ass to cap all asses, screaming your heehaws!" the parrot answered with relish.

"Don't encourage him," Briar said, laughing.

"Why on earth not?" Layla grinned back.

"Because we all know *far* too many quotes from a man who's been dead for five centuries," I said with a stern look at them both. "Now back to Committee business. Richard said he's looking for a family heirloom and won't leave until he finds it. It's somewhere in the house, but the boggart keeps wreaking havoc on his search."

I turned to Layla, who was an expert on magical lore. "Any idea what it might be? He didn't tell me."

She frowned. "Not a clue. A Ravencroft secret, I suppose."

"But that's good news, isn't it?" Briar put it. "If he doesn't find it, he can't sell the Hall."

I shifted guiltily. "I told him I'd help."

Briar's freckled face screwed up in thought. "Could you . . . not be very good at it? Lead him on wild goose chases? Buy us time?"

The suggestion made sense from a strategic standpoint, but something in me rebelled. "That feels dishonest. He's paying me for a job."

Layla patted my hand. "Then don't sabotage him overtly. Just . . . take your time. Show him all the nooks and crannies of the estate, the village, the Wild Wood . . ."

"Make him fall in love with it," Briar said, gazing at Layla, who flushed and grinned. "The way I did."

"I can do that," I said. "I just hope I don't muck it up."

Mrs. Deen waved this away. "Nonsense." She sprinkled garam masala into the pot. The scent bloomed in the air, making my stomach growl. "Sometimes the heart remembers what the mind forgets. His blood belongs to this land. You'll make him see what's worth fighting for."

I swallowed past a tightness in my throat and nodded.

"We'll spare you from work for as long as you need," she added. "Autumn is the slow season after all."

"I can still do mornings," I offered.

Mrs. Deen shook her head. "You help him, dear. The inn will manage."

She ladled the curry into a tureen and carried it into the dining room. The aroma set my mouth to watering—cumin, coriander, and garlic mingling with the sharp tang of tomatoes and the creaminess of lentils. She placed a basket of naan beside it, still warm from the oven.

Usually, supper was a long and leisurely affair, with stories and laughter, but it didn't feel the same without Nan and Dr. Singer. Layla and I wolfed down our bowls, then carried a smaller pot over to Dr. Singer's house. He was lying on the couch, tucked under a quilt, but he seemed in good cheer and ate a bowl of curry—though his cough was worrisome.

While Layla built up the fire, I pulled Nan aside and give her the latest update. "What if he finds his heirloom too quickly?" I whispered. "Or I can't convince him to stay?"

Nan took my hand. Her skin felt like tissue paper over bird bones, but her grip was strong. "The Wild Wood has survived worse threats than one reluctant wizard. And you have a way with difficult people." Her smile turned impish. "Besides, he seems to like you."

"Maybe a little," I admitted. "But mainly because I liberated him from the attic."

Nan grunted and exchanged a knowing look with Layla, who quickly pretended she hadn't overheard.

We played a few rounds of Old Maid before helping Dr. Singer off to bed. Layla hugged us all goodnight and headed to the flat she shared with Briar above Sugar & Sprites, while I walked Nan back to the inn.

I was halfway up to my garret room on the top floor when I heard footsteps behind me. Richard stood on the landing, clutching a brown paper bag.

"I bought supplies," he explained as I came back down.

I peered into the bag. It was filled to the brim with boxes of Saxa table salt.

"I cleaned out the grocer in Southlea Cross," he admitted. "Do you think it'll be enough?"

I considered the colossal dimensions of Ravencroft Hall. It would take about six truckloads of salt to cover every window and door, but Richard looked so hopeful, I hated to crush him.

"It'll help us make a few safe zones," I said, "but Layla told me we need to learn the boggart's name. Find out why it's so angry."

He sighed. "Very well."

"I'll come by the Hall tomorrow at nine," I promised. "We'll sort things out, don't worry."

He looked at me and for a moment, he seemed almost happy. "Thank you, Kitty. I can drive us both, if you like?"

I hesitated. I wanted to stop and see Nyx first. I had to persuade the dryad not to leave; to give me a chance to fix things.

"It's all right," I said, "I like to walk in the mornings. Start my day with a bit of exercise." I vigorously swung my arms in case he needed a visual illustration.

Again, that ghost of a smile. "I'll meet you there, then."

I watched him go, then climbed the stairs. The wind rattled the small, crooked windows, but Mrs. Deen had slipped a hot water bottle between my blankets and the bed was warm. I lay awake with my thoughts tangled around ancient magic and the terrible burden of being everyone's last hope.

Well, there are worse jobs than faerie consultant to a dashing wizard, I decided, and drifted off with a smile on my face.

8

MR. MONTFORT

I rushed down the stairs late to breakfast, still groggy from dreams of locked doors and shadowy attics. The common room was empty except for Silas Grimes, who occupied his usual table by the window.

He wore a paint-stained jacket, its pockets bulging with pencils and a well-thumbed field notebook. His gaze followed me from under bristly, overgrown brows.

"Morning," I said, because no matter how surly he was, Nan had taught me to be polite.

He grunted and returned to his kippers.

I was halfway to the buffet when he muttered, "You'll catch your death up at the Hall. Weather's turning and that place is a tomb."

"I'll bring a scarf," I replied, buttering two slices of toast. "How'd you know I was going to Ravencroft Hall, Mr. Grimes?"

He grunted again and gave a half shrug. Grimes was the sort of man who'd never admit to being interested in anyone's business but his own, yet he always seemed to know what the rest of the village was up to.

I poured myself a mug of coffee and surveyed the room. Mrs. Deen was visible through the window, cutting back dead tomato plants in the garden, and Nan must have gone to look in on Dr. Singer. Barbarossa the cat patrolled underfoot, stalking dust motes in the sunbeam that cut across the tiles.

"Did Lord Ravencroft leave already?" I asked, feigning nonchalance.

Grimes snorted. "Saw him just after sunrise, driving off like a lunatic. He'll run someone down, mark my words."

I shrugged and loaded up my plate with eggs and fried tomatoes, then carried it over to the table farthest from Grimes. He bent over his newspaper, though I could see him watching me in the glass.

I finished breakfast in silence, fending off Barbarossa's repeated attempts to plunder my vegetarian sausage, and readied myself for the day ahead. I would check on my faerie friend Nyx, then rendezvous with Richard at the Hall to commence Operation Boggart.

I left the inn bundled in my macintosh and a wool scarf, a heavy lunch hamper in one hand. The walk to the western edge of the Wild Wood took me past Sugar & Sprites, where the first batch of cinnamon rolls were already sending up a siren song. I waved at Layla, who was sweeping the stoop in her slippers, and she gave me a brisk salute.

I cut through the churchyard, past the weathered headstones and the old yew trees that leaned together like conspirators. Nyx's oak was on the way to Ravencroft Hall, not far from the bridge over the river. The world changed as soon as I stepped under the first arching branch: the light fell colder, and the air smelled of loam.

Nyx was waiting for me. Her silhouette was easy to spot, even with the leaves nearly gone. She stood half-twined around the trunk, eyes closed, hair wild with wind and seed fluff.

"Kitty," she said. "You come as the hour grows late."

I looked up at the branches of her oak. In the space of a single night, a whole new carpet of golden leaves had drifted down. My chest tightened. Less than a third remained.

Nyx stroked the bark of her tree with fingers slender as twigs. "When the last leaf falls, my time here will end and I must return to the Otherworld. We are bound, my oak and I. Even now, the magic runs thin."

"I know, Nyx. I swear to do all I can to stop it. Can you help me?"

She gazed upward, as if she could will the leaves to stay. "If the heir accepts his place, the roots will hold. If not, all will fade."

"Richard doesn't want the Hall," I admitted. "He wants to sell it and run off to London. He barely believes in any of this."

"He believes. But he is afraid."

A cold finger of wind worked its way into my collar, and I tightened the scarf. "Of what?"

Nyx leaned forward from the shadowy hollow of the trunk. "Of what he might become. Of the darkness in him."

"Darkness? He doesn't seem much like his parents," I protested.

"He is a Ravencroft," she replied, as if that explained everything. "But you must hurry. The doors are closing. And Richard is not alone."

I frowned. "You mean the boggart?"

But Nyx had already stepped back into the oak. I stood there for a moment, watching another brittle leaf detach and spiral to earth. Then I hurried up to Ravencroft Hall. It looked even more forbidding in the grey morning light, but I ignored the gargoyles at the entrance and marched up the drive with what I hoped was an air of confidence.

When I rounded the topiary, I saw Richard standing outside in conversation with a pink-skinned man whose blond hair had the texture of spun sugar. He must have used a whole can of hairspray for it didn't budge in the wind. He wore a pinstriped suit and shiny shoes. A valise sat at his feet.

Richard looked up with an almost guilty start when he saw me. "Oh, hello, Kitty! This is Mr. Montfort. He represents a firm that's interested in the—ah—potential sale of the estate."

"Ambrose Montfort, at your service," said the man, stepping forward and offering a hand. His grip was cold, like a freshly dead fish.

"Kitty Boot," I replied. "Local guide and faerie wrangler."

Montfort's smile showed a fence of white teeth. "How quaint! The villagers must be thrilled to see the Hall open again. So much potential for tourism."

"We have quite enough tourists as it is, Mr. Mortfort," I replied firmly. "No need for more. That would spoil the whole reason people want to come here."

Montfort's eyes narrowed. "Indeed. Well, we shall see what the market will bear. Lord Ravencroft, if we might continue our conversation in private?"

Richard shot me a look that was equal parts apology and embarrassment. "Kitty, would you mind? We shouldn't be long."

"No worries," I said with a stiff smile. "I'll try to keep the boggart at bay."

Richard scowled at me but Montfort only laughed, as if

he found the notion hilarious. "Boggart? What a delightful sense of humour our Miss Boot has!"

I wished the imp would appear and muss his perfectly coiffed hair—which looked fake, now that I was closer—but it stayed hidden. I headed around the corner of the house, towards the side entrance, then paused to eavesdrop the moment I was out of sight. The wind shifted and I caught a few scraps of conversation. Montfort's voice was urgent.

" . . . assure you, my backers are eager to proceed . . ."

" . . . unfettered access . . ."

" . . . as soon as the necessary papers are signed . . ."

Richard's replies were muffled, but his tone was clipped. He was obviously putting Mortfort off until he found his dangerous heirloom. But it was clear to me that Nyx was right; the hour was growing late to save the Hall.

I went around to the kitchen and let myself in, stowing the hamper on a side table. Richard had thickened the salt lines at the windows and doors, white crystals glittering in the morning light. I stepped carefully over the threshold, listening for the telltale giggle, but the air was still.

The kitchen remained in the same shambles as yesterday —shattered crockery across the floor, bags of flour split open, powdered sugar coating every surface like fresh snow. I rolled up my sleeves and set to work, figuring I might as well make the place habitable if we were going to hunt for a mystical heirloom all day.

I began sweeping, piling the broken plates and cups in one corner. The kitchen was massive, with copper pots hanging from ceiling hooks and an ancient oven built into the brick wall. In its heyday, it must have fed dozens of party guests. Did wizards wear black tie? Or just pointy hats and robes?

The door swung open and Richard appeared. His expression was tight with displeasure, but it softened when he saw me.

"You don't need to do that," he said quickly. "I didn't hire you to be a housekeeper."

I shrugged, not pausing in my sweeping. "You're paying me a generous sum, so I'd like to feel I've earned it. Besides, we need a base of operations that's not a complete disaster."

His shoulders relaxed. "Fair enough." He leaned against the doorframe, watching me work. "I apologise for Mr. Montfort. He wasn't supposed to come until next week. I would have warned you if I had an appointment."

I kept my voice casual. "What does he want, exactly?"

"He represents an investment group that's interested in the Hall. They have a development plan. A hotel, I think. It's all rather vague."

My stomach clenched. A hotel? "I hope you're not rushing into anything," I said.

"No, no," he assured me. "I haven't signed yet, and I won't until I find what I'm looking for. Montfort is just . . . persistent."

I whisked the broom so hard it sent a cloud of flour into Richard's face. He coughed and stepped back.

"Sorry," I muttered, not sorry at all. "Do you really trust the man? His shoes are so shiny I could floss my teeth in them."

That startled a laugh out of Richard. "I wonder if he polishes them between meetings?"

I grinned, relieved to see him smiling again. Perhaps there was hope after all. If I could just keep him from signing anything, buy us time to make him see what he would be giving up . . .

"The boggart seems to be behaving itself today," I said, changing the subject.

"For now." Richard glanced around warily. "But I'm not counting on it lasting. I should get back to my search. The ballroom is next on my list."

"Good luck," I said.

He nodded and strode out, leaving me alone in the kitchen. I turned back to my task with renewed purpose, scrubbing and sweeping. If I couldn't stop the sale directly, at least I could make this one room feel like a home again.

By lunchtime, the flagstone floor gleamed, the windows sparkled, and I'd even found some polish in a cupboard and rubbed it into the old oak table. The air smelled of lemon rather than curdled milk, and a fire crackled in the massive hearth.

I filled a copper kettle and hung it over the flames, pleased with my progress. There was still no sign of the boggart, though twice I'd heard distant, mocking laughter. Richard was out there somewhere, still hunting.

I found him eventually in the fabled dungeon, a dank, low-ceilinged space beneath the house accessed by a spiral staircase in a corridor off the billiards room. Richard was poking through a cabinet of rusty implements, dead spiders adorning his dark hair. He looked so wretched that I couldn't help but laugh.

He whirled around, startled. "What?"

"You have . . ." I gestured to his head.

He ran a hand through his hair and grimaced as it came away with cobwebs. "Lovely."

"I've made tea," I said. "And I'd packed us lunch from the inn, if you're hungry."

"Starving, actually," he admitted.

We adjourned to the kitchen. Richard's eyes widened as he took in the transformation. "This is remarkable. It looks almost—"

"Habitable?" I suggested.

"I was going to say 'cheerful,' but yes, that too."

I laid out the contents of my hamper. I'm a firm believer in substantial, fortifying meals, especially when battling supernatural forces, so I'd brought egg sandwiches on thick slices of Briar's sourdough, pasties filled with cheddar and sweet onion, cold potato salad, a jar of pickled gherkins, and for dessert, miniature treacle tarts.

"Good lord," Richard exclaimed. "Do you always eat like this?"

I frowned. "Don't you?"

He gave a happy laugh and dug in. We ate in companionable silence for a while, the only sounds the crackle of the fire and the occasional appreciative murmur. I kept the conversation light, telling him how Nan and I were saving up to take a trip together.

"She was born in Little Groating but ran away to sea when she was seventeen," I explained between bites of potato salad. "Nan eventually married a sailor, and they traveled all over the world. I thought it would be fun for her to have a last adventure. We've been planning it for years. First we thought the Polynesian islands, but now she wants to see Svalbard instead."

"How old is your Nan now?" Richard asked.

"Ninety-two," I replied.

He looked impressed. "She's a hardy woman."

"That she is." I learned forward confidentially. "I do want to go, but the best part is sitting by the fire and looking at all her old maps, hearing her stories. She swears she once saw a sea serpent off the coast of Gibraltar."

"What about your grandfather?" Richard asked, reaching for a treacle tart.

I felt the familiar pang of an old sadness. "Harry Boot

died in a storm. I never got to meet him. That's when Nan came back to Little Groating. I was four. It was around the same time my parents were discovered by an art dealer and began showing their work in London."

I shrugged, trying to keep my voice light. "They like the glamorous life. I haven't seen them in almost three years now, though they send the occasional postcard."

Something in Richard's eyes shifted—a kinship in abandonment. "I know something about that," he said quietly. "I haven't heard from my parents in twenty years. Not a single letter, though I wrote dozens to them."

The bitterness in his voice made me want to reach for his hand, but I restrained myself. "I'm sorry, that's awful."

He shook his head. "It's in the past now. I've made my own way." His face brightened. "I've just completed my training as a general practitioner. I plan to open a private practice in London."

"That sounds nice," I said. "Helping people."

"Exactly. It's important to me to—" He paused, searching for words. "To do something good with my life."

I could see how much it meant to him, this fresh start in London far from the ghosts of Ravencroft Hall. He had built a vision of his future that didn't include Little Groating or the Wild Wood or any of it. Nan was right. Arguing now would only make him dig in his heels deeper.

So I held my tongue and passed him another treacle tart, biding my time.

9

AN INSULT TO WORMS

The rest of the afternoon passed swiftly. Richard searched three of the upstairs bedrooms after lunch, finding nothing but dust and mouse droppings. I helped him salt the windows and doors of each room and he crossed them off his list.

"If you told me what you were looking for, I could help you," I ventured.

Richard stiffened. "It's not that I don't trust you, Kitty. But my parents swore me to secrecy."

I shrugged. "I don't care either way. In fact, you know my position. I'm hardly eager for you to find your heirloom and throw us all to the wolves!"

He sighed but made no response to this, moving from cabinet to drawer with the single-minded focus of a man convinced his salvation lay just behind the next door. I trailed along, keeping an eye out for the boggart, which had remained suspiciously quiet all day.

By the time we reached the east wing, with its faded tapestries and suits of armor, the windows had begun to darken. Richard stood in the middle of the billiards room, black hair disheveled and shoulders slumped.

"You should head back to the inn," he said. "It'll be night soon. Do you need a lift?"

"My own feet will do," I replied, "but thanks for the offer. Shall we expect you for supper?"

He shook his head wearily. "I'll tackle the library next, and that could take all night."

"Will you be all right here alone?" I asked, lowering my voice in case the boggart was listening.

"I survived ten years of public school," he said dryly. "I can endure one malevolent faerie."

All day, I'd kept my opinions to myself, instead praising the Hall's unique features—its bedposts carved with grinning imps, the way the stained glass on the third landing painted the walls with glints of purple and gold. Richard had barely noticed, so intent was he on his search.

Now I hesitated, wondering if I should again broach the subject of his plans to sell. But people rarely change their minds because you badger them, and Richard wasn't the sort of man you could persuade with words. If he was going to stay, it would have to be his idea.

"Very well," I said. " I'll be back tomorrow morning."

He nodded, already turning to the bookcase he'd been examining. "I'll be here."

I let myself out the kitchen door, carefully stepping over the salt line, and headed down the long gravel drive. The gargoyles always got you leaving as well as coming, but I felt only a mild twinge of unease as I passed their glaring eyes.

It occurred to me that in the old days, Mortfort never would have been allowed to find us. He would have wandered in circles until he ended up back at the train station in Southlea Cross. But the magic that hid Little

Groating and the Wild Wood from such men was failing—and it had been for years.

Twilight turned the sky indigo, with a scattering of bright stars. The meadow was a sea of pale gold rippling in the breeze. The Wild Wood stood dark along the hills, and I thought of the world that lay beyond its protective barrier. A world of mortal cities and machines and asphalt and no magic at all.

I breathed deeply, filling my lungs with crisp autumn air. The path curved downhill toward the bridge and I paused halfway across, leaning on the mossy parapet to stare at the water below. There was something hypnotic about the way it swirled and eddied around the rocks, carrying leaves downstream like time itself, sweeping us all along whether we liked it or not.

A flash caught my eye. I turned toward the Wild Wood, where a small, bobbing light moved between the trees. It winked once, twice, then vanished. A will o' the wisp? They weren't uncommon in these parts, especially at dusk, though I typically spotted them down by the Barrows.

I waited to see if it reappeared, but the woods remained dark. A chill ran through me and I hurried on toward the village, feeling suddenly alone on the quiet road.

My taut nerves eased as Little Groating appeared, smoke curling from chimneys into the darkening sky. Lamps were lit in every window, and the spire of the church stood silhouetted against a three-quarter gibbous moon. I could just make out the cheerful glow of the Dancing Toadstool at the bottom of the High Street.

My throat tightened with fierce love. Maybe because it was the only home I'd ever known, or maybe it was something deeper—a connection to the land, to the old magic that still lingered here when most of the world had forgotten.

As I walked, I turned over in my mind how to persuade Richard that selling the Hall would be a grave mistake. I understood him better now. He wasn't a callous man, just a wounded one. I had a feeling that he would be just as miserable in London as he was now, if not more so. He was still a Ravencroft, however much he wanted to turn his back on it all, and he belonged here.

I chewed my lip. His childhood home was failing to inspire a change of heart, but what about the rest of the estate? Richard zipped past the scenery in his car without truly seeing it. What he needed was to slow down, to walk the land his ancestors had tended for centuries.

That was it! I would convince him to take a ramble with me tomorrow. I'd show him the Wild Wood and the Barrows, where ancient kings slept beneath their grassy mounds. Perhaps I could persuade Nyx to come out, or at least show him her sickly oak. Only someone with a heart of stone could fail to be moved by her plight.

The more I thought about it, the more I liked the plan. Let him feel the earth beneath his feet, the whisper of the Wild Wood against his skin. Let him meet the Folk, not as pests to be eradicated but as neighbors who had honored and served his family for generations. There was a connection there, buried but not broken. I just had to help him find it.

By the time I reached the Dancing Toadstool, my spirits had lifted. The inn looked especially welcoming, its windows glowing amber against the gathering dark. I pushed open the front door, already anticipating warmth and laughter and a hearty supper.

Nan was in her usual chair by the fire, needles click-clacking as she worked on a tiny emerald jumper for Quince. She looked up as I entered, her bright eyes studying me.

"How was your day with the young lord?" she asked.

I shrugged out of my coat and hung it on the hook. "He's friendly enough, but I haven't changed his mind yet." I dropped into the chair opposite her. "At least he's not rushing to sign anything."

Nan's needles paused. "About that," she said, and something in her tone made my stomach knot. "Mr. Montfort has taken rooms here."

"What?" I sat bolt upright. "So you've met him. When?"

"This afternoon," she replied, resuming her knitting with a grim set to her mouth. "Mrs. Deen nearly threw him out once we realised his business, but we decided it would be smarter to keep our enemy close. At least we can watch him that way."

I imagined Montfort prowling around the village with his too-white teeth and his too-shiny shoes, and felt a surge of anger. "Where is he now?"

Nan fixed me with a stern look. "Don't do anything rash, Kitty."

I was about to protest when the door opened, letting in a gust of chill air. Layla stuck her head in. "You'd better come over," she said tightly.

I followed her back to Sugar & Sprites, which was unusually busy for a weekday evening. A small crowd had gathered near the bookshelves, where Montfort stood holding court, a stack of volumes on faerie lore tucked under one arm and several bags of sherbet lemons dangling from his fingers.

"Ah, Miss Boot!" he exclaimed when he spotted me, his voice carrying across the shop like a carnival barker's. "Just the person I wanted to see. I hear you're quite the expert on local folklore."

The way he said "folklore" made it sound like something quaint and slightly ridiculous. I pasted a stiff smile on my face.

"I know a bit," I said. "The owners of the shop know more."

Montfort beamed at me, that dazzling, artificial grin. "Splendid, splendid. I'm doing a bit of research myself. The investors I represent are quite excited about the entertainment angle of Little Groating. They see enormous potential in the place that will only be of benefit to all the villagers! Well, good evening, ladies."

He tipped his hat, gathered his purchases, and left in a waft of vile aftershave.

"What a worm," Briar exclaimed.

"That's an insult to worms," Layla muttered, "which are beneficial creatures. Let's call him what he is—a greedy human."

"Why is he buying all those books?" I wondered aloud. "It can't be for anything good."

Briar glowered. "He can stay at the inn, but he can't eat my cookies. I'm hanging up the closed sign if he turns up again. Did you see the way he looked at us with a proprietary eye? As if he already owned the place!"

"How can Richard have anything to do with such a man?" Layla demanded.

The shop erupted in a chorus of angry voices. Mrs. Whittlesby, who lived at Madame de Berry's boarding house and walked with two canes, thumped one of them on the floor for emphasis as she railed against "that pompous city fellow."

Three other elderly villagers clustered around her, nodding vigorously, while Madame de Berry herself stood with her arms folded across her shawl-draped bosom, lips pressed in a line of disapproval. I raised both hands, trying to establish a modicum of order.

"Everyone, please!" I shouted over the din. "One at a time!"

"What's going on, Kitty?" Madame de Berry demanded, her hazel eyes flashing with indignation. "That man was talking about investors and development plans as if we were a rundown seaside resort in Blackpool!"

I took a deep breath, weighing how much to share. The villagers deserved the truth, but panic wouldn't help anyone. "Richard Ravencroft is considering selling the Hall," I admitted. "But nothing's been signed yet. We still have time to change his mind."

A collective gasp went up. Mr. Hawkins, who'd played the church organ for fifty years, shook his head in disbelief. "A Ravencroft? Selling to outsiders? It's unthinkable!"

"The young lord doesn't understand what's at stake," I explained, trying to sound more confident than I felt. "He was sent away when he was just a boy. He doesn't remember the connection between his family and the land."

"Not to mention the faeries," added Mrs. Whittlesby darkly. "My garden gnomes have been cantankerous all week. They know something's coming."

I nodded, though I strongly suspected her "garden gnomes" were just that—painted plaster figures with pointy red hats. "Richard needs to be reminded of his responsibilities. If we present a united front, I believe we can convince him to stay."

"I don't see what the fuss is about," came a surly voice from near the door.

Silas Grimes stood there, paintbrushes jutting from his pocket like porcupine quills, his expression sour as usual. He never came to the shop. Claimed he had no sweet tooth, which Briar argued made him a likely serial killer.

"Progress isn't something to fear," Grimes continued, when we all stared at him. "Montfort's plans could bring prosperity to this backwater. Jobs. Tourism. Modern amenities."

"Modern amenities?" echoed Layla, hands on her hips. "Like what? A multiplex cinema?"

Grimes scowled. "Like reliable internet, for a start. And perhaps a bus service that runs more than twice a week."

"Who wants The Online?" someone shouted in a tone that suggested it was a contagious disease.

Canes banged the floor. "Not us!"

Madame de Berry stepped forward, her gaze narrowing. "What do you know about it, Silas? You've barely been here two years, and suddenly you're an expert on what our village needs?"

"I know enough," he muttered.

"Have you spoken with this Montfort before today?" she pressed, stooping towards him like a prosecutor challenging a hostile witness. "You seem well-informed about his plans."

A flicker of something—guilt? alarm?—crossed Grimes' face. "I merely overheard what he said just now," he said stiffly. "Anyone with half a brain could see the potential benefits."

"At what cost?" I asked. "The Wild Wood bulldozed? The faerie roads paved over? The entire reason people come to Little Groating is because it's not like everywhere else."

Grimes' mouth pinched even tighter. He muttered something under his breath about "backward thinking" before turning on his heel and stalking out, the bell above the door jangling discordantly as it slammed behind him.

The room fell silent for a moment as we all digested what had happened. I filed away Grimes' unexpected interest in Montfort for later consideration. There was something odd in his manner, a defensiveness that went beyond his usual curmudgeonly disposition.

"I never did trust that man," Mr. Hawkins announced. "He sits for hours by the bridge with his easel, but has he ever shown any of us a single painting?"

Madame de Berry nodded vigorously. "And he's always prowling around the edge of the Wild Wood, taking notes. What sort of notes, I ask you?"

"I say we go up to Ravencroft Hall ourselves," proposed Miss Carlisle, brandishing her walking stick like a rapier. "Talk some sense into the young lord. A delegation of concerned citizens!"

This suggestion was met with a chorus of approval, and they began to organise themselves into a geriatric strike force.

"That might not be the best approach," I said hastily. "If Richard feels cornered, he might dig in his heels even more. It could do more harm than good."

"Kitty knows him best!" Layla shouted over the din. "Listen to her!"

"Do you have a better plan, dear?" asked Madame de Berry, not unkindly.

I nodded, though the "plan" was hardly ironclad. "I'm working on it as we speak. I'm going to show Richard what he stands to lose—not just the Hall, but everything it protects. Trust me. It will all be fine."

My words sounded hollow, but the villagers appeared mollified. They trusted me, had known me my whole life. I couldn't let them down.

As the shop gradually emptied, with Madame de Berry herding her boarders back home for supper, I slumped against the counter. Briar locked the door behind the last customer and flipped the sign to CLOSED.

"Well, that was eventful," she said, tucking a stray ginger curl behind her ear.

"Silas knows more than he's letting on," Layla said, gathering up the other books Montfort had manhandled and left lying about.

I nodded, thinking aloud. "Keep an eye on him. But we must stay focused on Richard. If he won't change his mind, we need a Plan B. If I can't stop the sale through persuasion, then I'll have to find this heirloom and hide it myself."

Briar raised an eyebrow. "Do you know what it is?"

"Not yet. But I'll try to persuade Richard to tell me tomorrow," I said with more confidence than I felt. "He trusts me now, at least a little."

Layla shot me a worried look. "There's still the boggart to contend with."

"I'll cross that bridge when I come to it," I replied. "But I promised to fix this, and I will. One way or another."

I gave them both a reassuring smile and tried to ignore the knot of anxiety in my stomach. Tomorrow, I would drag Richard on an impromptu walking tour. And if the land itself couldn't change his mind . . . well, I still had a few tricks up my sleeve.

Let Montfort think he'd won. But Little Groating wasn't going down without a fight.

10

BLIGHT & PENHALIGON

I arrived at Ravencroft Hall the next morning eager to launch my new strategy. The manor loomed against the pale sky, windows glinting in the morning sun. It seemed peaceful, but yesterday's lack of boggart activity proved to be the calm before the storm.

As I crossed the threshold, the hairs on my neck prickled. All our carefully laid salt lines were gone, swept away by wind gusting through a cracked window. It was quite chilly. The fire in the hearth had died to embers, and the kitchen counters were dusted with floury footprints that marched up the wall and across the ceiling.

That little . . .

"Richard?" I called, setting down my lunch hamper. No answer.

He hadn't returned to the inn last night. I assumed he had simply slept at the Hall, but now I grew worried.

I ventured into the foyer, where the suits of armor had shifted position. One was missing a helmet; another held its sword upside down. The Ravencroft ancestors glowered from their gilt frames as if holding me personally responsible for the indignities befalling their home.

I called his name again. A muffled thump came from the entry hall, followed by what sounded like a strangled curse. I traced the noise to a door beneath the grand staircase—a cloakroom, as I recalled.

"Richard?" I ventured.

"Kitty?" His voice came through the heavy oak door. "Thank God. I've been trapped for hours."

I grasped the knob, which turned easily in my hand. "It's not locked."

"It is for me," he groaned. "And every time I touch it, it turns red hot. But don't come in!"

"Why not?" I was already pushing the door open when his voice rose to a desperate pitch.

"Because I'm not decent!"

I froze with the door wide enough to glimpse darkness beyond—and a pale figure crouched in the corner. "What do you mean?"

"I mean," he hissed through clenched teeth, "that the blasted boggart stole my clothes. Every stitch."

I bit my lip hard to keep from laughing. "Oh dear."

"I was searching through the old kennels when it began to rain straw down everywhere. I glimpsed it for a moment, Kitty, it's a hideous creature. The boggart led me on a merry chase back inside the house, flitting away each time I tried to seize it."

I eased the door shut and glanced around the shadowy foyer, wondering if the boggart was hovering nearby.

"Then I heard laughing behind a door," Richard contin-ued, "and found myself at the top of a narrow staircase I'd never seen before. I followed it down, thinking it might lead to the kitchen, but it emptied out here. The moment I stepped inside, my clothing simply ... vanished."

There was a long pause. Then he added with great dignity, "I've been trying to fashion a toga out of the cloaks, but they keep flapping away."

I could imagine it all too well—and a pretty picture he made, too. A snort of laughter escaped me before I could stop it.

"I'm glad you find my predicament amusing," he snapped.

"I'm sorry," I managed. "But you must admit it's rather funny."

"From your fully-clothed perspective, perhaps."

"Look," I said, getting my mirth under control, "there must be extra clothes somewhere in this enormous house."

"I've already thought about it," came the muffled reply. "There's a trunk in the attic. It belonged to the last gamekeeper. I found it yesterday while searching for—well, you know."

"The gamekeeper?" I asked. "That poor fellow who disappeared?"

"Yes, that would be the one. His name was Jasper Something-or-other. Before my time."

I'd heard stories about the last gamekeeper of Ravencroft Hall. He'd vanished one winter evening from his cottage near Nelly's Pond. The village consensus was that he'd met the same fate as so many others who'd wandered too close to the pond at dusk.

I shivered in the draughty foyer. "You must be freezing. Back in a trice," I promised, and headed for the stairs.

The attic was just as cluttered as the last time I liberated Richard. Thick beams crossed the ceiling at odd angles, and the floorboards gave creaks of protest with every step. I sighed and regarded the piles of trunks, hatboxes, and furniture draped in yellowing sheets. Faint light filtered through small, dusty dormer windows.

I'd brought a candle from downstairs, which now guttered in a draught. I held it higher, scanning the gloom for anything that might contain men's clothing.

"I know you're here," I said to the empty air. "I can feel you watching."

A soft, malevolent giggle echoed from somewhere to my left. I turned, but saw only stacks of old paintings leaning against a wall.

"We can't go on like this," I continued, picking my way between a harpsichord and a stuffed badger missing one eye. "Is your name Nettle? You can tell me."

The candle flame snuffed, plunging me into semi-darkness. I fumbled for matches in my pocket.

"Apparently not," I muttered, striking a fresh match. The tiny flame illuminated just enough to see a book fly off a shelf, pages flapping like the wings of a trapped bird.

I relit the candle and continued my search. "Look, I'm trying to help. You're obviously upset about something. Is it because the Ravencrofts left? Because one of them is back now, and—"

The candle extinguished again, this time accompanied by a sound like paper being ripped. When I relit it, I found myself standing next to a massive leather-bound ledger. It had fallen open to a page of household accounts, where someone had scrawled "LIARS" across an entry for "brownies' milk and honey."

"I see," I said softly. "You think the Ravencrofts deceived you. But I can assure you, they did not want to leave this place. And none of it is Richard's fault. Will you at least let me find some clothes for him? It's cold down there."

Silence, then a soft thump from the far corner of the attic.

My candle dimmed but didn't go out. Taking this as tacit permission, I made my way toward the sound.

There, wedged between two rolls of musty carpeting, was a wooden trunk, its brass fittings tarnished with age. A small brass plaque on the lid read "J. Hargreaves."

"Thank you," I said to the empty air.

I tried the lid; it was unlocked. Inside, neatly folded, were the earthly possessions of a country workman: flannel shirts in muted plaids, heavy woollen trousers with suspenders, thick socks, a tweed jacket with leather patches at the elbows, and a pair of sturdy boots. Everything smelled faintly of mothballs and pipe tobacco.

I wondered what happened to poor Mr. Hargreaves. Had Nelly truly claimed him? Or did he simply walk away, leaving his belongings behind? The trunk contained no personal items—no letters or photographs, nothing to suggest a life beyond service to the estate. It seemed a lonely sort of existence.

I considered carrying an armload of clothes down, but the trunk wasn't all that heavy. I managed to get it down the stairs without too much trouble, which is when I noticed that the family portraits were now hanging upside down and several suits of armor had swapped helmets with each other, giving them a distinctly cross-eyed look.

Of course, the trunk got heavier as I went. After much huffing and puffing, I dragged it to the cloakroom.

"I'll leave it here," I called, rapping on the door. "You'll find everything you need inside. I'll redo the salt lines and make some tea in the kitchen."

"Kitty, you're a saint," came Richard's muffled reply.

"I know," I said. "Take your time."

I retreated to the kitchen, where I rebuilt the fire and put the kettle on. By the time it boiled, I'd found two mugs and a tin of Earl Grey in the back of a cupboard. I'd just poured the tea when I heard footsteps in the hallway.

Richard appeared in the doorway. Gone was the tailored suit and starched white shirt. In their place, he wore the gamekeeper's woollen trousers, a flannel shirt, and a brown tweed jacket that strained slightly across the shoulders. He looked like he belonged on the moors with a pack of hounds at his heels—every inch the country squire, despite his obvious irritation.

"I look ridiculous, I know," he said, tugging at the collar of the shirt. "The trousers are too short and the boots are too big, but it's better than the alternative."

And what's wrong with the alternative?

I thrust the picture of a stark naked Richard from my mind with an effort and handed him a mug of tea. "Not at all. The clothes suit you." I leaned against the counter, warming my hands on my own mug. "Since the boggart seems to have decided what you'll be wearing today, I thought perhaps we might take advantage of it."

"How so?"

"Well, you're already dressed for it. Let's take a walk—a proper one, not just up and down corridors. There are parts of the estate you haven't seen in years. Aren't you tired of dust and dead spiders? Just for the morning, then you can resume the hunt."

Richard hesitated, but I could see he was tempted.

"I must admit," he said, "the thought of escaping the boggart's domain for a few hours has appeal." His dark eyes held mine. "And I happen to enjoy your company, Kitty Boot. Some fresh air might clear my head." He looked down at himself with a wry grin. "These clothes do seem suited for tramping about the woods."

My heart leapt. "Excellent! We can set out right now."

I was just rinsing the tea things when the distant sound of a car engine broke the quiet. Richard's head snapped up, his expression shifting from relaxed to alert in an instant.

I rushed to the window. A black SUV was winding its way up the drive. Even from a distance, I recognised the driver's blond spun-sugar hair gleaming in the morning sun.

"Oh no," I groaned. "It's Montfort."

Richard slapped his forehead. "I completely forgot. I promised to show his partners around today."

"What?" My voice rose to an octave Sir Francis Drake would envy. "So soon?"

"I'm sorry, Kitty. I meant to tell you, but with the boggart . . ." He gestured vaguely at his borrowed clothes. "I agree it's inconvenient—"

"Inconvenient? Richard, these are the people who want to turn my home into a resort! And you're giving them a tour?"

He scowled at my tone. "*You* give tours," he reminded me. "To tourists."

"That's different and you know it."

Richard sighed. "I haven't agreed to sell to them. I promised to give them a quick look, that's all."

I glared out the window as Montfort parked a Range Rover in the circular drive and two passengers emerged from the backseat. They wore the self-satisfied look of men who were used to getting their way.

"What about our walk?" I asked, not trying to hide my disappointment.

Richard looked regretful. "Later, Kitty, I promise. After they've gone. But they have an appointment, and I can't very well turn them away now that they're here."

"You absolutely could," I muttered. But I knew it was useless.

"You're welcome to join us," Richard said in a placating tone. "I hope you will."

I scowled. "I *am* your employee. I suppose I have no choice."

"Of course you have a choice," he retorted, cooler now. "But I leave it to you."

We locked gazes. I decided I would rather know what transpired and gave a brusque nod.

AMBROSE MONTFORT STRODE UP TO THE FRONT DOOR AS IF HE owned the Hall already. His smile widened at the sight of Richard in his borrowed clothes.

"Lord Ravencroft! How rustic you look today. Going native, are we?"

Richard's jaw tightened. "I was out walking the estate this morning," he said tersely.

"If only," I muttered, and he shot me a quelling look.

Montfort's backers introduced themselves as Mr. Blight and Mr. Penhaligon. Blight was ruddy and round with a receding hairline, while Penhaligon was thin and angular with a shuffling gait like a mummy.

"Do come in," Richard said heartily, stepping aside. "Welcome to Ravencroft Hall!" He cleared his throat. "This is Miss Boot, a local expert I've hired to help with some, ah, unique aspects of the estate."

"Charmed," I said sourly.

"Miss Boot gives walking tours of the area," Richard explained. "She knows the history of the Hall better than most."

"Then we ought to hire her as a concierge once it's

converted to a hotel!" Mortfort exclaimed, beaming as if he expected me to fall to my knees in gratitude.

"Er, yes, well . . ." Richard began.

"Ah, what a wonderful day for a viewing," Blight boomed, brushing past him to admire the grand staircase.

Richard went pale as the three men unwittingly demolished the line of salt at the threshold like toddlers kicking sand at the beach. He glanced at the ruined barrier with a look of dread.

"Gentlemen, if you'll follow me," he said quickly, herding them through the foyer.

He led them into the drawing room, where the boggart had been relatively restrained in its destruction. Only a few cushions were slashed, though the crystal chandelier swayed ever so slightly.

"You'll have to excuse the state of things," Richard said, tearing his gaze from the chandelier. "Local teenagers, I'm afraid. They've broken in to throw parties over the years."

"Little hooligans," said Montfort with an unctuous smile. "Empty properties are always at risk. Imagine the vandalism a new development would prevent."

"Indeed," said Blight, making a note in his portfolio. "Our security measures would be state-of-the-art. Anyone who trespasses will face the full force of the law, regardless of age." His jowls wobbled. "Juvenile delinquents ought not be coddled, eh?"

I noticed a small but heavy-looking bust inching its way across a side table. Richard saw it too and swiftly moved to block the view.

"Very authentic," Penhaligon observed, kicking at the wainscoting with a pointy wingtip shoe. "A few coats of eggshell and you'd never know it had been here since the Crusades."

"I'm told this is the oldest part of the Hall," Montfort added. "Spectacular for period detail."

We made our way back to the foyer, where the grand staircase swept upward beneath a ceiling painted with a religious motif. The angels, I noticed, had thick mustaches drawn in black marker, and several of the saints had been given monocles and elaborate facial moles.

Montfort squinted but chose not to remark on this.

"The wood paneling is original Tudor," Richard said loudly. "And the carpets are Axminster, of course—"

A priceless-looking ceramic urn flew from its pedestal and shattered on the tiles. Penhaligon jumped. "What was that?"

"Old houses," Richard said with a strained laugh. "They settle. Shall we see the second floor?"

I trailed behind the group, caught between delight and a helpless sense of the ridiculous. Richard's nerves were fraying; he kept looking back at me with an expression that said, "Do something!" To which I could only shrug apologetically.

He hurried his visitors into the library, which looked even worse than when I'd seen it last. Books lay scattered across the floor, and the boggart had used crumpled pages to spell out what appeared to be "SOD OFF" on the central reading table.

Before the men noticed, Richard knocked the balled-up paper aside with a sweep of his arm. "One of the finest private collections in Britain," he declared. "Mostly first editions."

Blight nodded as a leather-bound volume of Shakespeare's sonnets drifted from a shelf and hovered directly behind his head, its cover slowly opening and closing in an ominous way that made me think of a Venus flytrap.

"The library could be converted into a high-end cocktail

lounge," suggested Montfort, who along with Penhaligon was preoccupied jotting down the room's dimensions on a notepad. "We'd preserve a few volumes for atmosphere, of course. The rest can go to auction."

Richard lunged for the book just as it snapped shut with a thunderous crack. Blight whirled around, but by then it lay innocently on the carpet.

"Draughts," Richard explained weakly, picking up the volume and stuffing it into a shelf. "The windows need new seals."

"No matter," said Penhaligon with a dismissive wave. "It's all factored into our renovation budget."

As they continued discussing the "five-star luxury potential" of the house, I noticed a shadow darting along the wall —small and hunched, with spindly limbs.

Richard was sweating now, his borrowed flannel shirt damp at the collar. He herded the men toward the billiards room, stepping carefully over another salt line, which Montfort promptly scuffed with the heel of his gleaming shoe. The three of them paused in the doorway as a low moan drifted from the depths of the house. It started softly, then swelled to a keening wail that made my teeth ache.

"What," asked Penhaligon, "is that sound?"

"Pipes," said Richard, just as Montfort said, "The wind."

They eyed each other. "The plumbing is Victorian," Richard added. "Very temperamental. Let's have a drink, shall we?"

He strode to the sideboard, hands trembling slightly as he poured two fingers of brandy from a crystal decanter and tossed it back with a wince. It seemed to steady his nerves. "The house has a few . . . eccentricities," he managed, passing snifters around. "Some say it's haunted, but personally, I've never noticed anything unusual."

I let this absurd remark pass. In fact, I was wholeheartedly rooting for the boggart. Montfort knew something was off, but he was determined not to let it scuttle his deal.

"All part of the ambiance of Ravencroft Hall!" he declared, raising his glass. "The oddities are a selling point, wouldn't you say?"

Blight and Penhaligon exchanged a glance. "To a degree," Blight conceded. "As long as it doesn't get out of hand. There's no profit in scaring people away before they've spent their money."

I sipped my brandy and froze. There, perched on the decorative molding, was the boggart—a wiry, grey-skinned creature with black button eyes and a mouth stretched in a rictus of malice. As I watched, it picked up an inkwell and grinned with a mouth of pointy teeth.

Richard coughed loudly. "The library connects to the billiards room and the ballroom," he said, his voice too high. "It would make an excellent space for private events. And that concludes our tour, gentlemen."

"But we've scarcely seen half of the ground floor!" Mr. Penhaligon objected.

"You can come back another time," Richard said. "But I've just remembered, I have another appointment."

"A potential buyer?" Montfort demanded. "I thought we had an exclusive listing."

The boggart began to tip the inkwell above Mr. Blight's head. Richard's jaw set. His dark eyes flashed with fury. The fingers of his left hand gave a strange spasm and he muttered something under his breath. My ears popped with a rush of air and the boggart vanished. A look of surprise crossed Richard's face, but he swiftly regained his composure.

"I'll be in touch, gentlemen," he said, steering them back to the foyer.

"Delightful property," Blight declared, mopping sweat from his brow. "Absolutely unique."

"We'll need to do extensive renovations," Penhaligon declared, "but the bones are there."

Montfort managed a wan smile. "I look forward to drawing up the paperwork. You won't sell it out from under us, I hope?"

Richard muttered reassurances. It was obvious he couldn't get them out the door fast enough. I watched from the window as they drove away in a flurry of gravel, Montfort's blond toupee gleaming until the curve of the drive swallowed them.

Richard sagged against the banister. "Well," he said, "that was dreadful. I thought for certain the boggart would murder them outright."

I gave him a chilly smile. "Perhaps it's saving its best for next time. Odd how it just vanished before the final trick. You didn't have anything to do with that, did you?"

Richard glared. "How could I? You've seen how I'm at the vile creature's mercy." He drew a deep breath. "You despise them, don't you? Blight and Penhaligon?"

"Any thinking human would," I replied, adding spitefully, "But you can do whatever you want. It's your property."

He studied me, jaw ticking. "That's just it. I never asked for this burden. My parents were traitors. They abandoned me without a backward glance. Why should I preserve anything they valued?"

I bit my tongue, remembering his awful childhood. "You could at least try to make peace with the boggart," I said in a gentler tone.

Richard only gave a bitter laugh. We lapsed into silence.

After a while, I went to the billiards room, found the

decanter of brandy, and brought it back. We sat on the staircase and passed it between us.

"Richard?" I ventured.

He looked up.

"Are you any closer to finding the thing you're looking for?"

He hesitated. "No." He took a long pull of brandy. "Would you like to know what it is?"

"You don't have to tell me—"

His dark eyes settled on me. "We might disagree, but I trust you, Kitty. You're the only person who's been kind to me in . . . years, actually."

Guilt prickled. I'd been on the fence about whether to help him find the heirloom or hide it from him forever, but meeting Blight and Penhaligon had cinched it for me. I had to stop them by any means necessary.

"It's a moonstone amulet," Richard said. "On a silver chain. It's the key to the family's power, or so my parents said, though I'm not quite sure how." He shook his head. "I don't want the power. I don't want any of it. I just want the sale to go through, and to be free."

I nodded slowly. "I'll help search, if you like."

He gave me a searching look. "Thank you. And I . . . I'll think about all you've said. Perhaps we can find another solution."

It wasn't exactly victory, but perhaps it was progress. And if the magic of Ravencroft was going to end, I'd at least see it through to the last day.

11

CANDLES IN THE DARK

The search for the moonstone amulet began in earnest the following day. Still, Richard's trust only extended so far. Now that I knew his secret, he never let me wander alone through the labyrinthine corridors of Ravencroft Hall.

The house itself shifted like a slumbering beast, staircases appearing where none had been before, doors opening onto rooms that hadn't existed yesterday. Richard explained that the original architect had gone mad halfway through construction, and successive generations had taken this as an artistic motif.

"We need a system," he announced that first morning, "otherwise we'll waste time covering the same ground twice."

Richard still wore the gamekeeper's attire since his own clothes had never turned up. I privately thought flannel and tweed suited him far better than his London suits, but I didn't dare say so.

He spread a floor plan across the kitchen table, weighing down the corners with salt and pepper shakers. I leaned over his shoulder, catching a whiff of tweed and warm male skin.

101

"Bold of you to assume the rooms will stay where they're meant to be," I said.

Richard's brow furrowed. "The nursery moved quite often, I do remember that. Some days it was next to the music room, others between the apiary and the oubliette."

"There's an indoor apiary?" I arched a brow. "And a secret dungeon? Which I presume is worse than the regular dungeon?"

He nodded gravely. "Far worse. I fell through the ceiling hole once chasing a marble. Thank God Gilcarren found me and hauled me out."

"Gilcarren?"

A faint breeze ruffled the floor plan. Richard glanced around nervously. "One of the servants." He tapped his map. "Let's start with the attic. I only got halfway through the search last time. My parents would have hidden the amulet somewhere safe but accessible."

Richard armed himself with an ancient battery torch, and I carried a candle stub in a saucer. We spent the morning combing through the attic again, this time with a thoroughness that bordered on archeological.

"I'm not sure what's more alarming," I remarked, flipping through a folder of brittle receipts, "the amount your ancestors spent on French cheese, or the number of military-grade sabers they ordered in 1820."

"Don't judge them too harshly," said Richard. "They were locked in a feud with the wizards of Bohemia and the Camembert was a matter of morale."

We shared a laugh. Richard was growing less formal, and I caught a glimmer of what he might have been like if his life hadn't gone so spectacularly off the rails at age ten.

He was methodical, I'll give him that. He checked every loose floorboard, every off-kilter joint in the ancient beams.

I kept an eye out for the boggart, but it seemed content to lurk at the edge of sight, darting into shadows whenever I turned my head.

"Tell me about this amulet," I said as we pawed through mouldering hatboxes. "How big is it?"

Richard hesitated, wiping dust from his forehead with the back of his wrist. "The centerpiece is a moonstone the size of a robin's egg, set in silver filigree."

"Well, that helps," I said, poking at an old mouse's nest. "Sort of."

When we finished with the attic, we moved on to the servants' quarters. They had been left untouched since the days when the Hall was fully staffed. In one room, a perfectly preserved bellboard hung on the wall, still wired to every guest room in the house. Richard pressed a button at random, and somewhere above us a muted clang answered back.

"It must have been something to grow up with an army of servants at your command," I said.

Richard shrugged. Clearly, he took this fact of his existence for granted. "My mother gave me free rein to roam the estate, though I wasn't permitted to visit the village. I spent a lot of time in the Wild Wood."

This surprised me. "Did you? But it's dangerous."

"Not to Ravencrofts," he replied with a dry laugh. "What about you? Were you always fascinated by faeries?"

"They were just . . . there," I said. "Nan says I could spot the difference between brownies and pixies by the time I was four. Only because they let me see them. The Fair Folk are particular about which mortals they reveal themselves to."

He eyed me curiously. "How *do* you manage the walking tours?"

I pulled an apple from my pocket and bit into it. "The

Folk and I have a deal. The tourists leave gifts and the faeries permit a quick glimpse. If they're in the mood. No hard feelings either way."

"I knew I'd hired an expert," he declared. "You're far more than a tour guide, Kitty. You're an . . . ambassador to the fae."

This was generous of him, though the only faerie we encountered in our search was the boggart, whose campaign of terror continued unabated. It upped the ante by stacking the furniture in towering, precarious heaps. Richard acquired a collection of bruises defusing these hazards.

"Just tell it you're sorry," I advised, as I dabbed iodine on a scrape.

"I haven't done anything to apologise for," he muttered. "God's teeth, that stings!"

"Stubborn, both of you," I said, clucking my tongue. "Someone's got to make a start."

"Well, it won't be me," he said with a wince. "Why did I let you use iodine? It's medieval!"

He had beautiful hands, with well-formed, strong fingers. I told him this as I stuck a plaster on his wrist.

"I took piano lessons for years," he admitted.

"Play something for me!" I said, clapping my hands in delight. "We haven't searched the music room yet."

"I haven't in years, but . . ." A crooked grin. "For you, Kitty."

Rain pattered against the conservatory windows as Richard sat before the grand piano and tested a few keys, the black lid glimmering in the candlelight without a speck of dust.

"It's still in tune," he said with a note of wonder.

That surprised me. It had to be the boggart; perhaps the creature was protective of the Hall after all—or the memories it contained of happier days.

"What shall you play?" I asked.

He studied the sheet music on the ledge. "Bach's Piano Concerto No. 3," he said quietly. "It was my mother's favourite."

His fingers hovered above the keys for a breath, then descended. The opening chords were wobbly, but soon grew clean and sure-footed, weaving through the air. Richard leaned into the rhythm, shoulders swaying slightly, eyes half-closed.

My pulse quickened as the music built and turned, intricate as clockwork yet warm and alive. It sounded like silver birds taking flight. Like moonlight spilling through a casement. A sweet melancholy came over me.

Then, impossibly, other instruments joined in—the dark timbre of cellos, the bright answering voices of violins. I wanted to run out into the rain and dance. To spin in fevered circles on the wet grass. I gripped the lid of the piano as the music swept through me like a wind from the Wild Wood, hot and cold at the same time.

When the final notes faded, I stared at him. Either I was going mad, or Richard had just performed magic.

His eyes opened, slightly glazed. "How was that? I'm a bit rusty."

"Marvelous," I replied with a dry throat. "Thank you."

He drew a short, sharp breath, like a man awakening from a dream. "Let's get to it then, shall we?"

I debated telling him what I'd heard, but sensed he would not take it well. "*Carpe diem*," I agreed with a wan smile.

AFTER HOURS OF FRUITLESS SEARCHING ON THE SECOND DAY, we retreated to the kitchen, where I laid out a feast of savory ploughman's pie, Victoria sponge cupcakes filled with raspberry jam, and tart apples Layla had picked at the orchard. Richard sank into a chair.

"I never thought it would be this difficult," he admitted. "The Hall is enormous, and every room seems designed to hide things."

"The old families built these houses with secrets in mind," I said, pouring two glasses of lemonade. "Priest holes during the Reformation, smuggler's caches during the wars. Nan says the Ravencrofts were always particularly clever about such things."

Richard accepted the glass with a grateful nod. "What's your Nan like? You mentioned she sailed the world?"

And just like that, the conversation shifted. I found myself telling him about the time she and my grandfather outran pirates off the coast of Borneo, and how she'd taught herself to tie seventeen different knots by the time she was twelve.

"She sounds remarkable," Richard said, smiling over the rim of his lemonade. "You must take after her."

The compliment warmed me. "Hardly. I've never been further than London."

"But you want to travel?"

"Nan talks about seeing the Northern Lights. We're saving up for it."

His expression turned thoughtful. "I'd like to travel too. Not just for pleasure—there's so much medical knowledge in other cultures. Remedies and techniques we've never considered."

"Is that why you became a doctor?" I asked. "To pioneer new treatments?"

"Partly." He fidgeted with his glass. "Mostly, I want to do

some good in the world. Prove I can be useful, despite my . . . background."

I understood; he'd spent his life trying to distance himself from his parents' reputation, and medicine was as far from dark wizardry as one could get.

"So you plan to open a private practice in London?" I asked.

"It's not as mercenary as it sounds," he said quickly. "I want to help people, not just the wealthy ones. But I also want to pay off my debts and maybe take a holiday now and then." He gave me a long look. "What would you do if you had a windfall?"

"Buy Ravencroft Hall," I said without hesitation, "and keep it just the way it is. Though I don't think that would be enough to save us. The Hall is just a building. Without a Ravencroft living here, the magic would still fade."

Richard looked uncomfortable. "I'd sign over the deed if I could, but I haven't a farthing except what the house is worth."

I forced a smile. "Then I'd settle for a new pair of Wellies. Mine are getting leaky."

"Now that I can help with," he said, brightening.

Richard presented me with a thick envelope sealed with black wax. "Your first week's pay," he said. "And there will be a bonus if we find the amulet."

I considered making a joke about bribes, but thought better of it. Instead, I opened the envelope and peered inside. It was stuffed with crisp twenty-pound notes—far more than I'd ever seen excepting the till at Sugar & Sprites during the holiday rush.

"This is too much," I protested, but he shook his head.

"You've earned it." Richard eyed me seriously. "It would be awful to search this place alone. By my reckoning, you've saved me from at least two nervous breakdowns this week."

We had a chuckle over that, and I tried to forget that my life was on the verge of being auctioned off to the highest bidder.

"So," he said, after the raspberry cupcakes had been eaten. "Do you have a partner, Kitty?"

I choked on my last sip of lemonade. "Ah . . . no, not really."

He studied me, his eyes warm. "I'm surprised to hear that."

Well, you see, Richard, I'm still in love with the fae prince I met when I was seven, so I don't really date mortal men.

"Small village," I managed. "It's awkward when you remember all the boys throwing bogeys at you in primary school." I paused and gazed into the middle distance. "Did I just say that aloud?"

He burst out laughing. "I'm afraid you did. But I can sympathise. Not many women care to get mixed up with a Ravencroft."

It's awful of me, but I was glad he didn't have a glamorous fiancé tucked away in London. "That bad, is it? Even after twenty years?"

"The tabloids have a long memory," he said darkly. "They keep doing anniversary specials. Where are they now? That sort of thing."

I nodded. "Where *are* they now? If you don't mind my asking."

Richard sighed. "My parents have been the permanent houseguests of a Carpathian wizard family, old friends of theirs. I mean, the last I heard at least."

He lapsed into a contemplative silence and I kicked myself for broaching the worst subject possible. The dead air was finally broken by the boggart blowing a loud raspberry from somewhere up near the ceiling.

At least, that's what I hoped it was.

AFTER LUNCH, WE TACKLED THE LIBRARY, CHECKING BEHIND the shelves for hidden catches or compartments. There were hundreds of beautiful gilded volumes of the classics, as well as histories and scientific journals, but after a while I noticed something odd.

"There are no books on magic or the fae," I said. "Not one. It's just a boring old mundane library. Don't you find that peculiar?"

"Now *there's* a relative word," Richard said dryly. "But you're right, Kitty. It's because there's another library, a secret one, hidden behind a door somewhere in this bloody house, but I have no idea how to access it."

"Your parents never—"

"No. It was forbidden."

"What if the amulet is hidden in this secret library?"

"Then we'll find the secret door to the secret library and then we'll find the damned secret amulet," he muttered. "What's so funny? Just keep searching."

To pass the time, Richard told me stories about his grueling schedule in medical school, the caffeine-fueled nights and the terrifying first surgeries.

"I nearly passed out from nerves," he confessed. "The professor took one look at me and said, 'Mr. Ravencroft, if you're going to faint, please do it in the hall where you won't contaminate my operating theatre.'"

I grinned. "What did you do?"

"Locked my knees and stayed upright through sheer stubbornness." He shook his head. "It got easier after that. The human body becomes familiar after a while. Less mysterious."

"Unlike this blasted house," I muttered, rifling through yet another dusty book.

"Indeed." Richard leaned against one of the sliding ladders that ran along the shelves. "What about you? Have you ever considered leaving Little Groating?"

"Not really," I admitted. "Briar and Layla and I go to the cinema in Southlea Cross once a month, when they change the films. And I want to see Svalbard with Nan. But I love it here."

He looked a bit sad and said nothing more.

As the day wore on, I found myself studying Richard when he wasn't looking. The way his brow furrowed and made a little notch above his beaky nose, how his hands moved with nimble precision of a surgeon. By evening, we were both filthy and exhausted, having discovered nothing of consequence except three lost chess pieces, a cache of smuggled French wine from the Napoleonic Wars, and a collection of letters in cipher that Richard said were probably from his great-uncle's espionage days.

The next morning dawned grey and drizzly, perfect weather for staying indoors. We moved our search to the west wing, where the family bedrooms sprawled across the second floor. Richard seemed more relaxed, even making jokes about the garish wallpaper in what had been his third cousin Theodora's room.

"She was colour-blind," he explained as we stared at the violently clashing floral prints. "No one had the heart to tell her the truth. My father said visiting her room was like being trapped inside a nightmarish garden."

"Was she one of the nice ones?" I asked, lying on my side to peer under the four-poster bed.

"Oh, terribly nice. She gave the best presents—always extravagant, always completely impractical. When I was six, she gifted me a live peacock. The wretched bird terrorised the household for months. It had a particular hatred for my father's valet and would lie in wait behind curtains."

The mental image of a small Richard chasing a vengeful peacock through these grand corridors made me laugh aloud.

"Do you have any pictures from when you were a child?" I asked. "Family photo albums?"

I'll admit, I was curious about his parents. In the tabloid spreads, they always had their heads down or hidden behind umbrellas carried by their solicitors. I wondered what they looked like, but I also thought that seeing pictures of himself from happier times might make Richard reconsider. Desperate, I suppose, but I was willing to try anything.

He snorted. "Albums? No. My parents are not sentimental people. Besides which, there are spells you can cast on a photograph that affect the real person."

"Ah. Never mind then."

We worked through bedrooms, dressing rooms, sitting rooms and boudoirs. Also, the famed apiary—which had no bees, thank god, just a pair of ancient exercise bikes. Richard filled the hours with stories about his life with the Earl of Kilmarnock, who had taken him as a ward after his parents were sent away.

"The old man was as stiff as his collars," he said, demonstrating with an exaggerated posture that made his borrowed shirt strain across his shoulders. "He would write formal notes to his own wife summoning her to his study to discuss

God knows what. The poor woman never looked happy when she came out."

"Why didn't he just . . . ask her?" I wondered, checking beneath the cushion of a window seat for hidden compartments.

"Everything had to go through the proper channels." Richard affected a pompous voice. "Tradition, young Ravencroft, is what separates us from the beasts of the field."

I snorted. "You must have driven him mad."

A shadow crossed Richard's face. "I tried very hard not to." He cleared his throat. "Anyway, I learned to play by his rules. It was easier that way."

I felt curious about his upbringing, but instinct told me to tread carefully. "Did the earl have children of his own?"

"Three daughters, all grown and married by the time I arrived." His voice lightened. "They visited at Christmas with their husbands and broods of children. Complete chaos. It was my favourite time of year, when the house would come alive. The earl always retreated to his study with a bottle of scotch until it was over."

"He sounds like an unpleasant man."

"I'll put it this way," Richard said darkly. "Boarding school in Scotland with boys who despised me was a welcome reprieve."

He said nothing more and I let the matter drop. That night, we ate dinner by candlelight, which was partly romantic but mainly because the boggart had shorted out the electricity again. The French wine had turned to vinegar, so we dug out some pear brandy. Richard asked more about Nan and our planned trip to see the Northern Lights.

"I've heard they're spectacular," he said. "Like curtains of green fire in the sky."

"Nan says the Aurora sings sometimes, too, though she might be embellishing." I smiled fondly.

Richard leaned forward, elbows on the table. "You're very close to her."

"She raised me," I admitted. "My parents would sweep in to lavish me with gifts, then vanish again for months."

"And now?"

"I get postcards. They're in India, I think." I shrugged, trying to seem nonchalant. "It's fine. I have Nan, and the Deens. The whole village, really. They're all my family."

"Still," he said softly. "It can't have been easy."

Something in his tone—understanding without pity—made my throat tighten. "No," I agreed. "But I imagine you know something about that."

Our eyes met. The moment stretched, intimate and strangely comfortable.

"I've been thinking," Richard said.

My heart skipped. "Oh?"

"I'm not making any guarantees," he added quickly. "But perhaps there's a way to protect the magical aspects of the estate while still allowing me to move on."

It was just what I'd wanted, yet I found myself not as happy as I ought to be. "Such as?"

"I don't know yet." He gazed into the middle distance. "But I'm considering all options."

Hardly a promise, but it was more than I'd gotten from him since Montfort's visit. Speaking of which . . .

"Have you heard from Montfort since he brought those awful men round?" I asked.

Richard grimaced. "He's left three messages at the inn. I haven't returned them."

"Good," I said with feeling.

He gave me a sidelong glance. "Why are you helping me, Kitty? It's hardly in your interest."

The question was too direct to dodge. "Because I still hope to change your mind," I admitted. "But also because . . . I like you, Richard. More than I expected to."

A faint flush coloured his cheeks. "You're not terrible company yourself." He hesitated. "Do you really think the magic will disappear if I leave?"

I took a moment to consider my answer. "What matters is that you're here now, and you have a chance to do the right thing. That's all anyone can hope for, isn't it?"

He smiled a bit grimly. "You have more faith in me than I deserve."

We sat together until the candles burned down, listening to the wind rattle down the chimney. By the time I walked home, the sky was dark and the air tasted of frost. I clutched the envelope to my chest, feeling a little bit richer, but not in the way I expected.

These three days had shown me a different side of Richard—funny, thoughtful, wounded but resilient. The more I knew him, the more I wanted to know, and the less I wanted him to leave.

Which made my earlier decision to find the amulet and hide it even more morally dubious. If I truly cared for him, shouldn't I help him find what he needed? But if I did that, he would go back to London, and the magic would fade, and the Wild Wood would wither . . .

I pushed the thought aside. Tomorrow was another day. Perhaps by then, I'd know what was right.

When I reached the gargoyles, I looked back at Raven-croft Hall. For the first time in years, there was candlelight shining in every window.

1 2

A TURN FOR THE WORSE

The following day's efforts produced nothing. By nightfall, Richard was visibly frustrated, running his hands through his hair until it stood on end. The boggart had made off with his boots, forcing him to wear his great-aunt Theodora's fluffy pink bedroom slippers. Luckily, she had large feet.

"It has to be here somewhere," he muttered.

I sat on the floor of Richard's childhood bedroom, now a mausoleum draped in sheets, watching him tap methodically along the baseboards for hollow spaces. My own patience, which Nan said was my least evident virtue, was wearing thin.

"Could your parents have taken the amulet with them to Romania?" I asked.

He shook his head. "It cannot pass beyond the boundaries of the estate."

"The boundaries?" I exclaimed. "Then the necklace might not be in the house at all!"

"We'll start on the outbuildings," he retorted, black eyes flashing.

Something in his tone—bitter resignation and fury mixed —snapped my restraint.

"You look like a lunatic," I said, "crawling around on your hands and knees, tap-tap-tapping at the walls. It's like Poe's story *The Beating Heart*!"

Richard gave an unhinged laugh. "At least a corpse is large, Kitty. Easy to find."

I shook my head. "What exactly is so terrible about this place that you're desperate to escape it? Most people would be grateful for such an inheritance!"

The moment the words left my mouth, I knew I'd made a mistake. Richard's face went rigid, then icy.

"Most people," he said, his voice quiet but sharp as a blade, "don't have parents who tried to depose the queen of England."

I swallowed hard. "Look, I didn't mean—"

He stood, brushing dust from his trousers with jerky movements. "When I was shipped off to Scotland, the other boys knew who I was. They were waiting for me. 'Traitors' chick, hatched from the black nest.' That's what they called me. Or simply *Cravencroft*. Every day for eight years."

His eyes were flint-dark now. "My first night at Bromfield, four older boys dragged me from my bed and locked me in a storage cupboard. They said it was practice for when I followed in my parents' footsteps and was thrown in the Tower of London."

My stomach knotted. "Richard, I'm sorry, I didn't know—"

"I'll spare you the worst of it, but the masters looked the other way. Why wouldn't they? My father's picture was all over the papers, being led away in chains." A muscle in his

116

jaw ticked. "I wrote to my parents every week for the first year. Then once a month. Then on holidays. I never received a single reply. Not one. So forgive me if I don't share your romantic attachment to this house. To me, it's just a painful reminder of everything I lost."

I rubbed my forehead. We were both exhausted. "Look, I understand that you're angry—"

"You understand nothing," he cut in. "You've lived in the same village your whole life, surrounded by people who adore you. Yes, your parents were distant, but at least they didn't disgrace you. They didn't make your name synonymous with betrayal."

That stung, and my own temper flared. "So your solution is to sell everything to a man who'll pave over the Wild Wood and turn this house into a tacky hotel? You'd punish us all for something that's not our fault?"

"It wasn't my fault either!" he shouted, and I swore I heard the glass panes in the windows rattle. "I didn't ask to be born a Ravencroft! I didn't ask for magic or boggarts or—or responsibilities to a land I barely remember!"

"But you *are* a Ravencroft," I insisted, rising to my feet. "And this land is part of you, whether you like it or not. You can feel it—I know you can!"

"What I feel," he said, eyes blazing, "is an overwhelming desire to be free of all of this. The moment I turned thirty and inherited this place, I swore I would sell it and start fresh. Build a life that has nothing to do with wizardry or scandal."

"Even if it means destroying everything your family built?" I demanded. "Even if it means the faeries will leave us?"

"The rest of the world manages just fine without magic," he said coldly.

I stared at him, this man I'd begun to care for, and saw only the stubborn set of his jaw. "So that's it then? You'll just walk away? Let Montfort and his vultures pick over the bones?"

"I never claimed to be a hero, Kitty." His voice had gone flat. "I'm a doctor. I save people I can see, injuries I can treat. Not ancient pacts I never agreed to."

The unfairness of it all lodged like a sharp stone in my heart. "Your parents might have made mistakes, bad ones, but at least they knew what mattered."

As soon as I said it, I knew I'd crossed a line. Richard went still. "Please go," he said hoarsely.

Tears stung my eyes. I glared at him.

"You'll never understand, and I am tired of this pointless debate." His voice was calm, but his hands trembled at his sides. "I'll pay you for the next two weeks, but your services are no longer needed, Miss Boot."

Part of me wanted to shout at him, to make him see reason, but the raw hurt in his eyes stopped me. I'd pushed too hard, and now I'd lost him.

"Fine," I said. "I'll go. But this isn't over, Richard. You can't just erase who you are."

He turned away from me, shoulders rigid. "We'll see."

I stormed out of the room, down the grand staircase, past the upside-down portraits and headless suits of armor. The boggart was nowhere to be seen—perhaps it knew better than to poke its pointy nose into our row.

Outside, the sky was dark and starless. I marched down the drive, emotions churning. How dare he dismiss everything I held dear? How could he be so blind and callous?

But beneath my anger, I felt an ache of sympathy. A boy— small, frightened, bearing a name that had become a curse— alone in a strange place, waiting for letters that never came.

No wonder he wanted nothing to do with his inheritance. In his mind, Ravencroft Hall wasn't a birthright but a prison—the thing that had defined and confined him his entire life.

The rain caught me halfway to the village, fat drops soaking through my coat and plastering my hair to my face. I barely noticed. My mind was too full of the pain in Richard's eyes and the awful certainty that I'd just made everything worse.

The Dancing Toadstool was quiet when I arrived, dripping water all over the carpet. Mrs. Deen appeared from the kitchen with Barbarossa in her arms, absently stroking his massive head.

"There you are," she said, her voice low and worried. "We've been trying to reach you. Dr. Singer's taken a turn. His cough is much worse, and he's running a fever."

My heart sank. "Where is he?"

"We've moved him into Room 2. Nan's with him now."

I hung up my sodden coat and followed her down the hall to the guest chamber overlooking the garden. Inside, the curtains were drawn, and the air smelled of eucalyptus and camphor. Nan sat beside the bed, her silver head bent over a basin of steaming water. In the bed, Dr. Singer lay propped up on pillows, his chest rising and falling with labored breaths.

"Kitty," Nan said, looking up with relief. "Good, you're here. Could you fetch more ice from the kitchen? His fever's climbing."

I nodded, but paused to look at Dr. Singer. His face was flushed, his usually neat white hair damp with sweat. Even in sleep, his breathing sounded painful.

Dr. Singer's wife had died a few years ago. Nan sometimes called him "that young dandy" since he was "only eighty-seven." He was madly in love with her, everyone knew it. Nan was sweet on him, too. She said his Bay Rum Brilliantine Hair Tonic reminded her of a tropical beach.

"Has the doctor from Southlea Cross been called?" I asked, keeping my voice low.

"She was off attending a birth in the countryside," Mrs. Deen replied from the doorway. "Her assistant doesn't know when she'll be back."

"Damnit." I glanced at Dr. Singer. "Not that he hasn't been wonderful, but the poor man deserves to retire in peace. What do we do now that he's ill?"

For the first time in my life, I envied the villages farther from the Wild Wood that had emergency care services.

"The cold's settled into his lungs," Nan said grimly. "He's had it before, two winters ago, but not this bad." She dipped a cloth in the basin and wrung it out, placing it on Dr. Singer's forehead. "I should have made him stay here sooner."

"It's not your fault," I said, squeezing her thin shoulder. "I'll get that ice."

When I returned with the bowl of ice chips, Nan was coaxing Dr. Singer to take a spoonful of syrup. He swallowed with difficulty, then fell back against the pillows, exhausted by the small effort.

"Kitty," he wheezed, noticing me. His attempt at a smile dissolved into a coughing fit that left him gasping.

"Save your strength," Nan admonished gently.

I sat on the edge of the bed, taking Dr. Singer's hand. It felt hot and dry.

"We'll have you right as rain in no time," I said with a confidence I didn't feel. "Just think of all the candies you'll be handing out once you're back on your feet."

His rheumy eyes crinkled at the corners. "Saved the last one for you," he murmured, gesturing weakly toward the nightstand.

I looked over and saw a lavender mothball sitting on a handkerchief. A lump rose in my throat.

"Thank you," I managed.

Nan's gaze was knowing, her hands steady as she crushed herbs for a poultice. "How was your day with young Lord Ravencroft?" she asked, too casually.

"Terrible," I admitted, keeping my voice down so Dr. Singer could rest. "We had a fight. I pressured him about staying, and he . . . he told me to leave."

Her gaze softened. "Ah, Kitty. The heart can be stubborn when it's wounded."

"It's not just his heart," I said. "It's his entire life. He was bullied at school, Nan. Tormented for years because of his parents. I don't think he ever recovered."

"Few do," she said simply. "Childhood scars go bone-deep."

I rubbed my eyes. "It feels like everything is falling apart."

Nan's hand found mine. "Nothing lasts forever, my love. Not the good, not the bad. All we can do is tend what's in front of us and trust that spring follows even the hardest winter."

I tried to take comfort in her words, but as the rain lashed the windows and Dr. Singer fought for breath in the quiet room, all I could think was that some winters lasted too long, and some things, once lost, could never be recovered.

THE HOUSE CALL

B y the following evening, Dr. Singer's fever had climbed, and his breathing was a wet rattle that made me wince. Nan refused to leave his side except to brew more eucalyptus tea, her face pinched with worry.

Ambrose Montfort appeared once, asking about lunch, but I showed him my teeth and he scuttled back to his room like a cockroach fleeing the light.

We needed a doctor—and soon. As night deepened and the rain lashed against the windows with renewed vigor, I knew there was only one option.

"I'll go get Richard," I said, breaking the heavy silence that had fallen over the kitchen.

Mrs. Deen looked up from the pot of broth she was stirring. "Will he come? After yesterday—"

"He'll come," I said, certain of this despite his temper. I pushed my uneaten stew aside. "There's been no word from the doctor in Southlea Cross, and we can't wait any longer."

Sir Francis Drake chose that moment to shriek from his

perch near the window, "Man overboard! Too slow, too slow!" For once, his commentary was all too apt.

I slipped into Dr. Singer's room to see Nan before I left. She sat in the same chair as before, her fingers methodically darning a tiny pair of red stockings—though her eyes never left Dr. Singer's face.

"I'm going to fetch Richard," I told her.

Nan set her knitting aside. "It might do him some good to help someone besides himself." She reached over to squeeze my hand. "You're still angry too, I can see it, but you'll swallow your pride for Jacob's sake."

I glanced at Dr. Singer. He'd attended my birth, and those of most people in the village. When he'd listen to my heart with his stethoscope as a child, he'd pretend he heard mice scurrying about. Pitter-patter, pitter-patter, pitter-patter-pat!

"Anyone would," I said.

"Not scoundrels like Montfort," Nan said with a glower. "Now go, before this weather gets worse."

I donned my macintosh and leaky boots and stepped out into the storm. The rain fell in sheets, driven sideways by a wind that delighted in finding every gap in my coat. It was a long, miserable walk to the Hall. Most of the windows were dark, but a soft glow came from what I thought was the library. I imagined Richard, surrounded by dusty tomes, still searching for his blasted amulet.

By the time I reached the front door, my leggings were soaked through and my hands were so numb that it took two attempts to grasp the knocker. It felt like ice against my palm.

Finally, I heard footsteps, and the door swung open. Richard stood there, silhouetted against the warm light from the entry hall. His dark hair was disheveled, as if he'd been running his hands through it.

"Kitty?" He looked genuinely surprised. Then his expression shifted to concern. "Come inside, you look half-drowned—"

"Dr. Singer is ill," I interrupted through chattering teeth. "High f-fever and he c-can't breathe properly."

Richard's face softened. "I'll come at once. Let me fetch my medical bag." He held the door wider. "Please, Kitty."

I stepped across the threshold into blessed heat. He must have finally gotten the ancient furnace to kick on.

"I was going to come down and see you tomorrow," he said sheepishly. "To apologise."

I held his gaze. "You needn't worry about that right now," I said, though part of me warmed at his words. "Dr. Singer—"

"Of course. Does he have a cough?" Richard shouted over his shoulder, long legs already bounding up the staircase.

"Yes, a bad one," I called back. "Nan's been giving him eucalyptus tea and cold compresses, but nothing's helping."

He reappeared a minute later, black bag in hand, clad in an elegant Chesterfield overcoat. It clashed rather violently with his great-aunt Theodora's fluffy pink bedroom slippers, but I refrained from commenting. No doubt she would have approved.

"Where'd you get the coat?" I asked with admiration. "It fits you perfectly."

"It was my father's," he said in toneless voice. "All I could find at short notice."

"Ah."

Richard sighed. "I *am* sorry, Kitty. I said things I shouldn't have."

"True. But so did I."

His dark eyes caught mine. "You were right about some of it. I've been selfish." He grabbed an umbrella from its stand. "But that's not important now. Tell me more about Dr. Singer's symptoms."

I detailed everything I'd observed—the rattle in his chest, the fever that spiked in the evenings, the way he struggled for each breath. Richard listened intently, asking occasional questions about onset and progression that I answered as best I could.

His Mini was parked out front. He held the umbrella over me as I got in, then slid behind the wheel, tossed his bag onto the back seat, and started the engine. It sputtered to life on the second try, a small mercy.

We rolled down the drive in silence, the wipers beating a frantic tempo against the windshield. The headlamps carved twin tunnels through the darkness, and I found myself gripping the edge of my seat as Richard navigated the curving road at his usual Formula One pace. (Yes, I live in a village with no internet, but I do spend every weekend chatting with tourists. You learn all sorts of things that way.)

At last, the lights of the High Street appeared ahead. We skidded up to the Dancing Toadstool and Richard cut the engine.

"I'll do everything I can," he said. "But if needed, I'll drive him to the nearest hospital."

The strain of the last two days came to a head. My eyes grew hot and watery. "Thank you," I said, turning away.

Richard gathered his bag from the back seat and we dashed for the door. Mrs. Deen met us in the entry, her usually serene face taut with concern.

"It's very kind of you to come," she said to Richard.

"We've moved him to one of the ground floor guest rooms, just there." She pointed down the hallway.

Richard nodded and strode off, already in doctor mode. I started to follow, but Mrs. Deen caught my arm.

"Did you two make peace?" she asked quietly.

I gave a half-shrug. "We've called a truce. For Dr. Singer's sake."

She squeezed my hand. "That's something."

I went to the kitchen to put on the kettle, stripping off my sodden coat and hanging it by the fire. By the time I'd changed into dry clothes, Richard had been with Dr. Singer for nearly twenty minutes. I carried a tray with three steaming mugs down the hall, nudging the door open with my hip.

The small room was quiet except for Dr. Singer's wheezes. Nan sat in her usual chair, her eyes fixed on Richard as he listened to the old man's chest with his stethoscope. His face was serious, brow furrowed in concentration.

I set the tray on the small table, and Nan reached for my hand, squeezing it hard. Richard straightened up and hung the stethoscope around his neck.

"Well?" Nan asked.

"It's pneumonia, as I suspected. His left lung is congested." He opened his bag and began pulling out bottles and instruments. "I'll start him on antibiotics."

"Will he recover?" I asked anxiously.

Richard met my gaze. "At his age, pneumonia can be quite serious, but I'd prefer not to move him in this weather. I'll do everything I can here first." He offered a reassuring smile. "I'm not leaving until he's stable."

"Thank you," Nan said, her voice wavering.

Richard's expression softened. "You've taken good care of

him, Mrs. Boot. The eucalyptus was exactly right. Now let me take over for a while."

He turned back to his patient, rolling up his sleeves. Despite everything—the argument, the hurt, the uncertain future of the Hall—in that moment, I was fiercely glad that Richard Ravencroft had come home.

I WATCHED RICHARD CHECK DR. SINGER'S VITALS AGAIN, listen to his breathing and peer into his throat with a small light. His hands moved with gentle efficiency, nothing like the man who'd been flinging books across the library in frustration the day before.

"Deep breath in, if you can," Richard ordered, stethoscope pressed against the old man's back. "And out again, slowly."

Dr. Singer complied, then descended into a coughing fit that left him wheezing. Richard supported him through it, one hand on his shoulder.

"You've had quite enough excitement for one day, Dr. Singer," he said, helping him back against the pillows. "Though I must say, your heart sounds strong enough for a man half your age."

Richard winked at Nan, who gave him a devilish half-smile.

"We fellow practitioners must stick together," Richard added. "Mrs. Boot, would you mind fetching a glass of water? And perhaps another pillow?"

Nan looked reluctant to leave but nodded and slipped from the room. Richard turned back to his patient, his expression growing more serious.

"It's pneumonia," he told Dr. Singer, "but we've caught it in time."

"Thought as much," Dr. Singer managed. "Getting too old for this nonsense."

"Nonsense indeed," Richard said firmly. "You'll need to rest completely. No midnight house calls for at least two weeks."

He rummaged in his bag and produced a vial and syringe. I watched as he drew up a precise measure of cloudy liquid, tapping the syringe to eliminate air bubbles.

"As I'm sure you've guessed," he said to Dr. Singer, "we'll start with a broad-spectrum antibiotic." He swabbed the old doctor's arm with alcohol. "Small pinch now."

Dr. Singer hardly flinched as the needle went in. Richard disposed of it carefully in a small container from his bag, then jotted in a small notebook.

"I'll leave oral antibiotics with Mrs. Boot, to be taken twice daily," he said. "And I'll be back tomorrow to check on you. If your fever spikes again or your breathing worsens, I want to know immediately."

Nan returned with water and an extra pillow. Richard helped Dr. Singer sit up higher, explaining that it would make breathing easier.

"Keep up the eucalyptus tea, and make sure he drinks plenty of fluids—water, broth, weak tea."

"And whiskey?" asked Dr. Singer hopefully.

"Not until you're off the antibiotics," Richard replied sternly.

Nan shot Dr. Singer a look. "I'll make sure he doesn't sneak off and raid the liquor cabinet."

Richard packed his instruments away and stood. "Try to rest. I'll leave these pills with instructions." He turned to me. "Kitty, could I have a word outside?"

My heart gave a little stutter, but I nodded and followed him into the hallway. The door closed behind us with a soft click. Richard leaned against the wall, looking tired.

"It's not bad news, is it?" I asked, slightly terrified.

"No, nothing like that. I do think he'll recover fully, and I'm grateful you came to get me," he said, his voice low. "You didn't have to, after how I spoke to you."

"Of course I did."

Richard ran a hand through his hair, making it stand up even more wildly. "I owe you an apology. A real one." He met my eyes directly. "I was angry, but not at you. It was my parents, the whole situation. I shouldn't have taken it out on you."

I studied his face—those dark eyes so sincere, the stubborn set of his jaw softened by genuine regret. "It's all right."

"It's not, though," he insisted. "You were only trying to help. And I . . . I've been difficult."

"Well, you're not wrong there," I said, allowing a small smile. "But I understand, Richard. More than you might think. My parents are rather self-absorbed too, just in a different way. They chose celebrity over everything else, including me."

"It leaves a mark, doesn't it? Being second choice."

"A permanent one," I agreed. "But we muddle through."

He nodded, something unspoken passing between us. "Can you forgive me?" he asked, his voice soft.

"Already have," I said, and meant it. "Though if you really want to make it up to me, you could sign over the Hall and all its contents to me right now."

That startled a laugh out of him.

The tension between us dissolved, replaced by something lighter yet somehow deeper. I realised with a small shock how much I'd missed him in just one day.

"Will you be heading back to the Hall tonight?" I asked.

Before he could answer, Mrs. Deen appeared from the kitchen, wiping her hands on her apron. "Absolutely not," she declared. "Dr. Ravencroft, you must stay for supper. It's the least we can do."

"I wouldn't want to impose—"

"Nonsense," she insisted. "I've made my famous turmeric rice Pongal, and Layla's brought over sourdough fresh from the oven. She and Briar are both eager to thank you properly."

Richard glanced at me, a question in his eyes.

"Best not to argue," I advised. "Besides, I think you've earned a hot meal."

"Then I accept with pleasure," he said, a genuine smile warming his face. "I can check on Dr. Singer again later."

"That's settled then," Mrs. Deen beamed. "Come through to the dining room. Everything's nearly ready."

The private dining room glowed with candlelight. Briar was setting down a steaming tureen in the center of the table while Layla arranged glasses. They both looked up as we entered.

"The hero of the hour!" Briar exclaimed. "Is Dr. Singer going to be all right?"

Richard nodded. "With proper care and rest, he should recover fully."

"Thank goodness," Layla said fervently. "We've been so worried."

Nan joined us a few minutes later, reporting that Dr. Singer was sleeping peacefully. We all settled around the table, and for a while, the conversation flowed as easily as the strong, frothy beer Mrs. Deen ordered from Southlea Cross. Richard, looking more relaxed than I'd ever seen him, told amusing stories about London, and in turn listened with interest as Briar described her latest experimental pastry.

I watched him across the table, his face animated in the candlelight. Here, surrounded by warmth and conversation, he seemed like a different person—or perhaps the person he might have been all along, if life had been kinder.

For a moment, I allowed myself to hope that this might be enough to change his mind about Ravencroft Hall, about staying. But it was enough that he was here, passing the butter to Nan and complimenting Mrs. Deen on her excellent chutney. Tomorrow would bring its own troubles. Tonight, we had an unexpected peace in the midst of the storm.

AFTER DINNER, RICHARD AND I LOOKED IN ON DR. SINGER. His fever had dropped a few degrees, and his breathing, while still uneven, had lost that awful wet rattle. Nan's relief was palpable as she fussed with his blankets and tucked the hot water bottle more securely against his feet. Richard checked his patient's vitals once more, nodding with satisfaction at whatever he found.

"He's responding well to the antibiotics," Richard said quietly. "Keep up with the fluids and rest, and I'll return in the morning."

"You're a good man," Nan told him, patting his cheek like she might have done when he was ten. To my surprise, Richard didn't bristle at this; he merely smiled, a touch of colour rising to his face.

Mrs. Deen ushered Layla and Briar out with promises to call if anything changed. They gathered their coats and umbrellas, casting grateful glances at Richard before disappearing into the rainy night. Mrs. Deen herself retired soon after, moving with the stiffness of a woman who had been on her feet all day.

That left Richard and me alone in the common room. He built up the fire while I fetched a bottle of Amaretto cordial and poured us each a dram.

"To Dr. Singer's recovery," I said, raising my glass.

"And to unexpected reunions," Richard added, touching his glass to mine.

We sipped in companionable silence. The cordial was sweet and fiery, warming me from the inside.

"Richard," I said, feeling magnanimous. "I want you to know that whatever happens with Ravencroft Hall—whatever you decide—I hope we can remain friends."

Surprise flickered across his features. "Even if I sell?"

I traced the rim of my glass with one finger, considering. "I won't pretend I'd be happy about it. But I've come to . . . value your company."

Well, *that* sounded horrendously uptight. Like I was a sixteenth -century suitor addressing my child bride.

Yet when his dark eyes met mine, I could see he was touched. Worse, that he could see right through to the tangled mess of feelings I was trying so hard to contain.

"I value your friendship as well, Kitty," he said. "More than you know. And I promise you this—I'll consider everything you've said about the Hall, about my responsibilities. I can't promise what I'll decide, but I won't dismiss it."

"That's all I can ask."

We lapsed into silence again, but it wasn't uncomfortable. The fire popped and hissed. Barbarossa curled up beside the hearth and began to gently knead my stockinged feet with his needle claws. Outside, the rain settled into a gentle, hypnotic drumming.

It occurred to me that for the first time in a week, neither of us was on edge, waiting for the boggart to swoop down and pour a carafe of ice-water over our heads.

As if on cue, at that very moment, a soft clatter came from the kitchen—the splash of soapy water, cupboards opening and closing. This was followed by a loud hiss and yowl. Barbarossa came shooting out the door and streaked up the stairs.

Richard tensed. "Who's that? I thought Mrs. Deen went to bed."

There was no point in lying anymore.

"Nothing to worry about," I assured him. "That's just Quince, the house brownie. He helps keep the inn running smoothly."

"A faerie?" Richard sat up straighter, alarm on his face. "Here?"

I waved my glass. "It's no big deal, honestly. Most of the houses in the village have brownies. Quince has lived here for centuries." I took another sip of Amaretto. "He's quite particular about how things should be arranged, but as long as we leave him a bit of cream and honey, he's happy enough."

"But . . . the growling?"

I chuckled. "Quince does tangle with Barbarossa some-times. Cats can see faeries, you know. They have the eldritch sight, and creatures of the Otherworld can't hide from them. I won't say cats and house brownies are enemies exactly, but the relationship can be . . . fraught, since they're both territo-rial creatures."

Richard's expression shifted from wariness to curiosity. "I

remember brownies from when I was small. We had several at Ravencroft Hall."

"I don't suppose one was called Nettle?" I said. "Quince mentioned the name, but he wouldn't say more."

Richard slapped his knee. "Yes! Nettle used to sneak me hot chocolate when my governess wasn't looking. I wonder if she's still at the Hall? But I haven't seen any brownies there, just that infernal boggart."

He leaned forward, a maniacal light in his eyes I knew all too well. "If I could find Nettle, she might tell me where the amulet is hidden. She knew every nook and cranny of Ravencroft Hall. There's a secret library I've been unable to find."

His expression fell. "Or perhaps she *is* the boggart. Though I can't imagine Nettle turning so malicious." He leapt to his feet. "May I speak to Quince?"

"We can try," I said, setting down my glass. "Though brownies are cagey about the business of other faeries."

I led him into the kitchen. It was spotless, every surface gleaming, every pot hanging just so. At first, I thought Quince had finished his work and retired to his cupboard, but then a small shadow detached itself from behind the flour bin.

"Good evening, Lord Ravencroft," came a gruff little voice. "You've grown bigger since I saw you last."

Quince stood on the counter, a nutcracker hanging at his hip like a rapier. He bowed formally from the waist.

Richard stared, clearly taken aback. "You remember me?"

"The Folk remember all the Ravencrofts," Quince replied, his button-bright eyes gleaming. "Even those who choose to forget us."

I shot Quince a warning look. "Remember when you

mentioned Nettle? Well, Richard thinks she might be able to help him find something important."

Quince's small face grew sombre. "Poor Nettle. A sorry business, that."

"What happened to her?" Richard asked. "Is she the boggart at the Hall?"

Quince hesitated, looking from Richard to me and back again. "It's not my place to speak of such things."

"I beg you," Richard said, "just tell me where to find her."

The heartfelt plea in his voice seemed to sway the little brownie. "She's at the old game warden's cottage," Quince admitted reluctantly. "On the shore of Nelly's Pond."

The mention of the pond sent a shiver through me. Like every other village child who'd made it to adulthood, I'd given Nelly a wide berth my whole life—save for the close brush involving Archie, and that was not by choice.

"We'll go first thing tomorrow," Richard declared heartily. "Will you come along, Kitty?"

I stared at him. "You're wearing the clothes of Nelly's last victim."

"We don't know that for certain," he replied in a tone that struck me as far too casual. "And her pond is part of the estate. I'm not afraid of some aquatic hag."

I shook my head in disbelief. "You're terrified of a *boggart*. Nelly Longarms is a hundred times worse!"

Richard glanced at Quince. "Is it safe?"

The brownie's laugh held no humour. "No place worth going is ever entirely safe. But if you want Nettle, you'll have to pay a visit. Just don't venture too close to the water."

With that cheerful warning, he scurried off to his cupboard.

"I suppose you'll go alone if I don't agree," I said sourly.

Richard drained his cordial. "I must."

"Good grief. I ought to let her eat you."

"But you won't," he said happily. "You're my faerie ambassador."

My head began to pound. Too much Amaretto. "As I recall, you fired me yesterday," I reminded him. "I'm going to bed."

An avian cackle came from the common room. "Stir it slow, love—slow!" shrieked Sir Francis Drake in a thick German accent. "One sip for sleep . . . two for eternal silence!"

NETTLE

The next morning dawned clear and bright. I found Richard looking in on Dr. Singer, whose fever had broken during the night. We were both relieved to see him sitting up and sipping broth, though I was less enthusiastic about our planned visit to Nelly's Pond.

"You look terrible, Kitty," Richard observed with maddening cheerfulness, passing me a steaming mug.

"Bad dreams," I muttered, dumping three sugar cubes into the coffee and drowning them with cream. I took a sip, feeling better immediately. A strong cup of coffee works its own magic.

"Ah, I'm sorry," Richard said. "Well, best we get it over with, don't you think?"

I sighed and took my coat from the hook. At least it had stopped raining, and the sky was that vivid, freshly-washed blue that came after a storm. The village was already awake and bustling with activity. Mrs. Whittlesby swept her front walk, her two canes propped against the wall. She gave us a wave as we passed, and I knew by lunchtime, the entire village would be speculating about why Kitty Boot and Lord Ravencroft were walking toward Nelly's Pond.

Or we'd be dead by then and they'd be talking about the tragedy.

We turned onto the north lane, leaving the village proper behind. The countryside opened up around us, rolling green hills dotted with grazing sheep. In the distance, Ravencroft Hall brooded on its hilltop. To our left, stone walls crisscrossed the landscape, remnants of field boundaries set down centuries ago.

The breeze carried the scent of damp earth and sun-warmed grass. In the hedgerows, late wildflowers still bloomed—purple knapweed and the occasional stubborn foxglove. Yet bare trees stood along the fringes of the Wild Wood, and fewer faeries were about than usual.

Castigating Richard had got me nowhere, so I kept my mouth shut at these obvious signs of decay. But he wasn't a complete fool, and I'm certain he noticed the changes. His gaze kept straying to the wood, and the skeletal branches where green and gold leaves had once fluttered in the breeze. His jaw worked, but he did not remark on it.

At last, the path dipped down into a shallow depression, and there, spread before us like a black mirror, was Nelly's Pond.

Some stories claimed it had no bottom, that it dropped straight down forever. I could almost believe it. Though the sun shone brightly overhead, not a single ray penetrated the murky water. The shore was ringed with reeds that swayed slightly despite the absence of wind.

A heavy silence hung over the place. No birds sang. No insects buzzed. Even the sheep grazing on the distant hillside gave the pond a wide berth.

I pointed to a tumbledown structure. "That's it."

Just beyond the far shore stood the gamekeeper's cottage. Its thatch roof was in a sad state of disrepair, and swallows flew in and out of a crooked chimney. Moss grew on its northern wall. The single window was broken like an empty eye socket.

"Charming," Richard murmured.

As we began to circle around the pond, he wondered aloud if the monster had really taken Jasper Hargreaves.

"Well," I replied, "it's known that Nelly prefers children, but she hasn't gotten any in quite a while, so she's probably hungry—"

Ripples marred the dark pond, and from their center rose the very same water hag. At first glance, she looked almost human. Thin shoulders broke the surface, wet hair falling down her back like trailing weeds, but the illusion ended there. Her skin was the colour of clay, slick and mottled with patches of greenish scum. It was her arms that gave me the worst fright—each as long as a sea serpent.

Before we could run, they shot out, closing the distance in an instant. Cold fingers encircled my waist, lifting me into the air. Richard gave a shout of alarm, and then he too was caught, suspended several feet above the water in Nelly's other hand.

"Richard Ravencroft," she said in a slippery voice. "The little princeling returns."

Her eyes were wide and lidless and black as the bottom of an old well.

"Put us down at once!" Richard demanded in a fury.

Nelly made a sound like swamp bubbles breaking the surface—*blup-blup-blup*—which I took to be a chuckle. "The new lord gives orders? You have no power here. Not until you claim your magic."

I squirmed, trying to free myself, but her icy fingers only tightened.

"Give me a nice fat child," the hag proposed in a reasonable tone, "and I'll let you go."

"What?" Richard spluttered. "Are you mad?"

If he'd been near enough to kick, I would have done so. The man did not understand fae at all.

Nelly gave us a vigorous, affronted shake. "Mad? In the old days, the Ravencrofts didn't balk at giving me a plump bairn every now and then!"

"Times have changed," he said hoarsely. "I won't—one can't simply sacrifice a *child* for the sake of expedience."

"Then I'll have to make do," Nelly hissed.

Her grip on me tightened, and I gasped.

"Wait!" Richard cried. "Take me instead! Just let Kitty go."

My heart lurched. "Richard, no."

Nelly tilted her narrow head, regarding him with a curious expression. "What ho? A Ravencroft acting chivalrous? How novel." She leaned closer and gave him a thorough sniff, like Barbarossa inspecting a piece of questionable meat. "You wizards are stringy and tough. Thank you, but no." Nelly's slitted nostrils swiveled my way. "This one, however, smells soft and juicy."

It was all those cinnamon buns. Briar's fault, really.

I forced myself to meet her lidless eyes. My mind raced, searching for a way out. Nelly was ancient and terrifying, but she was also fae. Perhaps like her cousins she could be flattered and cajoled.

"Your skin, my lady," I stammered, "is the most remarkable shade of pearlescent green. I've never seen anything like it."

Nelly blinked, and I realised she did possess eyelids, they

were just cunningly concealed in the hollows of her eye sockets. "You truly think so?"

I nodded vigorously. "And your teeth! So sharp and jagged. They would make a barracuda envious."

She preened, running a long green tongue along the tips. "Well, I do take care of them. Thank you for noticing."

"I imagine you like to tear flesh," I said quickly, aware that this was dangerous territory, "but since there is a tragic shortage of plump bairns at the moment, perhaps you might like the pond to be stocked with some brown trout. I'm sure Lord Ravencroft would be happy to arrange it."

Richard nodded. "Yes, of course! The finest trout money can buy."

Nelly considered this. "Fish are not as succulent as children," she declared at last, "but they are less trouble. The screaming does hurt my ears."

She set us down on the bank with a gurgling sigh. "You may go," she said. "But Kitty, on your next walking tour, perhaps you could bring the group down to the edge of the pond for a nice close look."

The hag smiled, flashing her teeth, and I wasn't sure if she was joking.

"As for you, wizard," she added, fixing Richard with her unblinking gaze, "claim your magic, accept your birthright, or the bargain will fail. The Wild Wood will wither. The Fair Folk will depart. And I . . ." Her smile widened. "I will be very, very hungry."

With that, Nelly sank back into the dark water, disappearing without a ripple. For a long moment, neither of us spoke. Then Richard turned to me, his face ashen.

"Are you all right?" he asked.

I nodded, though my legs felt like stunned eels. "Let's move away from the water, shall we?"

We retreated, putting a good thirty yards between ourselves and the pond before I could breathe properly.

"Do you think my ancestors really gave her children?" Richard asked tightly.

"They might have done," I conceded. "But when a creature like Nelly talks about the 'old days,' it could mean centuries. Maybe even longer."

"God, I hope so," he replied with feeling. "That was quick thinking with the trout. If you hadn't come along . . ."

My cheeks warmed. "You must learn to think as they do. I doubt she really wanted to eat you. Just to toy with you a bit. But thank you for offering yourself on my behalf."

Richard regarded me with soft eyes and seemed about to say something. Then his expression turned grim. "Let's find Nettle and get this over with."

The cottage looked even more forlorn up close. The door —what was left of it—hung askew on a single rusted hinge. Richard hesitated, hand raised as if to knock, then seemed to realise the absurdity of the gesture and called out, "Nettle? Are you there?"

A scuffling came from within, like small feet hurrying across a wooden floor. Then silence.

Richard frowned. "Nettle, it's Richard Ravencroft. Quince at the Dancing Toadstool said I might find you here."

A small face slowly appeared in the gap between door and frame—wrinkled like a dried apple, with bright button eyes and tufted grey brows. The brownie was no taller than my knee, wearing what appeared to be a scrap of rough burlap with holes cut for arms.

"My lord?" her voice was high and reedy. "Is it truly you?"

"It's me, Nettle," Richard said, crouching down. "May we come in?"

The door creaked open wider, and the brownie stepped

back with a bow so deep her nose nearly touched the floor-boards. "Enter and be welcome, though our home is humble."

We ducked inside. The cottage's interior was even more wretched. Dead leaves had blown in through the broken window to form drifts against the walls. The fireplace gaped empty and cold, its hearth scattered with bird droppings. What little furniture remained—a three-legged stool and a sagging table—was furred with dust.

For brownies to permit their dwelling to fall into such state . . . Well, their circumstances must be dire indeed.

A dozen of them huddled in corners or peered from behind the cupboard. All were dressed in the same makeshift clothing—scraps of burlap, tattered dishcloths, and pieces of old sacking. They shivered in the chill air, small faces pinched with cold.

"My lord," Nettle said, gesturing to the stool. "Please, sit. I fear it's the best we can offer."

I gave Richard a pointed look; they would be deathly offended if he refused. He seemed to be learning for he gave me a tiny nod and accepted the offer as graciously as if he had been offered a king's throne.

A murmur ran through the assembled brownies. They shuffled forward, forming a semi-circle around us, staring up at Richard with such hope it made my heart ache for them.

"You must forgive our appearance," Nettle said in an abashed tone. "We've fallen on hard times since the family left."

"How long have you been living here?" I asked. All the village brownies were round-cheeked and well-dressed. These creatures looked like half-starved ragamuffins.

"Fifteen years," Nettle replied, her gaze downcast. "Ever since we were driven from Ravencroft Hall."

Richard's brow furrowed. "Driven out? By whom?"

Nettle's face darkened. "One of our own. He now styles himself Lord Gilcarren."

I felt Richard go still beside me. "Gilcarren?" he repeated in shock.

A look passed between Nettle and the other brownies—shared sorrow and anger. "Yes, my lord. The very same."

Richard shook his head. "That's impossible. Gilcarren was the most loyal servant at Ravencroft Hall. He was my—" He broke off, swallowing hard. "He was my friend."

"He was a friend to everyone," said Nettle sadly. "The most diligent and cheerful of us all. But after your parents were exiled, the Hall sat empty. Dark things began to creep in from the Wild Wood, drawn to the power of the place."

Another brownie, thin as a twig, stepped forward. "Gilcarren took it upon himself to defend the Hall. Night after night, he battled the wicked fae who sought to claim it."

"But such battles change a soul," Nettle continued. "Each victory hardened him. Made him colder. Crueler. Until one day, we barely recognised him."

"He turned into a boggart," Richard said, comprehension dawning in his eyes.

Nettle nodded. "He drove us out with vile curses, took our clothes for himself, and claimed the Hall as his own domain."

"He wears a dozen coats now," added a younger brownie, her voice trembling. "One atop the other, stolen from us."

I thought of the boggart's antics—the flying books, the upside-down portraits, the endless pranks and torments. Had that creature truly once been Richard's childhood friend?

Richard's face was a study in conflicting emotions—disbelief, sorrow, and a slow-kindling anger. "I remember him teaching me to climb trees," he said softly. "He would wait at the top, encouraging me when I was afraid."

"He was good once," Nettle agreed. "The best of us. But isolation and power are a dangerous combination."

Richard's gaze swept the dismal cottage. "This is no place for you." He moved toward the cold hearth. "Let me at least build a fire to warm you."

Nettle stepped forward quickly. "No, my lord. We cannot."

"What do you mean?"

"We can enjoy neither fire nor proper clothes until we return to our rightful place," she explained. "Those are the rules that bind us. We are house brownies without a house. Until we return to Ravencroft Hall, we must live as outcasts."

Richard's jaw tightened. He looked around at the shivering brownies, and I saw real pity in his eyes. "I'm sorry," he said. "This is my family's fault."

"Not yours, my lord," Nettle said firmly. "You were but a child."

I remembered the thermos and buns wrapped in a kerchief I'd tucked into my pocket that morning. I knelt down to offer them to Nettle.

"It's not much," I said, "but the tea is still hot, and the buns are fresh from Sugar & Sprites."

The brownies' eyes widened. Several made small, involuntary movements toward the food, then checked themselves, looking to Nettle.

She accepted the thermos and buns with great dignity. "Your kindness is gratefully received, Miss Boot."

As she distributed the modest feast among her companions, Richard pulled me aside.

"This is worse than I imagined," he murmured. "They've been living like this all these years . . . it's awful!"

I squeezed his arm gently. "Make things right then."

His dark eyes were troubled as he turned back to Nettle. "The moonstone amulet," he said. "Do you know where it is?"

Nettle brushed crumbs from her long fingers. "Gilcarren has hidden it away, my lord. Out of spite."

Richard nodded slowly. "If I can reclaim the Hall, drive out Gilcarren, would you and the others return?"

Nettle brightened. "We would be honored to serve the Ravencroft line once more. To return to our proper duties. Our home."

The other brownies nodded eagerly.

"We would keep the Hall in perfect order," said one. "Clean the chimneys and fix the roof."

"Polish the silver till it gleams," promised another.

"Mend the plaster and dust the books," added a third.

Richard gave a strained smile. "Let me see what I can do."

The brownies crowded the doorway to wave us off. Richard walked toward the Hall in silence, his hands thrust deep into the pockets of his father's coat. His expression was distant, brooding.

"Are you all right?" I asked finally.

He gave a short, humourless laugh. "Not really." He kicked at a stone in our path. "My whole life, I've thought of Ravencroft Hall as just a building. A place I could sell and be free of. But it's more than that, isn't it?"

I didn't answer. I didn't need to. The truth was written all over his face.

"Gilcarren," he murmured. "I used to follow him every-where. He showed me secret passages no one else knew about. Told me stories of the grand fae courts. And now . . ." Richard stopped walking and turned to face me. "What a godawful mess they left me, Kitty. I must set it to rights."

I felt a flutter of hope. "Does that mean . . . you may not sell the Hall?"

"It means," he said carefully, "that I have far more to consider than myself."

It wasn't a promise, but as we continued toward Ravencroft Hall, I allowed myself to believe that the tide might be turning in my favour.

15

LORD GILCARREN

When we entered the Hall, the portraits in the foyer were all crooked, their expressions somehow even more disapproving from that angle. I wondered which of them had given Nelly her "plump bairns," then forced the macabre thought from my mind.

"Tea," Richard announced. "With lots of whiskey."

I followed him to the kitchen, which remained the only habitable room in the house. The fire had gone out in our absence, but Richard knelt to restart it while I filled the copper kettle.

"Do you think he's watching us?" I whispered.

Richard straightened, dusting ash from his hands. "Almost certainly."

I felt a prickling on the back of my neck. The air in the corner near the pantry shimmered slightly, but I pretended not to see it. Instead, I busied myself with the tea things. The kettle began to sing, and I poured boiling water over the leaves, breathing in the fragrant steam.

"It's strange," Richard said with a dry laugh. "I feel like an interloper, and you move around this place as if it were your own."

I snorted. "Well, I've spent enough time here." I shook my head. "Those poor brownies . . . But I imagine you know what it's like to be exiled. To lose everything you've ever known."

He was silent for a long moment. "Honestly, I would have preferred to stay with Nettle. She's far kinder than the people I was sent to live with."

"Her world is still here," I said gently. "Waiting to come back to life."

"Yes, but I'm not the same boy who belonged in it." He traced a whorl in the wooden tabletop with one finger. "Even before my parents were accused of treason, I was a lonely child. They wouldn't allow me to play with the village children. Said they were beneath my station."

I raised an eyebrow. "I suppose they thought wizards ought to keep to themselves."

"Precisely." He gave a sad smile. "There was one girl I liked very much, but . . ." He shook his head. "Never mind. It was a long time ago."

I felt a peculiar twinge in my chest—a sharp little stab of something like jealousy. Which was ridiculous. He'd been a child, for heaven's sake.

"The house faeries were my friends," Richard continued. "Especially. . . you-know-who. He would play games with me when my parents were busy with their parties. Hide-and-seek in the secret passages. Treasure hunts in the attic. When I had nightmares, he'd sit on the end of my bed and tell me tales of the Court of Silver Shadows until I fell back asleep. If I'd known what would happen to him—to all of them—I would have . . ." Richard broke off, his voice thick.

The air in the corner by the pantry condensed, like mist

forming on a cold window. For just a moment, I glimpsed a small, hunched figure with too-long arms and a face half-hidden beneath the brim of a miniature top hat. Then it was gone, dissolving back into the shadows.

Richard stared at the spot, his dark eyes reflecting a storm of emotions. "I think," he said with careful deliberation, "that I may have been too hasty in my plans to sell the Hall."

My heart gave a hopeful flutter. "You're considering staying?"

"I'm considering . . ." He frowned, searching for words. "I'm considering my responsibilities. To the land. To the faeries. To the village."

His intense gaze met mine. "I think, Kitty, that I've been running for so long that I forgot what I was running from. And what I might be running toward." He took a deep breath. "There's something I need to tell you. About the amulet."

"The moonstone?" I set down my teacup. "What about it?"

"It's not just a family heirloom," Richard said. "It's a key."

"A key to what?"

His voice dropped to nearly a whisper. "To the land of Faerie. Specifically, the realm of the Court of Silver Shadows. It can open a doorway between our world and theirs."

I stared at him. "My God, Richard."

Now it all made sense. I understood why he didn't dare to leave it for anyone to stumble across—especially Montfort and his ilk. The thought made me shudder.

He ran a hand through his hair. "The Ravencrofts have been guardians of that doorway for centuries. It's part of the bargain." Richard stood, pacing the length of the kitchen. "I've been trying to convince myself that it doesn't matter.

That the world has moved beyond magic. That no one would miss it if it were gone."

"But you don't really believe that," I said.

"No. Not anymore." He stopped pacing and leaned against the counter, arms folded across his chest. "All I know is that I can't let the amulet fall into the wrong hands. And I can't find the bloody thing without help."

"You know what you have to do, Richard."

He stared at me without speaking.

"Apologise," I added, in case it wasn't obvious.

He stared at me as if I'd suggested he swim naked in Nelly's Pond. "Apologise? He's terrorizing my house! He stole my clothes! He nearly dropped a crystal chandelier on my head!"

"He's hurting," I said simply. "He waited for you, Richard. Year after year. He protected the Hall long after everyone else had abandoned it. And what did he get for his loyalty? His spirit twisted. His very nature changed."

Richard opened his mouth, closed it again.

"He needs to hear that you're sorry," I continued. "That you understand what he's been through. That you see him— not as a boggart but as your old friend."

A sugar bowl whizzed past Richard's ear, smashing against the wall behind him. He ducked, then glared at the corner where the air shimmered.

"Very mature," he muttered.

"Richard." I gave him a pointed look.

He sighed, shoulders slumping. "You're right. I know you're right." He ran a hand through his hair again. "But what if it doesn't work? What if he's too far gone?"

"Then at least you'll have tried." I reached across the table to touch his hand. "And who knows? Maybe there's still enough of your friend left in there to remember what it was like before."

For a long moment, Richard was silent. Then he straightened, squaring his shoulders like a man preparing to face a firing squad.

"Very well," he said, the Ravencroft pride warring with resignation in his voice. "I'll try."

"It doesn't need to be graceful," I said. "It just needs to be sincere."

As if in response, the air in the corner solidified once more into the hunched shape of the boggart. This time, it didn't fade away. Instead, it crouched there, watching us with button-bright eyes that gleamed with malice. Then it leapt away down the hall. With an exasperated sigh, Richard followed.

The boggart skittered ahead of us, sometimes running on all fours, sometimes upright, its thin limbs moving with the uncanny grace of a spider. It led us from the kitchen through the drawing room, up the grand staircase, and down a corridor I'd never seen before. Paintings watched our passage with ancient eyes, their subjects seeming to lean forward in their frames as we rushed past.

"Wait!" Richard called. "We need to talk!"

The boggart cackled and slipped through a door that swung shut with a bang. By the time we reached it, the door had vanished, replaced by an unbroken stretch of wall.

"Blast!" Richard slapped his palm against the paneling. "Where did he go?"

"These are his tricks," I said, catching my breath. "He's testing you."

Richard's jaw clenched. "I'm tired of games."

He turned slowly, taking in the hallway, which seemed to stretch endlessly in both directions.

"Call his true name," I whispered. "He cannot refuse."

Richard's voice assumed a hard edge of command I hadn't heard from him before. "*Gilcarren*. Show yourself."

The air grew thick and heavy. Dust motes froze in the thin shaft of light from a nearby window. Then, with a sound like tearing silk, the boggart materialised directly in front of us. It was taller now, its spindly frame stretched to nearly Richard's height. The creature wore a dozen mismatched coats layered atop one another—a patchwork of stolen clothing that made its body appear lumpy and misshapen. The top hat remained, tilted at a rakish angle over eyes that burned with cold fire.

"You remember my name?" The boggart's voice dripped with contempt. "After so many years?"

Richard held its malevolent gaze. "I never forgot you."

The boggart circled us. "Yet you left. All of you left." It jabbed a bony finger at Richard's chest. "Left me to guard the Hall alone."

"I was a child," Richard said helplessly. "It wasn't my choice."

Gilcarren grunted. "Well, I chose to stay. To fight. To protect what was yours."

Richard flushed. "You're right. And I . . . I want to thank you for that. For defending Ravencroft Hall from the wicked fae of the Wild Wood. I know it couldn't have been easy."

It wasn't exactly an apology. Gilcarren regarded Richard with narrowed eyes.

"Pretty words," he said at last. "But words are wind. What will you give me in return for my service?"

"Give you?" Richard frowned. "What do you want?"

Gilcarren's mouth thinned to a line. "Recognition. I know, a title! Lord Gilcarren, Master of Ravencroft Hall. I like the ring of that!"

"That's absurd," Richard snapped, then visibly reined himself in. "I mean, surely we can come to a more reasonable arrangement. Perhaps your own chambers? With servants?"

The boggart's eyes glittered. "Not enough. I want a seat on your council. I want to be consulted on all matters pertaining to the Hall. And I want a feast held in my honor every year, with all the village in attendance."

I could see Richard's patience wearing thin, a muscle ticking in his jaw.

"I could provide you with a permanent position as head of household staff," he offered. "With authority over the other brownies. And any chambers you choose."

"No!" Gilcarren stamped his foot, and the floor trembled beneath us. "I am not a servant! Not anymore. I have earned the right to stand at your side, not below you."

"You overreach," Richard said, his voice hardening. "I am grateful for your service, but you've forgotten your place."

The boggart's face twisted with fury. "My place? I MADE this place! While you were gone, I ruled here. I kept out the dark fae. I sacrificed everything—my form, my kin, my very nature!"

"And I am trying to make amends," Richard insisted, his composure slipping. "But I cannot give you what you ask."

"Then give me what is mine by right!" Gilcarren shrieked. "The token you seek! The moonstone key!"

Richard's patience finally snapped. "Enough!" he shouted. "I command you to produce the moonstone amulet at once! It is mine by birthright, and you will return it or face the consequences!"

The boggart went still. For a heartbeat, I thought Richard had won. Then Gilcarren's mouth curved into a terrible smile.

"Consequences?" he whispered. "I'll show you consequences."

His spindly fingers curled in the air, and something groaned from the wall behind us. I turned just in time to see an ancient halberd tear itself from its bracket. The weapon—a wicked axe blade mounted on a long wooden shaft—hung suspended for an instant, then flew straight at me.

I didn't have time to scream. The blade whistled past my ear, so close I felt the wind of its passage, and buried itself in the floorboards with a mighty thunk. A lock of my hair drifted to the carpet.

Richard stared at the quivering weapon, then at me, then at Gilcarren. His face went white as frost. Something shifted in his eyes—darkness blooming behind them like ink spreading through water.

"You dare?" he whispered, his voice no longer his own. It came from everywhere at once, vibrating in the walls, the floor, the air itself.

The temperature in the hallway plummeted. My breath made a white fog. The candles in the sconces flared high, then guttered to nothing.

A terrible wind rose from nowhere, swirling around Richard. It lifted his hair and the edges of his coat, though nothing else in the corridor moved. His hands came up, fingers splayed, and darkness gathered between them—not the absence of light but something more solid, like black honey.

"Richard," I gasped. "Don't—"

But he was beyond hearing. His lips moved, muttering silent syllables. The darkness shot from his hands, enveloping Gilcarren in bonds of pure shadow. The boggart shrieked as it was lifted from the floor, turned upside down, and shaken so violently I heard its teeth rattle.

"Where is it?" Richard demanded, his voice still that terrible, resonant thing that wasn't quite human. "WHERE IS MY AMULET?"

He shook the boggart again, harder. Gilcarren's screams were pitiful now, his limbs flailing uselessly against the dark bonds.

I couldn't bear it. I seized Richard's arm, feeling a shock of cold that burned like dry ice.

"Stop!" I cried. "You're killing him!"

For a moment, I thought he hadn't heard me. Then his gaze swung to mine, and I saw a strange exultation, as if the power flowing through him was a drug he'd been denying himself for too long.

"Richard," I said firmly, though it chilled me to the marrow. "This isn't who you are."

Something flickered in his eyes—recognition, uncertainty. The wind died down. The darkness binding Gilcarren wavered, then dissolved like smoke. The boggart fell to the carpet in a heap, sobbing wretchedly.

Richard staggered back, staring at his hands as if they belonged to someone else. His face crumpled. "Oh God," he whispered. "I . . . I didn't mean . . ."

His legs gave out, and he slumped against the wall, breathing hard. I knelt beside Gilcarren, who had curled into a tight ball, his many coats tangled around him. He whimpered when I touched him.

"It's all right," I murmured. "It's all right."

I looked up at Richard. His face was a mask of self-loathing.

"I'm no different than they are," he said hollowly, and I knew he meant his parents. "The darkness is in my blood."

I wanted to reassure him, but I had glimpsed something ancient and terrible in his eyes—the legacy of generations of dark wizards who had wielded power without mercy. This was exactly what Richard had feared all along—not just that he might possess magic, but that the magic might possess him.

It was, I realised with dread, the very worst thing that might have happened.

16

THE NOBLE THING

Richard stared at his hands as if they belonged to someone else—a stranger he'd woken to find wearing his skin. The darkness that poured from his fingertips had dissipated, but its memory hung in the air like the scent of a thunderstorm.

"Are you all right?" I asked him, still kneeling beside the huddled form of Gilcarren.

Richard's laugh was harsh, scraping against the silence like a knife on stone. "All right? I nearly killed him."

"You stopped yourself," I pointed out.

"Because you were here. If you hadn't been—" He cut off, refusing to complete the thought.

Gilcarren stirred beneath my hand, uncurling slightly from his protective ball. One bright eye peered up at me, then at Richard. The boggart's many coats rustled as he shifted.

"Is he hurt?" Richard asked, not moving any closer.

I examined Gilcarren. He was trembling, but there were no visible injuries. "I don't think so."

Richard took a deep breath. When he spoke again, his voice was flat and distant. "I'm done."

"What?" I stood up, brushing dust from my skirt. "You can't—"

"I can and I will." His jaw was set in that stubborn line I was coming to know all too well. "I'll call Montfort from the village. Tell him to bring the papers. I don't care about the price anymore—I'll take whatever he offers."

My heart plummeted. "And the moonstone amulet?"

"To hell with it." Richard's eyes were hard, feverish. "If I stay here any longer, something worse will happen. I'll become . . ." He swallowed. "I'll become like them."

"Richard, please—"

But he was already turning away, striding down the corridor with the desperate energy of a man fleeing a burning building.

"At least wait until morning!" I called after him. "We can talk about this."

"There's nothing to talk about," he flung over his shoulder. "It's over, Kitty. I'm sorry."

And then he was gone, his footsteps receding down the grand staircase.

I turned back to Gilcarren, who had managed to sit up, his spindly limbs poking awkwardly from the tangle of stolen coats. The malice had drained from his face, leaving him small and vulnerable.

"Well," I said, crossing my arms. "I hope you're pleased with yourself."

The boggart tilted his head, regarding me with those bright, inhuman eyes. "It could have been worse."

"Worse?" I sputtered. "You nearly got yourself killed! And now Richard's going to sell the Hall to those awful men."

Gilcarren straightened his topmost coat. "Richard's

parents would have turned me into a moth and laughed as I caught aflame in the nearest candle," he said. "So all told I got off lightly, miss."

I stared at him. "That's awful."

Gilcarren only shrugged. "The Ravencrofts have never been known for their mild temperaments."

He stood, swaying slightly, and adjusted his top hat. The transformation was remarkable—from a cowering victim back to the haughty, self-possessed creature I'd glimpsed before.

"I had to know," he continued, "if the blood still ran strong in the son. And now I do."

Understanding dawned on me. "You provoked him deliberately?"

Gilcarren's thin lips curved. "His magic would have surfaced sooner or later. I merely hastened the process."

I wanted to shake him. Instead, I took a deep breath, trying to channel Nan's infinite patience. "That was cruel and dangerous. You drove him to this—to the very thing he fears most about himself."

"It was time for him to face the truth."

"Which is what, exactly?" I demanded. "That he's destined to become a dark wizard like his parents? That he's doomed to this legacy of cruelty and power?"

Gilcarren cocked his head. "Magic is neither good nor evil. It simply is, like the tides or the changing seasons." His gaze drifted to the window where afternoon light slanted through dusty panes. "But it is unpredictable. Mercurial. Like those who wield it."

"What do you mean?"

The boggart sighed, a sound like papers rustling in a forgotten drawer. "The magic has been dormant in him for twenty years. Coming home awakened it. But without the proper training, it will be volatile. Dangerous."

I recalled the black energy that had flowed from Richard's hands, the way his voice had changed, becoming something ancient and terrible.

"He must affirm the bargain," Gilcarren said, "with the Court of Silver Shadows."

I remembered the name. "Go on."

Gilcarren nodded. "Nine centuries ago, the first Ravencroft wizard, Matthias, sought power to protect his lands from the northern invaders. The Lord and Lady granted it, but at a price." The boggart's eyes gleamed. "Every Ravencroft heir must renew the bargain upon coming of age, or the magic turns against them."

I thought of the way Richard had staggered after his outburst, as if physically drained. "Is that what's happening to him now?"

"It's only beginning," Gilcarren said grimly. "The longer he denies his heritage, the more unstable his power will become. The magic will leak out in bursts he cannot control."

My mind raced. "But he's leaving for London."

Gilcarren's laugh held no humour. "It won't matter. The magic is part of him now, awakened and hungry. It will follow him wherever he goes."

"Then we have to stop him," I said, already turning toward the stairs. "I have to make him understand—"

"He won't listen," the boggart called after me. "Not yet. The fear is too fresh." His voice dropped. "But perhaps you might succeed where I failed. You seem to have a certain . . . influence on the young lord."

I paused at the top of the stairs, looking back at the strange mercurial creature who had been both Richard's childhood friend and his tormentor. "The moonstone amulet," I said. "Where is it?"

Gilcarren's expression grew sly. "Safe. Hidden where only a true Ravencroft can find it."

"That's not helpful."

"It wasn't meant to be," he replied with a mocking bow. "Some things must be earned, not given."

I bit back a retort and hurried down the stairs. Richard paced back and forth across the foyer, his borrowed coat flapping around his legs, hands thrust deep into his pockets.

He looked up as I approached, his expression wary. "If you've come to change my mind—"

"Just listen," I said, holding up a hand. "Please."

Something in my voice must have reached him, because he stopped pacing and waited, arms crossed over his chest, as I descended the last few steps.

"I spoke with Gilcarren," I began.

"And I suppose he's sorry," Richard said sarcastically.

"Not exactly." I leaned against the newel post. "But he did explain a few things about your magic."

Richard's face closed like a door slamming shut. "I'm not interested."

"Well, you should be," I insisted. "Because running away won't solve anything."

"I'm not running away," he said stiffly. "I'm starting fresh."

"The magic will follow you, Richard. It's part of you now."

He shook his head vehemently. "No. It's this place. These walls. Once I've sold it, the power will subside again."

"Don't be so sure about that."

Richard paled slightly, but his jaw remained set. "I'll manage."

"How?" I demanded. "By hoping it doesn't happen during surgery? While you're operating on someone?"

That struck home. I saw the doubt flicker across his face, quickly suppressed. "I'll find a way."

"There is a way," I said, stepping closer. "The Court of Silver Shadows."

He went very still. "What do you know about them?"

"Only what everyone in the village knows. That they're ancient and powerful. That they made a bargain with your family." I took another step toward him. "Gilcarren says you need to affirm it, like all the Ravencroft heirs before you."

"And if I don't?"

"The magic will turn against you."

Richard ran a hand through his hair, making it stand on end. "I can't believe I'm even having this conversation," he said. "Two weeks ago, I was a rational man of science. And now here I am, discussing faerie bargains!"

"They're real," I said quietly. "You know they are."

He was silent for a long moment. "Even if I believed you," he said at last, "I have no intention of binding myself to some archaic pact I know nothing about. My parents made their choices. I make my own."

"But—"

"No, Kitty." His voice hardened. "I won't become like them. I won't surrender to this . . . this darkness inside me. The best thing—the only thing—is to leave Ravencroft Hall behind."

Anger flared in my chest, hot and sudden. "So you'd rather let Montfort turn this place into a tacky hotel?"

"Better that than become a monster!" he shouted, his control finally slipping. "You didn't feel it, Kitty. The power. The rush of it."

"So you're a coward," I said.

Richard flinched as if I'd slapped him. "What did you say?"

"You heard me." My hands had curled into fists at my sides. "You're running away because you're afraid of yourself. Afraid you won't be strong enough to wield your power responsibly."

"You have no idea what you're talking about," he said, his voice low and dangerous.

"Don't I? I've watched you these past two weeks, Richard. I've seen how desperately you want to be free of your name, your family, your history. But you can't escape who you are. Not by selling this house, not by moving to London, not by anything."

"So what would you have me do?" he demanded. "Embrace the dark magic that destroyed my parents? That made them into the kind of people who would plot treason?"

"I would have you face it," I shot back. "Learn to control it, not let it control you. Be better than they were."

For a moment, I thought I'd reached him. Something flickered in his eyes—not anger but a deeper emotion I couldn't name.

Then his expression hardened again. "I've made my decision, Kitty. I'm calling Montfort as soon as I reach the village."

"Richard—"

"No." He held up a hand. "I understand that you care about Little Groating. About the Wild Wood and the faeries. But I have to care about the people I might hurt if I stay."

The finality in his voice stole the fight from me. He truly believed he was doing the right thing—the noble thing, even.

"Fine," I said, stepping back. "Do what you think is best. You know, I actually liked you, Richard. But now I know who you really are."

It was a cheap shot, and I regretted it immediately.

Richard's face went blank, all emotion carefully tucked away behind that mask of Ravencroft pride.

"Yes, you do," he said coolly. "Goodbye, Kitty."

He strode past me to the front door, his shoulders set in a rigid line. Part of me wanted to call after him, to try one more time to make him see reason. But another part—the hurt, angry part—let him go.

The door closed behind him with a soft click that somehow felt more final than a slam would have.

I stood alone in the vast foyer, surrounded by portraits of Ravencrofts long dead, their dark eyes seeming to judge me for my failure. What would happen now? To the village, to the Wild Wood, to Nelly's Pond and all the faeries who called this land home? What would happen to Richard himself, when the magic he was so determined to deny forced its way out again?

As if in answer to my thoughts, a chill breeze swept through the foyer, guttering the candles. The day had started with such hope. Now, as I gathered my coat, I felt only a hollow ache. Time was running out for Little Groating, for the magic, for all of us.

And there wasn't a damn thing I could do about it.

17

AN UNHOLY ALLIANCE

The walk back to the Dancing Toadstool felt twice as long as usual. Dark clouds gathered overhead, matching my mood, but the rain held off—small mercies.

I kept thinking of Richard's face when his magic had erupted, that terrible mix of exhilaration and horror. By the time I pushed open the inn's door, I felt like someone had scooped away all my insides and left only a thin shell of resolve. I needed tea—or something stronger. What I got instead was the sight of Ambrose Montfort and Silas Grimes huddled in the corner, their heads bent together.

I paused in the doorway. Montfort was speaking in low, urgent tones, jabbing his finger at what appeared to be a map spread between them. Grimes nodded, his sour face unusually animated. Neither had noticed me yet, though Barbarossa stared at the pair with slitted eyes, his tail swishing testily. He'd always been a good judge of character.

Seeing Montfort rekindled my anger like a match to dry tinder. All my helplessness transformed into hot fury. Richard might be surrendering, but I certainly wasn't.

Mrs. Deen emerged from the kitchen, wiping her hands on her apron. "Kitty! You look like you've seen a ghost. Come warm yourself by the fire and I'll fetch you some—"

"In a moment," I said, not taking my eyes off the two men. "I need to have a word with our guest first."

She followed my gaze, her expression darkening. "Those two have been thick as thieves all afternoon. I don't like it one bit."

"Neither do I," I muttered, shrugging off my coat.

I strode across the room. Montfort spotted me first, his too-white smile appearing as if by reflex. He straightened, nudging Grimes, who hastily folded the map and tucked it inside his jacket.

"Miss Boot!" Montfort exclaimed. "What a pleasure. We were just—"

"Discussing old times?" I suggested, coming to a stop at their table. "Reminiscing about shared acquaintances? Planning the destruction of my village, perhaps?"

Montfort's smile never faltered, though it grew strained around the edges. "I beg your pardon?"

"Don't play innocent," I said, planting my hands on the table and leaning forward. "I want to know how you two know each other."

Grimes scowled, his default expression, but there was a flicker of something else beneath it. Nervousness? Guilt?

"Mr. Grimes and I are old college chums," Montfort said smoothly. "We happened to reconnect by chance when I arrived in Little Groating."

"How fortunate," I said. "And which college would that be?"

"Cambridge," said Montfort, just as Grimes muttered, "Oxford."

They exchanged a quick glance. Montfort gave a forced

laugh. "Dear me, have we been at this argument again? You know perfectly well it was Cambridge, Silas. Though he did a term at Oxford, didn't you?"

Grimes cleared his throat. "Exchange program."

"I see," I said, pulling out a chair and sitting down uninvited. "And when exactly was this? Because Mr. Grimes here appears to be at least a decade older than you, Mr. Montfort."

Montfort scoffed, causing his hairpiece to retreat like a small, skittish animal trying to avoid notice. "Appearances can be deceiving," he said. "Silas has always looked older than his years. It's the artistic temperament, isn't it, old boy? All that brooding and scowling weathers a face."

I turned my attention to Grimes. "You know, it's strange. In the two years you've lived here, you've never once shown anyone your paintings. No exhibitions, no displays at village fairs. For an artist, you're remarkably private about your work."

Grimes' face flushed an ugly red. "I don't need to justify my creative process to anyone, least of all to you."

"No, but you might explain why you were so quick to defend Mr. Montfort's plans for Ravencroft Hall the other day, when you'd supposedly only just met him."

Montfort's smile had grown brittle. "Really, Miss Boot, this inquisition is most unbecoming. What Mr. Grimes and I discuss is our business."

"It becomes my business when it involves the fate of my village," I shot back. "You two have been planning this for a while, haven't you? Long before Richard inherited the Hall."

Grimes shifted in his chair. "This is absurd. I need to be going."

"Yes, I imagine you do," I said, not moving. "Back to your cottage—the one that's positioned between the village and the Hall. How convenient for keeping an eye on things."

Montfort laid a placating hand on Grimes' arm. "Now, now. No need to rush off, Silas. Miss Boot is simply concerned about changes to her little community. It's perfectly natural."

"What's not natural," I said, "is how an unknown water-colour artist with no visible means of support managed to convince my parents to rent him their cottage. Or how he just happened to arrive not long before Richard turned thirty and inherited the estate."

Grimes stood abruptly, knocking his chair backward. "I don't have to listen to these wild accusations!"

He stormed off, shouldering past a startled customer at the door. Montfort maintained his composure, folding his hands on the table.

"Miss Boot," he said, his voice taking on a patronizing tone, "I understand your attachment to tradition. Change is difficult for small, isolated communities. But I assure you, the development of Ravencroft Hall will bring nothing but benefits—jobs, tourism, prosperity."

"At what cost?" I demanded. "The extinction of the fae? Not to mention all the poor animals who live in these woods. Hares and foxes and . . ." My mind went blank for a moment, distracted by his slowly slipping toupee. "Badgers!"

Montfort chuckled, the sound as artificial as his blond hair. "You speak as if these fairytales were real. I must say, it's an excellent angle for marketing. We'll certainly preserve that colourful local folklore in our promotional materials."

"They are real," I said flatly. "And you know it. That's why you've been buying all those books on faerie lore. You're not interested in preserving anything—you want to exploit it."

Something cold flickered behind his eyes, there and gone in an instant. "You have quite the imagination, Miss Boot. It will serve you well when you're giving tours at Hogwarts Wizarding

World, or wherever it is you end up." He stood, straightening his perfectly creased trousers. "Now if you'll excuse me, I believe I should prepare for Lord Ravencroft's call."

I remained seated, glaring up at him. "You won't get away with whatever you're planning," I said. "This place has protected itself for centuries."

Montfort's smile turned condescending. "How quaint. Well, we shall see, shan't we?" He gave a small bow. "Good evening, Miss Boot."

He sauntered away, pausing to bid Mrs. Deen goodnight at the bar before ascending the stairs to his room. My hands had curled into fists so tight my nails bit into my palms. There was no longer any doubt in my mind—Montfort and Grimes were working together, had been for some time. This wasn't a simple case of a developer spotting an opportunity; this was a calculated plan.

But why? What did they want with Ravencroft Hall that went beyond its value as real estate? The map they'd been studying, Grimes' strategic position in the village, Montfort's interest in faerie lore . . . none of it added up to a straightforward hotel development.

As I sat there, mind racing, Nan appeared from the back room where Dr. Singer rested. She took one look at my face and made her way over, settling into the chair Montfort had vacated.

"You look like you're plotting murder," she observed.

"Close enough," I admitted. "Did you know that Grimes and Montfort are old friends? Or so they claim."

Nan's eyebrows rose. "Are they indeed?" She glanced toward the stairs. "That slippery toad has made himself quite at home. Asking about the village history, the Hall, the Wild Wood."

"He's up to something, Nan. They both are. And Richard is going to sell the Hall to them without even knowing what they really want."

She patted my hand. "The night is darkest just before dawn, my love."

"I'm not sure dawn is coming this time," I said, the weight of defeat pressing on me again. "Richard's magic surfaced today. It scared him so much he's running away as fast as he can."

"Ah." Nan nodded sagely. "The Ravencroft blood asserting itself. It was bound to happen sooner or later."

I stared at her. "You knew?"

"I suspected," she admitted. "The family has always been unpredictable." She lit her briar pipe and exhaled a puff of smoke.

"He's a study in contradictions," I said, watching Sir Francis mutter in his sleep on the perch by the fire. "Kind and gentle one moment, taking a hammer to the walls the next. He has quite a vile temper, Nan!"

She smirked around her pipe and gave me a pointed look. "Sounds like someone else I know."

"I'm serious. He's like two different people, and I never know which one I'm going to get."

She nodded sagely. "The Ravencrofts are like that. Not all good nor all bad, but somewhere in the middle." She stabbed the stem at me. "Mercurial is what they are. They choose whichever path best serves the moment. Now tell me what's happened."

I filled her in on the latest disaster, from Gilcarren's provocation to Richard's magical outburst and decision to leave. "We have to stop him," I finished. "And we have to figure out what Montfort is really after."

Nan took my hand, her fingers dry and warm. "Sometimes the best way to win a battle is not to fight it head-on."

"What does that mean?"

She smiled, a hint of her old mischief lighting her eyes. "It means you need reinforcements."

18

OUR FINAL ROW

I woke before dawn and dressed quickly, my fingers clumsy from lack of sleep. If Richard had made up his mind, then today was my last chance to stop him.

I headed down the hallway toward Dr. Singer's room, meaning to check on him before breakfast. I'd just rounded the corner when the door opened and Richard emerged, medical bag in hand. He stopped short at the sight of me. He looked as exhausted as I was, but his shoulders were set in that familiar stubborn line.

"Kitty," he said, his voice neutral. "Good morning."

"You came back," I said in an equally flat tone.

A frown creased his forehead. "I couldn't leave without looking in on Dr. Singer."

Of course he couldn't. For all his talk of escape, Richard was, at his core, a healer. He wouldn't abandon a patient, even as he prepared to abandon everything else.

"How is he?" I asked.

"Much improved. The antibiotics are working nicely. His

fever's down, and his lungs are clearer." Richard glanced back at the closed door. "He's a tough old bird. Reminds me of my anatomy professor at Oxford—too stubborn to retire until he'd terrorised at least three more generations of medical students."

I smiled despite myself. "That sounds like him. He'd be horrified to think he might die before he gets a chance to propose to Nan."

Richard's eyebrows shot up. "Are they . . .?"

"Going on a decade of mutual pining," I confirmed. "The whole village has bets on when he'll finally pop the question."

Richard laughed, a genuine sound that made the air between us a little lighter. Then reality reasserted itself, and his expression shuttered.

"I should go," he said, taking a step back. "I have . . . arrangements to make."

My smile died. "Richard—"

"Please don't." He held up a hand. "I've made my decision, Kitty. Montfort promised me the changes would be small-scale. That they would respect the wishes of the villagers—"

"He's lying! My god, isn't that obvious?"

His jaw tightened. "It's for the best."

"For whom, exactly?" I demanded. "Not for the village. Not for the Wild Wood. Not for the brownies living in that awful cottage. And not for you, Richard!"

His jaw tightened. "How can you say that after what I did? If I stay, it's only a matter of time before I hurt someone. And if it . . ." He drew a steadying breath. "If it was you, I'd never forgive myself."

I was taken aback. "That's not—"

"Montfort will be at the Hall this afternoon to conduct a final walk-through," he interrupted, his voice taking on that clipped, formal tone I'd come to recognise as his armor. "The solicitors have already wired the down payment to an escrow account. The sale will be finalised by week's end."

The words hit me like stones. I'd feared this was coming, but hearing it with such finality stole the breath from my lungs.

"So quickly?" I managed.

"There's no reason to delay." His gaze dropped to the medical bag in his hand, fingers tightening around the handle. "The sooner this is done, the better for everyone."

"You can't possibly believe that," I said, my voice rising despite my best efforts to keep it level. "You know what's at stake."

"I do," he said grimly. "That's precisely why I'm leaving."

"Richard, what happened yesterday—it wasn't your fault. Gilcarren admitted to me that he provoked you deliberately!"

"And I tortured him for it." Richard's voice cracked slightly. "That power . . . The way it surged through me. It was . . ."

"Frightening," I finished.

"Yes. But also . . ." His eyes met mine, dark with self-loathing. "Intoxicating."

I reached for him, but he stepped back again. "That's why I have to go," he continued. "Before I do something I'll regret forever."

"You wouldn't hurt me, Richard." I insisted. "I know you wouldn't! You have a good heart."

"I'm sure my parents started with the best of intentions. Power corrupts, Kitty. And apparently, my family is particularly susceptible."

I wanted to grab him by the shoulders and shake him. "You're not your parents," I said firmly. "You're the man who dropped everything to come treat Dr. Singer in the middle of the night. The man who offered himself to Nelly in my place. The man who played Bach so beautifully that the music itself took shape around you."

A flicker of surprise crossed his face. So he'd known after all.

"It was beautiful," I said. "And it was magic, Richard. *Your* magic."

He shook his head. "It's not that simple."

"It could be," I insisted. "With practice."

"And who will guide me?" he demanded. "The same capricious fae who made the original bargain with my ancestors? I'd sooner trust a cobra not to bite."

I bit my lip. How could I make him understand when he was so determined to run away?

"I have to get back to Hall," he said, glancing toward the stairs. "I'm sorry, Kitty. Truly."

"So that's it? What about the amulet? What about Gilcarren?"

"He tried to kill you," Richard snapped. "Or have you forgotten?"

"He was aiming the halberd at you," I retorted. "And he was trying to provoke you, not kill you."

Richard sighed, running a hand through his already disheveled hair. "In any case, I've left instructions for Nettle and the others. They can return to the Hall once I'm gone. Montfort has agreed to maintain the grounds as they are for at least six months during the planning phase."

"You do realise he's lying about everything," I said coldly.

His eyes hardened. "This isn't easy for me either, Kitty."

"Isn't it?" I challenged. "Because from where I'm standing, it looks like you're taking the easiest path available. Running away rather than facing your heritage. Selling to the highest bidder rather than considering alternatives."

"There are no alternatives!" he snapped, his voice rising. "The magic is in my blood, whether I want it or not. If I stay, I put everyone at risk."

I followed him up to his room, where a single suitcase lay open on the bed, half-filled with neatly folded clothes. He didn't acknowledge my presence as he continued packing, his movements methodical and precise.

"What about Dr. Singer?" I asked finally. "He still needs medical attention."

"I've spoken with Dr. Harlow in Southlea Cross," he replied, not looking up. "She'll be checking in on him daily. And I've left detailed instructions for his care."

Of course he had. Ever the responsible physician, even as he prepared to flee.

"And what about me?" I asked.

His hands stilled over the suitcase. "What about you?"

"I thought we were friends. Was any of it real? Or was I just a convenient distraction while you finalised Montfort's offer?"

Richard turned to face me, his expression pained. "Kitty, don't. You know it wasn't like that."

"Do I?" I pressed. "Because right now, it feels like none of it mattered. Not the things we shared. Not even—" I broke off.

"Not even what?" he asked, his voice soft and careful.

"Not even the fact that I was foolish enough to care for you!" I finished, cheeks burning. "And that I might be worth staying for."

The look he gave me then twisted the blade—tender and tormented all at once.

"You are worth more than I can ever say," he admitted.

"And in another life, I would have . . ." He shook his head. "But I won't put you in danger."

"I'm not afraid of you," I said fiercely.

"Well, you should be."

He closed the suitcase with a decisive click and lifted it from the bed. I stepped aside to let him pass, my throat tight with unshed tears. This wasn't how it was supposed to end.

Richard paused at the door. "I left an envelope with Mrs. Deen. Two weeks wages. I hope that's sufficient."

I stared at him in disbelief. "I don't want your damned money!" I shouted. "Keep it!"

He cast me a wounded look and then he was gone, his footsteps receding down the stairs. I stood frozen for a moment, then jolted into action, racing after him. I couldn't let him leave like this. Not without one last attempt.

I caught up to him at his car, where he was stowing his suitcase in the boot.

"Richard, wait," I called, rushing up to him. "One more day. That's all I'm asking. Give yourself one more day to consider alternatives."

He shut the boot with a firm thud. "Please don't make this any harder than it is. My mind is made up."

"Then you *are* a coward," I said, desperate enough to try anything, even cruelty. "Your parents ran away when things got difficult. Now you're doing the same."

His jaw tightened, but he didn't rise to the bait. "Think what you will," he said, moving around to the driver's side. "It doesn't change the facts."

I followed, standing between him and the door. "The fact is, you're needed here. By the village. By the Wild Wood." I swallowed hard. "By me."

For a heartbeat, he wavered. I saw it in his eyes—a flicker of doubt, of longing. Then he gently moved me aside.

"I'm sorry," he said again, sliding into the driver's seat. "More than you'll ever know."

The engine roared to life, drowning out my final protests. I stepped back as he put the car in gear and sped toward Ravencroft Hall as if a pack of hellhounds were snarling at his heels.

19

COLD IRON

I watched Richard's car disappear around the bend in the road. A numbness spread through me—not the merciful kind that dulls pain, but the paralyzing sort that keeps you rooted in place while your mind races in useless circles.

I couldn't face my friends, couldn't bear to admit that I'd failed. Richard was gone, and with him our last hope of saving Little Groating. Then I thought of what Nan had said about reinforcements.

And I turned toward the Wild Wood.

The path to Nyx's home was worn by my feet alone. Village children were sternly cautioned to stay clear of the forest's fringe, but I'd been visiting the dryad since I was eleven, drawn by her wisdom and laughter.

Her oak stood at the edge of a clearing, its trunk wide enough for six men to clasp hands. Even in the depths of winter the limbs would spread wide and green, sheltering birds and squirrels and a fox den under the roots.

Now, the branches stood bare. A single leaf clung on,

trembling in the slight breeze. The sight made my chest feel like I lay beneath a heavy stone.

"Nyx?" I called hoarsely. "It's Kitty."

I wasn't sure what I planned to say. Goodbye, I suppose. But she didn't appear. I pressed my forehead against the bark. "Has it happened already?" I whispered. "Have you gone back to Faerie?"

My knees gave out and I collapsed among the ancient, majestic roots. There, with no one to see me, I indulged in a good ugly cry. When I was done, I wiped my face on my sleeve and clambered to my feet.

"I'll come back tomorrow and sit with you, old friend," I said to the oak, "until your last leaf falls."

Then I turned, eyes stinging again, and delved into the Wild Wood. It had been my refuge since childhood. Walking the faerie roads was what I'd always done when problems seemed insurmountable.

They unwound like dry riverbeds, sunken paths with high mossy banks that twisted through the oldest part of the wood. The ways appeared and vanished according to the whims of the Fair Folk, and I never knew where they would take me. Part of me wished they'd whisk me away to the Otherworld where Nyx had gone, though that was a coward's way out.

I followed one such path as it wound among silver birch trees. Here, in the heart of the wood, no decay had yet taken hold. The branches were thick with leaves and sunlight spilled golden coins across the soft earth. The air smelled of rocks and moss and green growing things.

If Richard wouldn't stay, perhaps there was another solution. My thoughts drifted to the fae prince I'd met when I was seven and ventured into the Wild Wood on a reckless quest to find Layla's father. Instead, I'd met Fenwick, who saved me from wicked faeries and spent a glorious day with me, climbing trees and splashing in bright pools.

I'd been half in love with him ever since, though he'd never shown himself again. I hadn't tried summoning him in years . . . but if ever I needed a fae prince's aid, this was the moment.

"Fenwick," I called softly. "Fenwick, if you can hear me, my need is dire."

The wood remained silent save for the soft hoot of an owl. I hadn't really expected him to appear, but disappointment still pinched my heart. I was about to turn back and find my way out of the wood when I heard a thin, miserable cry.

I froze, listening. It came again, a pitiful mewl like an abandoned kitten.

Of course, it could be a trick. There were faeries in the wood who took pleasure toying with mortal trespassers. But the sound tugged at my heartstrings. I couldn't turn my back without finding the source, so I followed it downhill into a dale sheltered by yews whose branches intertwined overhead like clasped fingers.

The lament grew louder. Someone was weeping, I realised, quietly but unceasing. At the bottom of the dale, in a small clearing carpeted with ferns, I stopped in my tracks.

A cage sat on a flat stone, about the size of a shoebox. It was forged of dull black iron. Inside, a faerie no larger than my thumb flitted frantically back and forth, its blue wings a blur. Iron was anathema to the Fair Folk—everyone knew that. To imprison a faerie in an iron cage was unthinkably cruel.

It babbled at me in a language I didn't understand, though

the meaning was clear. I hurried over and knelt beside the cage.

"Who did this to you?" I demanded, rage building in my chest.

The faerie only repeated its plea, tiny hands outstretched. Its reddish skin was dull. Dark scorch marks marked its wings where they had brushed the iron bars.

"Don't worry, I'll get you out of this vile contraption," I muttered, examining the cage. It had a simple latch. Whoever had set the trap hadn't expected anyone to find it.

I fumbled with the mechanism and the latch gave way with a faint click. I swung the door open and put my hand inside. After a moment, the trembling faerie alit on my finger. I drew it out of the cage.

"You're free, poor thing," I said. "Now tell me—"

But the terrified creature had already vanished. I couldn't blame it—after such an ordeal, the last thing it wanted was to answer a mortal's questions.

I peered into the cage. There were wrappers inside for sherbet lemons. The very same kind of boiled sweets Montfort had bought at Sugar & Sprites a couple of days ago.

I thought of Montfort and Silas Grimes, their heads bent together, voices low and secretive. The books on faerie lore Montfort had been buying. Grimes' strategic position in the village, watching and waiting. The lantern I had spotted one night, moving through the wood.

I stuffed the wrappers in my pocket. It was fortunate for them both that they weren't here now, because I felt entirely capable of strangling them with no remorse at all.

I needed to tell Layla and Briar. If Montfort was experimenting with ways to capture faeries, then his plans for Ravencroft Hall were far more sinister than a tacky hotel.

I tucked the cage under one arm and climbed out of the

dale, moving quickly. The Wild Wood seemed to sense my urgency; the faerie road widened and ran straight before me.

For the first time since watching Richard drive away, I felt something other than despair. Anger, yes—burning hot beneath my ribs—but also purpose. Whatever dark scheme Montfort was hatching, he would not get away with it.

20

LOTHIAN COTTAGE

I clutched the iron cage to my chest as I raced through the village toward Sugar & Sprites. Thoughts tumbled through my mind like leaves in a gale—Montfort and Grimes with their heads together, Montfort's sudden interest in faerie lore.

On the High Street, Madame de Berry was walking her three-legged spaniel. She called out a greeting, but I had no breath to answer and gave her a distracted wave. The iron cage banged against my ribs with each step.

I skidded to a halt in front of the shop. Today's window display featured cheddar and chive scones next to a faerie ring of mushrooms made from marzipan. The sign—a pixie stirring a steaming cauldron—creaked in the breeze.

The bell jingled as I burst through the door, startling a young couple who were examining a display of iced biscuits. The warm, yeasty air inside wrapped around me like a comforting blanket, thick with the scent of cinnamon and vanilla and that indefinable magic that was Briar's special touch.

"Sorry," I gasped to the startled customers. "Bakery emergency."

I pushed through the swinging half-door that separated the shop from the kitchen, nearly colliding with Briar, who was emerging with a tray of fresh-baked raisin loaves.

"Whoa there!" she exclaimed, deftly shifting the tray to avoid a collision. "What's got you tearing about like—" Her eyes fell on the cage in my hands, and her jovial expression vanished. "What the hell is that?"

"Where's Layla?" I demanded, my breath still coming in short gasps.

"Inventory." Briar set down her tray and wiped flour-dusted hands on her apron. "Kitty, why are you carrying an iron cage?"

"You won't believe it," I tossed over my shoulder, charging toward the small office in the back. Layla was hunched at the very edge of an ergonomic chair scrolling through a laptop with a pencil tucked behind her ear. Her long-sleeved t-shirt said *Equal Rites,* which was an all-girl goth band from Southlea Cross.

"I found this in the Wild Wood," I announced, setting the cage on a crate of flour. "There was a crying faerie inside. It was horrible!"

Layla stared at the cage, spots of pink flushing her brown cheeks. "Who would do such a thing?"

Briar had followed me in, her face grim. "It has to be Montfort."

"I'm certain of it," I said. "I've seen him with Grimes, chatting like they were old friends. Montfort's been buying books on faerie lore—you already know that much. And I saw lights in the wood a few nights ago—I bet that was one of them setting traps."

Layla closed her laptop and peered at the cage. "This is

bloody barbaric," she muttered. "The iron would burn the poor fae with every touch."

"Bastards," Briar growled. "How many are out there, do you think?"

"I only found the one," I said. "But I fear there could be more."

"You have to tell Richard," Layla said firmly. "Whatever his plans for the Hall, he would never sell to someone who would capture and mutilate faeries!"

The mention of Richard sent a fresh wave of anger through me. "He's already made up his mind," I said bitterly. "He's meeting with Montfort this afternoon to finalise the sale."

"But this changes everything!" Layla insisted. "Richard may be stubborn, but he's not cruel. You said so yourself! If he knew what Montfort was planning . . ."

"Which is what, exactly?" Briar cut in, her practical nature asserting itself. "We need more than suspicions, my love. We need proof."

I paced the length of the storeroom. "Montfort's staying at the Dancing Toadstool. Let's confront him directly."

Briar untied her apron and hung it on a hook. "I'll get my coat." Her blue eyes hardened to chips of ice. "No one fucks with our faeries."

Two minutes later, we were marching abreast to the Dancing Toadstool. Briar was not a small woman and she militantly carried an eggbeater in one hand—for what purpose I didn't dare ask. Layla strode alongside, wrath in her eyes.

"If Montfort really is capturing faeries," she said, "it must violate the compact between the Ravencrofts and the Court of Silver Shadows. Not to mention basic decency."

"I don't think decency is high on his list of concerns," I replied.

The inn was quiet, most guests out enjoying the afternoon. Mrs. Deen looked up from polishing glasses behind the bar, her eyebrows rising as we burst through the door.

"Montfort," Layla said without preamble. "Is he here, Mum?"

She shook her head. "He left . . . oh, an hour ago. Said something about meeting his associates in Southlea Cross before heading to the Hall." Her gaze shifted to the cage in my arms. "What on earth is that?"

"A faerie trap," Briar said with disgust. "Kitty found it in the Wild Wood."

Mrs. Deen's expression darkened. "And you think Montfort—"

"We know he's involved with Grimes," I cut in. "And given Montfort's sudden interest in our local faeries . . ."

Sir Francis Drake came flapping in and roosted on Mrs. Deen's shoulder. "Betray the cap'n and meet the deep!" he screamed. "He sold us for a shiny coin! A shiny coin!"

"What's that?" Nan voice drifted from Dr. Singer's room.

I started down the hall to fill her in, but Briar grabbed my arm. "Grimes," she said. "If Montfort's not here, let's interrogate his accomplice. There's no time to mess around."

I nodded grimly. "Lothian Cottage."

"Be careful," Mrs. Deen warned. "That man strikes me as dangerous when cornered."

"So are we," Layla growled.

Her mum gave a firm nod. "I'll tell Nan and Dr. Singer what's happened."

Layla, Briar and I hurried back outside, taking the lane that led to my childhood home, now rented to a man I felt certain was tangled up in something despicable. Lothian

Cottage stood alone, a stone's throw from a stream that marked the boundary of the Wild Wood.

Its quiet locale, set apart from the rest of the village, made it an ideal artist's retreat—or the perfect spot for a man with foul deeds to hide.

"Well, look at that," Briar said flatly. "Someone's nervous."

New iron horseshoes had been nailed above the door and windows, gleaming in the morning light. I pounded on the door.

"Silas!" I shouted. "Open up!"

No response came from within. I fished in my coat pocket and withdrew a ring of keys. "As the owners' agent," I said, "I have every right to enter the premises if I suspect wrongdoing."

Layla and Briar gave me tight nods. The key stuck a moment, then turned in the lock. I pushed the door open, wincing at the smell—stale food, unwashed clothes, and something else, a sickly-sweet odor that reminded me of burnt sugar.

We stepped inside. The cottage I'd grown up in was barely recognizable. Where my parents had filled it with light and colour, Grimes had transformed it into a dim, cluttered space that felt smaller than it was. Dirty dishes were piled in the sink, newspapers and sketching materials covered every surface, and the walls were papered with crude drawings of what I assumed were meant to be faeries, though they bore little resemblance to the real things.

We spread out, moving cautiously through the small cottage. I headed for my parents' old bedroom, heart sinking at what Grimes had done to it. Gone were the bookshelves and wide, sunny window seat where I'd spent countless hours reading. In their place stood a workbench littered with tools—pliers, wire cutters, a small anvil, and most disturbing of all, a soldering iron.

"Kitty!" Layla's voice, high with alarm.

I hurried into the kitchen, where Layla and Briar stood before the pantry. Inside, stacked on shelves where my mother had once kept preserves and flour, were iron cages—a dozen at least, identical to the one I'd found in the wood. And inside each one, a faerie.

They were different species—some with colourful dragonfly wings, others with skin like tree bark, still others with tiny antlers sprouting from their heads. A few flitted weakly back and forth. Others crouched motionless, their natural glow dimmed. All stared back at us with pleading eyes.

"Oh, god," I whispered, bile rising in my throat.

Briar was already reaching for the nearest cage. "We have to get them out," she said, her voice tight with fury.

We worked quickly, opening cages and setting the faeries free. Some fled, vanishing into cracks in the walls. Others had to be lifted out. Layla spoke to them in soothing tones using the Faerie tongue, which she'd taught herself the rudiments of from books.

As the last faerie recovered enough to flit away, I heard a floorboard creak in the study. I strode through the doorway, ready to throttle Silas Grimes with my bare hands, but it was just Briar.

"He's been keeping records," she said, holding up a leather-bound notebook. "Dates, locations, species descriptions."

"Inventorying the merchandise," Layla said grimly from behind me. She moved to a desk in the corner and rifled through a stack of papers. "Here's something—letters with Montfort's letterhead."

I peered over her shoulder. The topmost bore the seal of

the Blight & Penhaligon Development Company, addressed to "Mr. A. Montfort" and signed by someone with an illegible scrawl.

" . . . delighted with your progress," Layla read aloud. "The specimens you've obtained will make excellent attractions for the menagerie. Our investors are particularly interested in the luminous varieties, which would create a spectacular nocturnal display."

"They're planning a zoo," Briar exclaimed in disbelief. "A fucking faerie zoo!"

Layla shuffled through more papers. "Here's a blueprint," she said, spreading out a large sheet. "Look—they're planning to build it right next to the hotel they want to make out of Ravencroft Hall."

The plans showed Ravencroft Hall converted into a luxury hotel, with an adjacent structure labeled "Enchanted Encounters"—a sprawling complex of glass domes and iron-barred enclosures.

"This is what Grimes has been doing?" I said, my voice rising. "Testing out their sick plans by capturing faeries from the Wild Wood?"

"He's their local agent," Layla agreed, gathering up the most damning documents. "Probably reporting back on which species are easiest to capture, how they respond to captivity."

"How they respond to iron," Briar added grimly, glancing at the empty cages. "The bloody fools. Don't they realise what will happen if they anger the Court of Silver Shadows?"

I grabbed the blueprint and several of the letters. "We need to show these to Richard. Immediately, before he signs anything."

"Will he listen?" Layla asked, her voice gentle but doubtful. "After what happened between you—"

"He has to," I cut her off. "Whatever he thinks of me, whatever he fears about his own magic, he cannot—will not —allow this." I stuffed the papers into my coat. "Come on. Montfort's meeting him at the Hall this afternoon. We have to get there first."

For all his flaws, I felt sure that Richard would do the right thing when faced with the evidence of Montfort's barbarity. Somewhere beneath his stubborn pride and his terror of his own magic, there beat the heart of a wizard.

21

COMSLUG'S NEW MEMBER

Twilight was falling by the time we reached Ravencroft Hall. Purple shadows lengthened along the drive as the last rays of sunlight vanished behind the Wild Wood. Layla clutched the plans we'd pilfered from Grimes's cottage, while I lugged one of the vile iron cages.

"Shit," Briar gasped, her red curls damp with sweat. "Isn't that Montfort's car out front?"

His black Range Rover was parked next to Richard's dented blue Mini. We rushed up to the door and burst into the foyer. Montfort's booming voice drifted from the library.

"—a pleasure doing business with you, Lord Ravencroft."

My heart clenched as we all spilled through the library door. Richard sat behind the massive desk, fountain pen poised above a stack of papers. His dark eyes flicked up to meet mine, narrowing in puzzlement as they slid to the iron cage. Montfort's toothy smile dimmed for a fraction of a second before reasserting itself.

"Miss Boot! And her friends, how delightful," he exclaimed, spreading his arms as if to embrace us all. "You're just in time to congratulate Lord Ravencroft on making a sound business decision."

I strode forward, slamming the cage down on the desk with enough force to make both men jump. "We found a dozen of these in Grimes's cottage—full of captured faeries. Trapped in iron, Richard. Do you understand? They were suffering horribly."

Richard frowned and turned to Montfort, who cleared his throat. "Now, now, let's not be melodramatic—"

"Shut up," Briar snapped. She dropped the stolen documents onto the desk beside the cage. "Blueprints for your 'development.' Letters from your investors. You're planning to build a faerie zoo, you bastard!"

Richard stared at the cage, then at the blueprints, his face draining of colour. "Is this true?" he asked Montfort.

Montfort sighed, adjusting his cufflinks. "I had intended to disclose the full scope of the project once the sale was complete. But yes, we envision a menagerie of the more fantastic elements of the estate. Visitors are fascinated by folklore, and what better way to celebrate it than by showcasing real faeries."

"Showcase?" I sputtered. "You mean imprison them until they die!"

"Die?" Montfort chuckled, shaking his head. "Nonsense. We'll treat them well. I'll admit, the cages Silas Grimes made are crude. We simply needed to test the idea. But the final version of the theme park will have climate-controlled habitats, regular feedings—"

"You're a monster." Layla's voice was low and furious. "They're sentient beings who tend this land. Part of a delicate ecosystem you couldn't possibly understand."

Montfort waved a dismissive hand. "The public will be enchanted. Think of how happy we'll make all the children."

"Happy?" Briar echoed in disbelief. "Those kids will be traumatised for fucking life!"

Something in me snapped. I lunged at Montfort, but Layla and Briar caught me, pulling me back as he stumbled away.

"Control yourself, Miss Boot!" he spluttered. "Or I'll press charges against all of you!"

I turned to Richard. "You can't go through with this," I hissed. "Not now."

He looked up at me, and I saw the ruin in his face. "It's already done, Kitty. The money's wired. The keys are his."

My gaze fell to the papers on the desk. Richard's bold signature shone damply on the final page. A wave of sickness rolled through me.

"The faeries aren't your property!" I shouted, straining against my friends' grip. "The Wild Wood isn't your property!"

Montfort straightened his coat, a dangerous gleam entering his eye. "Actually, according to the ancient charter, everything within the boundaries of the estate belongs to the owner. Which is now the Blight & Penhaligon Development Company."

"Just the house," Richard said, his voice tight. "And the immediate grounds. Not the Wild Wood."

Montfort's smile turned predatory. "I'm afraid you're mistaken, Lord Ravencroft. Your solicitors should have explained the full extent of your holdings." He tapped a section of the contract. "Under the ancient feudal code, the village of Little Groating is part of the estate. As is the Wild Wood, the pastures to the east, and even that charming little pond with its . . . unusual inhabitant."

I held Montfort's smug gaze. "Would you like to meet Nelly? I can introduce you to her right now."

He laughed. "Thank you, Miss Boot, perhaps another time. The point is, my investors now own all of it—the Hall, the woods, the village." His tone hardened. "And anyone who doesn't cooperate with our development vision can leave."

"You can't just evict an entire village," Briar protested.

"Can't I?" Montfort's smile didn't reach his eyes. "The leases will need to be renewed, of course. And I'm afraid the rents will have to reflect the property's new status as a premium tourist destination."

I watched Richard as the full weight of what he'd done sank in. He slumped in the chair, gripping his head in his hands. Montfort turned away from us and began to gather the papers, humming to himself.

"Do something," I hissed at Richard. "Use your magic!"

He looked up at me. For a moment, the old fire lit his eyes. He whispered something under his breath . . . and slumped back. "I can't . . . I . . . it's gone, Kitty."

Montfort snapped his briefcase shut. "You've made the prudent choice, Lord Ravencroft. Walking away with a fortune, no connection to the estate you despise, and with the prospect of a brilliant medical career in London. Everything you ever wanted."

Richard stared at him with hollow eyes. "Everything I wanted," he repeated softly.

"Precisely," Montfort continued. "You're free of this awful burden. Free to build a life unencumbered by your checkered past." He seemed genuinely mystified. "Isn't that what you've been seeking all along, my lord?"

Richard's gaze traveled around the library—the shelves of ancient books, the portrait of his ancestors above the mantel, the window with a view of the Wild Wood in the distance. Then his gaze moved to me and lingered. "No," he said. "No, I don't think it is."

Montfort's smile faltered. "I beg your pardon?"

"I said no," Richard repeated forcefully, rising to his feet. "I don't want any of that anymore."

Layla and Briar exchanged glances. Montfort flushed an ugly red. "It's rather too late for a change of heart. The sale is complete. In the meantime, I suggest you begin packing."

With that, he swept for the door. I exchanged a glance with Briar and we chased him outside. "This isn't over," I shouted as he rushed to his car.

Montfort whirled to me, face mottled with rage. "It absolutely is," he shouted back. "The money has changed hands. The contract is signed. There is nothing—nothing—any of you can do about it!"

He yanked open his car door and flung his briefcase onto the passenger seat. "I'd start looking for new accommodations if I were you, Miss Boot. I doubt the Dancing Toadstool will remain an inn for much longer. Perhaps we'll make it a spa. Or a fast food franchise!"

Briar lunged, but this time I was the one who caught her arm. "Let him go," I muttered.

Montfort slid into the driver's seat and slammed the door. The engine roared to life, and he sped down the drive, gravel spitting from beneath his tires.

We trudged back inside to find Richard pacing the library. "You must hate me," he said grimly. "And I deserve it. But I'll make it right somehow, I swear to you—"

"We don't hate you," Layla interrupted with a frown. "Montfort used you. He's a greedy, evil man, but not a stupid one. He manipulated your weakness to get what he wanted. But if we all work together, we can still stop this."

"My love speaks true." Briar wrapped an arm around Layla's waist and kissed her temple. Layla snuggled her head against Briar's shoulder.

"Kitty?" Richard asked hoarsely. "Can you forgive me? I know I keep saying that, but I mean it this time. Give me one more chance and I swear you won't regret it."

I was still angry, more than I'd ever been in my life, but the abject misery in his face made me relent. After a moment, I stepped forward and gave him a hug.

"We'll find a way," I whispered against the wool of his coat. "Together."

Richard pulled me closer, his chin resting against my hair. I felt the steady beat of his heart and knew that somehow, against the odds, everything would turn out right. The wizard of Ravencroft Hall had finally come home.

THE HALL FELT GLOOMY AND UNWELCOMING AS IF IT KNEW what he'd done, so I persuaded Richard to drive us all down to the village. We piled into his Mini, no one speaking much.

The inn's common room was nearly empty save for the corner by the fire. There, to my happy surprise, sat Dr. Singer in an armchair, wrapped in a thick blanket. His colour was improved and though he still looked frail, the worst danger had passed. Nan sat beside him, her knitting needles clicking as she worked on a pair of tiny mittens.

They both turned as we entered. I watched a series of expressions cross Nan's face—relief at our safe return, curiosity about our grim faces, and finally, a sharp assessment of Richard, who hung back as if contemplating flight.

"Well," she said, setting down her knitting. "You've been through the wars."

Richard stepped forward, his whole body rigid. It reminded me of the time Layla thought it would be fun to give Barbarossa a bath. The cat had the same look of resigned dread.

"Mrs. Boot, Dr. Singer," Richard declared. "I'm afraid I've made a terrible mistake."

He drew a deep breath and confessed everything—the sale of Ravencroft Hall, the discovery that this included the entire village, and Montfort's plans for a faerie zoo.

"I was a fool," he finished. "I let fear cloud my judgment, and now I've endangered everything and everyone. I understand if you want nothing more to do with me."

Nan clucked her tongue. "Sit down," she said. "You look ready to collapse."

He blinked. "You're not . . . angry?"

"Oh, I'm furious," Nan replied, her brows drawing together. "But not at you. At that snake oil salesman. He played you like a fiddle, taking advantage of your vulnerabilities." She patted the chair next to Dr. Singer. "Now sit. A mistake is only fatal if you refuse to correct it."

Richard sank into the chair, looking dazed.

"She's right, my boy," Dr. Singer added, his voice raspy but steady. "The measure of a man isn't whether he stumbles, but whether he picks himself up afterward."

Mrs. Deen emerged from the kitchen, a tray balanced in one hand. "I heard voices," she said. "What's happened?"

As Layla and Briar filled her in, Richard sat hunched forward, elbows on his knees, staring into the fire. His face was a study in misery.

"You know," Nan said, breaking the silence, "this reminds me of a time off the coast of Sumatra. The year would have been 1954, I believe."

Richard glanced up as Nan launched into her tale.

"We were caught in the worst storm I'd ever seen. Waves high as houses, wind that screamed like a banshee. Our main sail was torn to ribbons, the rudder damaged. We'd lost our navigational equipment, and our radio was dead." Her eyes grew distant with memory. "Skipper thought we were done for. Said his goodbyes to the crew, told us it had been an honor."

She smiled. "But I wasn't ready to die. Neither was Harry —my husband. We rigged up a sea anchor from what was left of the sail to keep us from capsizing. Then I remembered something an old fisherwoman had taught me in Singapore. The sea has currents beneath the storm. If you can find them, they'll carry you to safety."

Richard straightened, drawn into the story despite himself. "What did you do?"

"We watched the water, not the sky. There was a pattern to the swells, you see. We followed it, using what little control we had, and do you know what? By morning, we'd drifted into the lee of a small island. The storm was still raging behind us, but we were safe." Nan's sharp blue eyes fixed on Richard. "Sometimes salvation comes from the most unexpected quarters, if you're willing to look for it."

Richard gave her a wan smile. "I appreciate the sentiment, Mrs. Boot, but I'm not sure there's an easy way out of this particular storm. I've . . . lost my magic, too."

She nodded slowly. "It's tied to the estate. When you renounced your legacy—"

"The magic renounced *me*," Richard finished.

He rose abruptly and began to prowl the length of the common room. His power might be gone, but the Ravencroft temper was perfectly intact. He muttered to himself, vile oaths interspersed with dire threats.

"I'll do whatever it takes to stop Montfort," Richard declared, his black eyes sweeping across us all. "That I vow on my honor as a Ravencroft!"

Barbarossa hissed and ran under Nan's chair. For the first time, I glimpsed what his magic truly might be—not darkness, but passion.

"That's good," I said, "but you'll need help, starting with the house brownies."

Richard stopped his pacing. "Nettle, you mean?"

"All of them. Including Gilcarren."

He grimaced. "Yes. I suppose I'll need to make peace with him if we're to have any chance."

"And I'll research the lore," Layla offered. "Dunmorra makes several references to the Court of Silver Shadows. I've got a spreadsheet on it, just have to dig it out. There might be a way to invoke your family's pact against Montfort. Get your magic back."

"And I'll bake," Briar declared. Everyone looked at her, and she shrugged. "What? You'll need to win over the brownies, and the surest way is through their stomachs."

Mrs. Deen had been listening quietly, her hands folded before her. Now she straightened. "What we need," she said, "is a proper war council. I find they're best convened with curry." She regarded each of us in turn. "Half an hour, in the private dining room."

Supper proved to be a feast worthy of the occasion—turmeric rice steaming with ghee and black pepper, a rich veg curry that filled the room with its fragrance, and a mountain of samosas with tamarind chutney. We gathered around the table, the weight of the day temporarily lifted by good food and better company.

"First order of business," Nan said, "I propose we induct Lord Ravencroft into COMSLUG."

"I'm honored," Richard said. "Ah, what's COMSLUG?"

"The Committee to Save Little Groating," I explained.

"Excellent!" he shook out his linen napkin and spooned rice onto his plate. "But . . . where does the U come from?"

"See?" Leyla elbowed me. "I told you it ought to be *COMSLIG*."

I opened my mouth to argue but Briar, ever the diplomat, intervened.

"Which is why we agreed to refer to ourselves as simply the Committee," she reminded everyone.

"Very well." Layla raised her wineglass. "To our newest member!"

The rest of us joined the toast as Sir Francis Drake soared in and alit on the sideboard. "Don't drink that!" he screamed. "No antidote!"

Richard froze mid-sip.

Sir Francis gave a raspy chuckle, then added in a deeper voice, "Taste it, taste it, be brave!"

"Don't mind Sir Francis," Briar said, casting a reproachful look at the cackling parrot. "He had some shady owners before Nan bought him."

For the next hour, we strategised between bites. Dr. Singer offered insights about the history of the Hall. Nan recalled tales about Richard's parents that even he hadn't known. Layla sketched out her plan of research, while Briar kept our spirits up with ribald jokes.

Through it all, Richard spoke little but listened closely, asking questions and taking notes on his prescription pad. When the meal ended and we began to drift upstairs toward our beds, he caught my arm. "Could I have a word, Kitty?"

We stepped into the small garden behind the inn. The night was cool but not cold, with a scattering of bright stars.

"I wanted to thank you again," Richard said. "All of you, but especially you. You had every right to wash your hands of me after what I did. Instead, you stood by me. It means more than I can say."

His face was in shadow, but his voice was laced with strong emotion. "I've spent my whole life running from who I am. From *what* I am. I was so afraid of becoming like my parents that I refused to see any other possibility. But you did."

I clasped his hand. "I don't believe the essence of magic is dark or light. It's the intent that matters. Your parents might have misused their gifts, but that doesn't mean you will. And it will take magic to save us all, Richard."

He considered this. "Even if we find the moonstone amulet, faerie courts are not known to show mercy toward mortals who break bargains. And I *have* broken the ancient pact, Kitty."

"You won't face them alone," I reminded him. "We're your family now. I'll be at your side every step of the way, Richard."

His fingers tightened around mine, warm and strong. "Together," he said, and for the first time since I'd known him, he sounded like he truly believed it.

22

PITY HE WON'T COME CLOSER

I found Richard in the kitchen the next morning, nursing a cup of strong black coffee while Briar packed a basket with freshly baked treats. Cinnamon and brown sugar filled the air.

"Just one," she admonished when I reached for a swirled bun. "They're for Nettle."

"Sure," I replied, the word garbled through a mouthful of fluffy bliss.

Richard's eyes were bloodshot from what had obviously been a sleepless night, but determination had replaced yesterday's despair. When he smiled, it was like ice cracking on a frozen pond—tentative, but with a hint of life beneath the surface.

He pushed a steaming mug toward me. "Briar's been up since four."

"The brownies deserve my best work," she said, tucking a cloth over the basket. "If we're going to war against capitalist vultures, we need allies who are well-fed and happy."

I sipped the coffee. "The Folk remember kindness."

Richard nodded, his dark eyes serious. "And slights," he added.

Briar handed him the basket. "Don't drop it," she warned. "The apricot tarts took me an hour to glaze."

We set out for the gamekeeper's cottage, walking side by side up the High Street. A misty drizzle hung in the air, hardly enough to merit opening our umbrellas. Richard matched his long stride to mine, the basket swinging between us.

"Do you think they'll help?" he asked.

"The brownies? Of course they will. They've been waiting for a Ravencroft to return to the Hall for twenty years."

Richard frowned. "I don't mean Nettle and her kin. I mean the Court of Silver Shadows."

I tripped over an exposed root and he caught my wrist. The touch sent a shiver along my skin.

"That's a different matter," I said. "But I know little about them."

"Nor do I," Richard admitted. "My parents would have taught me the essentials once I got older, but they never had the chance."

"Layla will find something," I said. "She has a vast database of lore on her laptop. Honestly, the woman is probably one of the leading fae experts in England, if not Western Europe."

He frowned. "I thought there was no internet in the village?"

"There's not. She goes to the library in Southlea Cross. They have free wi-fi."

We turned onto the path to Nelly's Pond, which lay flat upon the landscape like a dark mirror in the distance.

"It would be quite satisfying if the pond hag ate Montfort," Richard remarked. "But that wouldn't solve our problem."

"No," I agreed. "We'd still have Blight and Penhaligon to deal with. Not to mention their army of solicitors."

Richard's laugh was grim. "Solicitors. More terrifying than any boggart."

"The only way to truly stop them is to void the sale some-how," I said. "And for that, we need a power greater than theirs."

We walked the rest of the way in silence. As we neared the reedy shore, I felt that familiar prickle of unease.

"Look," Richard murmured, pointing.

At the far edge of the pond, among a cluster of late-blooming water lilies, Nelly floated lazily on her back.

"She knows we're here," I whispered. "We mustn't be rude."

As if in response, one eye opened, fixing on us with predatory interest. I waved and called a greeting. Nelly rolled over, her serpentine arms propelling her slowly toward us. Richard stiffened but held his ground. She stopped a few yards from shore and gave us a jagged grin.

"I saw the man with the false hair," she said, water streaming from her green skin. "Pity he didn't come closer."

"When was that?" Richard asked.

"Early this morning. He's gone now." She kicked off the bottom and drifted backward into deeper water. "He was taking photos of my pond. I don't like that. Wish he'd come a bit closer. In the old days, eating one idiot was enough to discourage the rest. Good luck to you."

With that, she sank beneath the surface, leaving only ripples to mark her passage.

"Montfort probably wants to drain it to build an Olympic-sized swimming pool," I said.

Richard shook his head. "Christ, I *do* wish she'd eat him."

We continued around the edge of the pond toward Nettle's cottage. Small faces peered from the broken windows, disappearing when they realised they'd been spotted.

"They're still wary," I said.

"Or angry," Richard said, clutching the basket tighter.

We stopped before the crooked door. He made an elaborate bow from the waist, as I'd told him to.

"Nettle," he called. "It's Richard Ravencroft. I've come to speak with you, if you'll permit it."

There was a great whispering inside. Then the door creaked open and the brownie peered up at us. "Sir," she said, in a cooler tone than the first time we'd visited.

Richard set the basket down. "I bring gifts. Briar Godwin sends her regards."

A murmur rippled through the brownies. Nettle lifted the cloth, and a chorus of appreciative gasps arose as the scent of fresh-baked treats wafted out.

"Most generous," Nettle said, her button eyes gleaming. "Come inside and share our hearth, such as it is."

The brownies had made efforts to tidy the dismal cottage, sweeping the dead leaves into a corner and clearing away the cobwebs. Yet no fire burned in the hearth and it was quite cold. They swarmed around the basket, exclaiming over each treasure as Nettle unpacked it—scones glazed with honey, miniature tarts filled with bright apricot preserves, tiny seed cakes studded with caraway.

Pity swelled my heart as I watched the thin, ragged creatures, and I know Richard felt the same. When the last crumbs were devoured, Nettle stood on a three-legged stool and fixed him with a penetrating stare.

"What is it you want from us, sir?" she asked.

Richard knelt before her. "I need your help to rectify a terrible mistake. Ravencroft Hall has been sold to men who mean to destroy the Wild Wood and imprison the Fair Folk for profit."

Her gaze went flat. "We already know this. But I fear we cannot aid you."

"Why not?" Richard demanded. "Surely you don't want to serve these monsters!"

"Want has nothing to do with it," Nettle replied sharply. "We are bound to Ravencroft Hall. Until you claim your birthright at the Court of Silver Shadows, we cannot recognise you as our rightful master."

Richard looked stricken and her expression softened. "Forgive us, but the fact remains that you have not affirmed the ancient pact. You have lost your magic, sir. Until you get it back, we are required to serve whoever owns the Hall."

"Oh no," I muttered. It was worse than we'd thought.

"However wicked the new owners may be," Nettle added with evident distaste. "It is the way of things."

"But if I were to affirm the pact?" Richard asked. "If I were to reclaim my magic?"

"Then we would serve you with great delight, my lord. We would help you reclaim your ancestral home and drive out these interlopers."

Richard fell silent. At last, he looked up, jaw set in that familiar mulish line.

"Then I will do it," he said firmly. "I will go to the Court of Silver Shadows and claim my birthright. Do you, er, have any advice on how to accomplish that?"

Nettle regarded him solemnly. "You must begin with the moonstone amulet. With Gilcarren."

Richard gave a resigned nod. "Thank you, Nettle. All of you. I will return when it is done."

WE REACHED RAVENCROFT HALL AS THE RAIN BEGAN IN earnest, dashing up the front steps and huddling together under an umbrella.

"Speak from the heart," I advised. "He fears you now, but it's loyalty given freely that you need. Gilcarren was your friend once. He can be so again."

He sighed. "I know. I will try, Kitty."

Montfort hadn't yet changed the locks, and Richard had wisely kept a spare key. We entered the house, and he drew himself up to his full height. "Gilcarren," he commanded. "Make yourself known."

From the shadows beneath the grand staircase a figure emerged—hunched, spindly, swathed in layers of stolen coats. "You called, my lord?" His voice was rough and scratchy, as if unused to conversation.

Richard stepped forward. "I owe you an apology, Gilcarren. You protected this house at great cost to yourself, and I repaid you poorly."

Gilcarren's bony shoulders slumped. "You were but a child when it happened, sir."

"And I am one no longer," Richard replied. "I should have thanked you. Sought your counsel. Instead, I lashed out and used my magic against you. For that, I am truly sorry."

The brownie stared at Richard for a long moment. Then he removed his top hat, kneading the brim with long, bulbous fingers. "I, too, must beg forgiveness, sir. I stole your clothes. Provoked you deliberately." His eyes flicked to me. "Almost harmed Miss Boot, though that was an accident. I *was* rather horrid, sir, but I only wanted to test your magic."

"Well, you succeeded in that," Richard said dryly. "And now I need to get it back."

Gilcarren's face split in a homely grin. "Then I must give you what is rightfully yours, sir."

From some pocket in his outer waistcoat, he withdrew a pendant on a silver chain. The setting held a moonstone the size of a robin's egg, nestled within an intricate silver filigree that formed a pattern of interlocking crescent moons. The stone pulsed with an inner light.

"The amulet," Richard breathed.

Gilcarren hobbled over and placed it in his palm. "Hidden where only a true Ravencroft could find it—with the one who loved him best."

Richard's fingers closed around the moonstone and for a heartbeat, the air around him seemed to shimmer, then fade. His dark eyes met mine over Gilcarren's hunched form.

"Now," he said, "we must find the doorway."

OF COURSE, THIS PROVED EASIER SAID THAN DONE. WHEN Richard asked where to seek the Court of Silver Shadows, the brownie—for he had returned to himself and was no longer a boggart—shook his head.

"I was never privy to such secrets, my lord," he said. "The way to the Court is knowledge passed only from one Ravencroft to another."

Richard's expression darkened. "And my parents are in Romania, if they're even still alive. I haven't heard from them in twenty years."

"Could we call them and ask?" I suggested desperately.

"There won't be phones where they are. And even if I

knew where to send a letter," Richard said, "there's hardly time to wait for international post."

"How much longer do you own the hall for?" I asked.

"Until the 15th of November."

Three days from now.

"Nettle said I must affirm the pact before she can help me." Richard slipped the amulet around his neck. The moonstone pulsed once with a faint white light as if it recognised and approved of him. "But how am I supposed to affirm a pact when I don't even know where to find the other party?"

I thought for a moment. "What about the secret library? There's bound to be some good stuff in there."

Richard slapped his forehead. "The secret library! Gilcarren, surely you know where *that* is."

Gilcarren brightened, his blue-tinted ears twitching. "I do indeed! Follow me."

He led us to the billiards room and paused in front of the fireplace with the solemnity of a priest at the altar. "Observe, sir," the brownie said, and twisted the beak of a stone griffin at the end of the mantel, a half-turn clockwise, then a full turn counterclockwise. There was a grinding sound and the entire firebox swung forward, revealing a passage behind it.

"Good heavens," I said. "That's ingenious. We might have looked for our whole lives and never found it."

Richard eyed the narrow, pitch-dark opening with suspicion. "Are you sure there's a library down there and you're not sending us to the oubliette?"

Gilcarren laid a wizened hand over his heart. "I swear, sir, my days of mischief-making are behind me now. I regret that I cannot accompany you further. The secret library is warded against fae. If I entered, I'd be reduced to a pile of salt and soot before you could sneeze."

With a flourish, he produced a candle from somewhere

about his person and handed it to Richard. "Godspeed, milord. Miss Boot."

We ducked into the passage, Richard holding the candle high. Its flickering light illuminated stone walls just wide enough for us to walk single file. The way led to a spiral stair that felt far longer than the depth of the house should allow, our footsteps echoing. At the bottom, we found a plain wooden door with an antique brass handle. Richard hesitated, then touched the amulet at his throat. He seemed to brace himself, as if expecting a jolt of power or perhaps an explosion.

He turned the handle and stepped through.

I've seen pictures of fantastic libraries before. Trinity College in Dublin. The Bodleian at Oxford. That insane one in the Vatican with all the frescoes. Layla calls it her "library porn" and she uses them as screensavers on her laptop.

But I was still impressed by the sheer audacious splendor of the Ravencroft Library. It was four stories tall—yes, four, though the Hall itself was only three stories aboveground—and lined from floor to dizzying ceiling with books.

Hundreds of thousands, perhaps millions, shelved in dark walnut that gleamed like polished stone. Spiral staircases wound upward at dizzying intervals, and ironwork balconies hung suspended over the air like delicate spiderwebs.

Each level was lined with plush carpets woven in cosmic patterns: constellations, planetary orbits, and zodiac wheels. Rolling ladders tracked the walls, their brass rails burnished by centuries of use. Hanging lamps—some glowing with natural gas, others with a soft magical radiance—bobbed overhead, adjusting their intensity in direct response to the movement of a reader below.

There were also windows, tall as cathedral doors,

showing not the actual landscape of the Hall but a perpetual scene of gentle snowfall over towering fir trees.

In the center of the chamber, a fire blazed in a hearth larger than the dining room table at the Toadstool. An enchanted tea trolley, burdened with delicate porcelain and ever-replenishing cakes, drifted through the room with a cheerful clatter. There were armchairs, some of which appeared to be reading books on their own; when you approached, they politely yielded their seat.

Richard and I simply stood there for a moment, mouths agape.

"If this is real magic," I managed, "sign me up now."

He gave a low whistle. "It's like a bloody TARDIS."

I wanted to rush everywhere at once, to climb ladders and eat cakes and curl up in a chair forever and ever, but we had a mission. I forced myself to focus.

"I suppose we start by looking for a catalogue," I said.

Richard's eyes scanned the room. "There," he said, pointing to a podium at the base of the nearest staircase. I rushed over and found not a catalogue but a map—one that shifted and flickered in and out of focus, reordering itself as if the Library couldn't quite decide where everything belonged.

"Look at this," I said, turning so he could see. "The stacks rearrange themselves. You think of what you want, and the map tries to show you."

He stared at the surface, then said in a loud, clear voice: "The Court of Silver Shadows."

The map rippled, then settled on a narrow aisle in the uppermost gallery. "I suppose we go up."

We began the climb, which was not as simple as it appeared. The stairs changed their grade and length depending on the whim of the library. At one landing, we found ourselves at a dead end, confronted by a portrait of a disapproving old man with a wand and a particularly aggressive beard.

"Great Uncle Matthias," Richard said, and the painting snorted and turned its face away.

We backtracked, found another stair, and eventually reached the fourth floor. The air here was thinner, colder, and the books themselves gave off a faint silvery gleam, as if dusted with frost. The spines were labeled in a dozen languages—Latin, Old English, something that looked like cuneiform, and a neat, spidery script that sent a chill up my arms.

The shelf we sought was labeled simply: "Faerie Affairs—Advanced."

The first book I pulled was wrapped in what looked very much like human skin, though the touch was dry and not at all unpleasant. The title, embossed in faded gold, read: "A Concordance of Courts: From Avalon to Zenobia's Retinue."

Richard flipped through it, shaking his head. "Nothing. Only treaties and bloodlines. The Ravencrofts get a footnote, but it's all about some inter-court rivalry in the thirteenth century."

I grabbed another book, this one chained to the shelf. When I asked nicely in my best library whisper, the chain released with a courteous click. The book was heavier than expected, and as I opened it, I saw a warning inscribed on the inside cover: "Knowledge Has a Price."

"Doesn't it always?" I muttered, and began scanning the index for references to the Court of Silver Shadows.

We worked for hours, the fire below never waning and the tea trolley materializing at our side every half hour. Pages turned, notes were taken. I learned more about the savage, byzantine politics of the fae in a single afternoon than I had in all my years as a village busybody.

But the actual ritual? The step-by-step process for affirming a pact, regaining one's magic, and opening the way to the Court? If it was here, it was well hidden.

Richard's optimism faded by degrees. At one point, he slumped into a red velvet armchair and let his head fall into his hands. "This is hopeless," he said. "There are thousands of books here. Montfort and his cronies could bulldoze the entire Hall before I find the right volume."

"Then we need more eyes," I said, rising from the step-stool where I'd perched. "I should have just dragged Layla here straight away. She'll sort it out. So will Nan and Briar. We'll bring the whole Committee. If we all search, we might have a chance."

He looked up, a glimmer of hope reappearing. "Thank you, Kitty. I don't deserve your faith, but—thank you."

I patted his arm and Richard managed a crooked smile.

"I'll go fetch reinforcements," I said, stretching. "You keep looking. But for God's sake, don't try any ritual you find in these books until the rest of us are here to supervise."

He saluted me with a teacup, and I wound my way up the four flights of stairs, into the secret passage and out the final door, towards the hopeful smell of coming rain.

2 3

_____

THE LAST LEAF

B y the time I rounded up the Committee and led them through the billiards room fireplace, the library looked as though it had hosted a competitive séance: books scattered everywhere, the lamps blazing at full brightness, and Richard bent over a table, his black hair in disarray.

"Thank god," he said, glancing up. "I was about to start in on the section marked *Adepts Only*, and I don't trust myself not to end up cursed, ensorcelled, or trapped in a snow globe."

Briar deposited a tin of shortbread cookies on the nearest table. Nan made a beeline for the trolley and demanded a whiskey sour. Layla inhaled so sharply at the sight of the shelves that her glasses fogged up.

"I could die here," she announced. "And it would be a good death."

"Not before you help us save the village," I said, dragging her toward the stack where Richard was assembling books with any reference, however obscure, to the Court of Silver

Shadows. "We have less than two days before Montfort turns the Wild Wood into a petting zoo for hedge fund managers."

Layla shuddered and attacked the shelves with missionary zeal. Briar hopped on one of the sliding ladders and took it for a spin down the towering wall of shelves. A while later, Layla returned with an armful of fat volumes and dumped them on a table. "These look promising. What have you found so far, Richard?"

He sighed. "Every reference to the Court of Silver Shadows is buried under three feet of riddles, and the family codex is written in a hand that's actively disputing the concept of legibility."

"Can't be worse than a doctor's," Briar quipped from the depths of a plush fainting couch.

"Let me see it," Nan said, seizing the codex and flipping through its pages with the arrogance of someone who'd once outdrunk a Norwegian herring magnate.

They settled into a rhythm: Layla scanning indices and dispatching Briar to ferret out particular volumes from the stacks, Nan deciphering spidery script with one crooked finger, and me bouncing along them, assembling any promising fragments. Richard methodically worked his way through his own piles, muttering to himself and jotting in a notebook.

Hours passed this way. After drinking four cups of tea, I discovered that the loo was lavish as well, with a sunken marble tub filled with scented pink bubbles for those who preferred reading in the bath.

There were no clocks in the library, but the simulacrum of weather outside gradually shifted from "charming snow-fall" to "full-blown howling blizzard." At some point, Briar threw a tart at the nearest window just to see if it would bounce. It did, returning in a slow arc and landing neatly on the tea trolley.

It must have been shortly before dawn when Layla let out an excited yelp. "Listen to this!" She held up a fat volume titled *Bartering With the Unbowed: Traditions of Fae Oaths and Their Prices*. "'The Court of Silver Shadows, once invoked by mortal bargain, will honor the letter of their bond, but never its intent. They may only be reached at the place where old kings lie sleeping.'"

Richard blinked. "That could be anywhere in Britain, Layla. This country is basically built on a substratum of dead kings."

She jabbed the page. "It gets better. 'The entrance to their court is guarded by the one who slew his father, and cannot be opened save on the night when the moon is full and cold.'"

I did a quick calculation. "That's tomorrow night. A full moon in November is called a Frost Moon."

Nan, who had been scribbling notes on a cocktail napkin, nodded. "Old kings, patricide, and a moonlit key. That's a reference to the Barrows."

Briar looked up. "You mean the burial mounds south of the village?"

Nan nodded, looking grimly satisfied. "Specifically, the so-called Mordred barrow. Legend says King Arthur and his bastard son are both buried there."

Layla had already moved on to another book. "It says here—" She pointed to *The Ninefold Courts of Winterglass*— "that the only way to open the door is with a true token of the original bargain. Which would be . . .?"

She looked to Richard, who produced the moonstone amulet from under his shirt.

"This," he said.

Layla's eyes widened behind her glasses. "May I?" She held out her hand.

Richard hesitated, then unfastened the chain and handed it over.

Layla examined it closely, turning the amulet this way and that. "I've seen this kind of work before. I mean, read about it in books. Look, there's a hidden catch. Hang on . . ."

She twisted the moonstone and the backing popped open. Layla held a silver skeleton key up to the firelight. It was about half the length of her thumb, with an ornate bow at one end. "Bloody hell," she murmured. "Do you know how rare these things are?"

I stared at the key, my heart drumming in my chest. It suddenly felt all too real. A key that opened a door to the Otherworld. What I'd always dreamed of—

Briar noisily drained her chocolate milkshake through a fancy straw, courtesy of the trolley. She set the tall, fluted glass down on a table, where it promptly vanished. "What happens once you get inside?"

Richard shrugged. "I have no idea. But if it's anything like the rest of my legacy, it will be complicated, dangerous, and embarrassing."

"You'll need someone who knows how to navigate faerie courts," I said. "Plus, I've already seen you in several embarrassing situations, including public nudity."

"How did I miss that part?" Briar demanded.

Layla regarded us sternly. "It's not a joke. The Court of Silver Shadows is High Fae. They're ancient and powerful, and they'll turn on you in a heartbeat if you misstep. You might not come back, and there's no use pretending otherwise."

A hush fell over the secret library, broken only by the

gentle popping of the fire and Nan's snoring. She had, apparently, fallen asleep mid-conversation.

"So," I said, "any ideas on where the Mordred barrow might be? Because I walk there all the time and I've never seen anything like a tomb or a door."

Layla chewed her lip. "Perhaps it's only visible on the night of the full moon to someone who has the key. I mean, the Ravencrofts wouldn't want random people just stumbling over it, would they?"

"I suppose not," I said doubtfully. "But let's keep looking. Maybe we can find something else useful."

For what remained of the night, we sifted through books, mapping out every rumour and warning. For the first time since this ordeal began, I felt not just hope, but a strange, giddy anticipation. It was one thing to dream of magic when you were a child, quite another to meet it face to face.

By dawn, the Library had settled into a soft blue glow, the storm outside having given way to a pale winter sunlight. Nan was napping facedown on the tea trolley, Briar and Layla sprawled together on a heap of cushions, and Richard sat staring into the fire, the moonstone amulet—now equipped with its tiny key—dangling from his fingers.

I slipped away and made for the secret passage. Gilcarren was waiting patiently by the fireplace when I emerged.

"Any luck, Miss Boot?" he asked.

"I believe so, Gilcarren."

He held my gaze. "I don't wish to serve those men," he said quietly. "Blight and Penhaligon."

"Nor shall you," I replied firmly. "Lord Ravencroft will sort it all out tonight."

Gilcarren swept a formal bow that made him look dignified despite his ragged collection of coats. "I am bound to the

Hall, but I can deploy a few tricks if the new masters appear before the sale is final."

I thanked him and walked outside into the chill morning light. The Wild Wood at dawn was a different creature than by moonlight or midday—the trees dissolving into fog and the old paths blurring until you could forget whether you were coming or going.

A terrible weight pressed down on me as I approached the clearing to Nyx's mighty oak, but my heart lifted when I saw that the tree still stood, its single leaf clinging stubbornly to the lowest limb.

"Nyx?" I called.

No answer came. I hadn't expected one. I sat at the base of the trunk, my back against the wise old being that had given home and shade to untold generations of woodland creatures. I fancied that I could feel the tree's spirit, still present, though it drowsed like an elderly cat before the hearth.

"Do you remember when Edward Turner stole my book-bag? I sat up in that notch and cursed him all afternoon." I smiled wickedly. "You dropped acorns on his head the next day."

A breeze rustled the branches, making the last leaf dance. I patted the trunk. "I'm going to the Barrows tonight, old friend. There's a door to the Court of Silver Shadows, and we mean to make a new bargain. So . . . please don't go yet."

I sat with the oak until the sun rose above the trees and the birds began to sing. Nyx never turned up, but as I stood to leave, I could have sworn the last leaf grew a little brighter.

WHEN I RETURNED TO THE HALL, I FOUND RICHARD STILL bent over a stack of books.

"Where is everyone?" I asked.

"Layla, Briar, and your Nan went back to the inn to get some rest," he replied without looking up. "Where did you go?"

I approached the table and sank down in the opposite chair. "To visit a friend."

His dark eyes caught mine and read my mood at a glance. "I will fix this, Kitty. I swear to you."

"I know you will." I looked at the large tome in his hands. "Find anything else useful?"

He stretched. "A few odds and ends. But we know where to find the door." He touched the amulet around his neck. "And we have the key."

We sat for a minute, watching thick flakes drifted past the windows.

"It's odd," Richard said quietly. "I spent my whole life running from this place, from magic and family and obligation. And now it's all I want—to keep it alive."

"It's not odd at all," I said. "It's who you really are."

He hesitated. "Kitty, if I don't come back tonight—"

"Then neither of us will," I interrupted. "Since I'm coming along. You'll need someone who knows the correct forms of address and how to avoid being turned into decorative statuary."

He reached across the cushion and took my hand. "Thank you," he said simply.

"For what?"

"For believing in me. For not letting me be a coward even when I desperately wanted to."

I squeezed his hand back. "You were never a coward, Richard."

He smiled.

"Just unspeakably selfish," I added with a smile.

He burst into laughter. "What would I ever do without your blunt honesty, Kitty?"

We sat and watched the snow sift down on the fir trees, which glimmered with tiny white lights. Eventually, Richard returned to his *Hierarchies of the British Faerie Courts*. I sat with my head snugged against his shoulder until I finally drifted into restless sleep.

24

THE BARROWS

I awoke to find that Richard had tucked me under a blanket on one of the library's cosy sofas. The lord of the manor himself was slumped at the kitchen table, where Gilcarren had assembled a lavish brunch. I stuffed myself with eggs and hash browns and pasties, trying not to feel like a condemned prisoner relishing their last meal before the gallows.

Rain sheeted off the windows, but by late afternoon the sky had cleared, and the world outside had the grey, washed-out look of late autumn in the shires. By seven, Richard and I had joined the others in the common room of the Dancing Toadstool. We wore our coats inside out to protect against glamours, and carried twigs of broom tucked into our pockets—also a charm against fae enchantments.

The plan was to find Mordred's tomb and the doorway to the Court of Silver Shadows; beg forgiveness for the broken pact; and hope that the fae court would graciously accept a new bargain instead of flaying us alive and using our bones for croquet mallets.

Layla sat on the floor with her laptop, reviewing spread-sheets. "Tell me again," she demanded.

Richard sighed. "Don't eat or drink anything. Don't agree to the first offer if possible, or if the terms aren't specified in precise language. Don't accept gifts. Answer questions with questions."

She nodded. "Good. And the last one?"

"No matter what, keep the amulet around my neck."

She gave a brisk nod. "They already know your name. Nothing we can do about that." The firelight glinted off her glasses. "But guess what? I managed to find out *their* names. Lady Seraphine Vael and Lord Thalen Vael. That's who you'll be negotiating with."

"Or groveling to," Briar added cheerfully.

Richard drew a deep breath. "That's brilliant, Layla, thank you."

"It only took me hours of cross-referencing and a dozen calls to some other folklorists I trust. You're lucky the phone lines were up." She scanned her notes. "Not much is known about either of them. Expect slippery and enigmatic, like all the High Fae."

Mrs. Deen came over with the final addition to our arse-nal: a flask of wine that contained frankincense, myrrh, and a bit of shaved agate stone.

"Drink that before you go through the doorway," Layla said. "It'll help you keep your wits about you."

Richard nodded. "We'd better be going. The full moon's already risen."

"Just . . . give a moment with Kitty, would you?" Layla asked.

He nodded. "Of course."

Layla drew me aside, out of hearing of the rest. She took a

deep breath. "When you reach the Court of Silver Shadows, will you keep an eye out for my Dad?"

She hadn't spoke of him in a long time. I knew it wasn't because she'd forgotten, or given up hope. It was just too painful. I took her hands in mine. "You know I will. And if he's there . . . well, maybe we can find a way to work him into the new bargain."

She gave a short nod. Layla knew as well as I did that mortals who lived with the fae, even for brief periods, rarely came back the same—if they came back at all. It had been two decades since Mr. Deen walked into the Wild Wood hunting for mushrooms. But I didn't say any of that. There was no need.

"I haven't talked to Mum about it," she added softly, glancing over at Mrs. Deen. "Don't want to get her hopes up, you know?"

"I know."

Briar came over and they both gave me fierce hugs. Nan summoned Richard, and when he leaned down she cupped his chin and peered into his face. "Your parents made regrettable choices," she said, "but you won't do the same. Remember that, and take care of our Kitty."

Richard nodded seriously. "I will, Mrs. Boot."

She patted his cheek, then pulled me down into an embrace that smelled of tobacco and wool. "Come back in one piece. And make sure this one doesn't agree to be anyone's footman for eternity."

"I'll do my best," I promised.

Dr. Singer rose with some difficulty and offered Richard a handshake. "I'll not insult your intelligence by giving advice, but every bargain can be broken and remade if you find the right loophole." He winked. "And if you come back a hedgehog, I'll treat you at half price."

Richard laughed, then turned to Mrs. Deen, who simply gave him a quick squeeze and said, "We'll see you soon, dear."

With that, Richard and I donned our scarves and set out into the dusk.

THE PATH TO THE BARROWS LED PAST THE OLD ABBEY, ITS ruined arches stark against the darkening sky. Presently, the ground began to rise beneath our feet and a dense mist appeared. It curled around our ankles, cold and clinging, as if reluctant to let us pass. In the distance, pale lights bobbed among the marsh south of Nelly's Pond—will-o'-the-wisps.

"Ignore them," I warned. "They'll lead us astray."

"I know the stories," Richard said grimly. "Travelers lured to their deaths in bogs."

"Or to the edge of Nelly's Pond," I mused. "I wonder if they work together? Maybe she pays them a commission for every poor soul they coax to her domain." I shuddered. "Imagine that black water closing around you. No one would hear your cries for help. And then, the touch of an icy hand on your leg . . ."

Richard glanced at me. "Thank you, Kitty, just what I needed to hear right now."

I patted the twig of broom in my pocket. "Sorry."

The air grew colder as we left the lights of the village behind. Somewhere in the distance, a fox barked. Richard tugged the moonstone amulet out from under his jumper and studied it, running his thumb over the silver filigree. The stone gleamed, catching every scrap of light.

"Do you think they'll hear me out?" he asked.

I sighed. "There will be a price set upon any new bargain

—a high one, you can be sure. But since none of us have ever met the king and queen of the Court of Silver Shadows, there's no way to anticipate what they'll demand in return."

"That's the worst part," he muttered. "The not knowing."

This hardly merited a reply, so I kept my mouth shut. The mist thickened as we passed the old abbey, its crumbling stones looming black against the sky. My heart thudded with each step, though I felt better with Richard at my side.

We crested a hill and stopped. The Barrows stretched before us, a series of grassy mounds rising from the earth like the backs of sleeping giants.

"Do they all contain tombs?" Richard asked in a hushed voice.

"Not all," I replied. "Some are just hills. But yes, local legend holds that some are the ancient resting places of British kings."

We moved among the Barrows, searching. Clouds scudded across the face of the moon, casting shadows that shifted in queer ways from the corner of one's eye. We each took a bracing sip of Mrs. Deen's anti-enchantment wine. It warmed my chest, but I didn't see any way inside the grassy knolls.

"The tomb should be marked," I said. "A cairn or a dolmen or *something . . .*"

"There," Richard said, pointing.

On the side of a small barrow, half-hidden by a tangle of shrubs, I glimpsed a flat stone slab—one that I swore hadn't been there a minute ago—carved with a cross above a dragon.

"King Arthur's sigil," I murmured. "He and Mordred supposedly killed each other at the Battle of Camlann. Most stories say Arthur was taken to the Isle of Avalon to be healed. That he'll return to Britain in her hour of greatest need. But Nan said one rumour claims they were buried in the same crypt. Mordred was his illegitimate son, after all."

Richard examined the stone. "This feels right, Kitty," he said with excitement.

As if in answer, the clouds parted and the Frost Moon's cold, bright light fell directly on the barrow. For a moment, nothing happened. Then, slowly, a thin silver line appeared, tracing the outline of a door in the earth.

Richard removed the amulet from around his neck. With a deft motion of those surgeon's fingers, he pressed the hidden catch and the backing sprang open. Inside nestled the tiny key. It was a thing of beauty, a sliver of starlight forged in silver, but it was also laughably small. The door's keyhole was at least three times its size.

We stood there, twin jesters in reversed coats, staring at the mismatch. "Try it anyway," I suggested.

Richard did so. The tiny key rattled around uselessly.

"Give it a wiggle," I suggested with a grin. "It's not the size, it's what you do with it."

He turned to me and arched a brow just as a tart voice drifted from the mist. "Having trouble?"

I whirled. Nyx stood behind us, looking annoyed. My heart soared to see her.

"I thought you'd gone back to Faerie!" I cried.

"Not just yet," she hissed. "And keep your voice down. The wind has many ears—and many tongues."

"I'm sorry," I whispered. "But can you help us?"

Nyx crossed her thin arms. They were cracked and shiny with sap, as if the coming winter had settled beneath her bark. "The key grows to fit the lock," she said grudgingly, "if you have the magic."

I managed to stop myself from making another terrible joke.

Richard stared at the dryad in amazement. Then he gave an embarrassed cough. "My magic. Yes, well—"

"I know what you did," Nyx interrupted. Never had I seen her so angry.

"He's trying to fix things," I soothed. "We both are."

She gazed up at the fat yellow moon. "The law of the court is clear. Only a Ravencroft may pass—and only by using his or her own magic."

"Miss Boot is my faerie consultant," Richard said. "I require her presence. And I *will* get my magic back." The last was said with ferocity.

Nyx muttered under her breath. "If it were anyone but Kitty . . ."

"Please aid us," I begged her. "For the sake of your tree."

She paused, then spread her wings and flitted to Richard. Nyx touched her finger to the key. There was a low, humming sound like a hive waking at dawn. The key stretched and grew until it was the length of my hand and twice as thick. This time when Richard tried, it slid home and turned without resistance.

Nyx stepped back. Her face was impassive, but I saw both hope and fear in her eyes. "If you return, do not forget who opened the way for you, Ravencroft."

She made the name sound both a curse and a kingly title.

Richard nodded gratefully. "I will remember it always, Nyx, thank you."

She turned to me. "Don't let this feckless mortal do anything stupid."

"That's literally my job," I replied.

The door rumbled, damp earth crumbling from its lintel. When I turned back to bid Nyx farewell, she was already gone.

The way into the tomb yawned before us, a rectangle of

darkness. I hesitated on the threshold. Above us, the full moon peeked between scudding clouds like fish scales, impossibly bright and close.

"Shall we?" Richard said.

"Yes," I said. "But first . . ."

I lifted up on my tiptoes and kissed him. Just a soft, fleeting press that lasted only a moment, but he made a startled sound, like a man who's been gently struck on the head by a brick.

"For luck," I said. "And well . . . we might die in the next hour or so, and I've wanted to do that for a few days now."

Richard pulled me into his arms and gave me a proper kiss that made my toes curl in my waterlogged boots. He caught my hand, our fingers twining.

"Had I known facing certain death was all it would take," he said roughly, "I would have sought out mortal peril ages ago. Kitty, I must have been mad to ever let you go."

"Yes," I agreed, squeezing his fingers. "You were."

We turned to face the doorway together. The darkness beyond seemed to wait with bated breath, eager as a spider in its web. Richard pulled out an electric torch, playing its beam over the walls of the tomb.

It smelled of cold stone with an underlying hint of something ancient and indefinable. A simple chamber fifteen feet square, with a large stone bier in the center. Unadorned save for a cross above a dragon, just as on the outer door.

"King Arthur," I whispered. "Do you think he's really in there?"

I wondered if he would be bones by now, or more like a preserved wax figure.

Richard eyed the bier with clinical detachment. "We need Mordred's tomb. Are you sure they're buried near each other?"

"No. But that's what one of the books said."

We both circled the small room, groping along the walls for another door. "Perhaps the moonstone itself is the key?" I suggested.

Richard nodded, removing the amulet from around his neck. He held it up to catch the shaft of moonlight that spilled through the open doorway. He tried touching it to the symbols on the bier, then to each corner of the room. Still nothing.

"Perhaps there's an incantation?" I offered. "Or a specific place where the moonlight must strike?"

"If there is," Richard said grimly, "it died with my parents."

I was about to suggest we try setting the amulet on the floor when a soft scraping sound froze me in place. It came from inside the stone bier. Probably a nest of field mice.

Or something stirring after centuries of sleep.

Richard's head snapped up. "Did you hear—" he began.

"Yes," I said tightly.

The sound came again, louder this time. A chill crawled along my spine and curled up at the base of my skull. "Richard," I said, "I'm beginning to think this was a mistake."

He had that feverish, obsessive look in his eye. "Perhaps Mordred and Arthur are buried in the *same* bier."

"That's mad," I snapped. "They hated each other."

"And they're dead," he pointed out, "so they wouldn't have had much say in the matter, would they? We need to look, Kitty."

"Why?" I was whispering, but my voice still sounded too loud. "Why do we need to look?"

"Because the door to the Court of Silver Shadows might be inside. Don't you want to save the village? The Wild Wood?"

I glared at him. "Fine," I muttered.

The scraping stopped as soon as we began forcing the heavy lid to one side, which was worse than if it had continued. We shifted it just enough to peer inside. A skeleton, mostly intact, draped in rusted mail and what remained of a red and gold surcoat. Its hands were clenched around the hilt of a broadsword.

"Is that Excaliber?" I breathed, impressed and terrified at the same time.

The skeleton's skull was tilted slightly, as if listening. It did not move, but I fancied that the scraping would resume the moment we put the lid back.

"Only one corpse," Richard said in a disappointed tone, apparently immune to standing within reach of the most famous sword in English history. "I suppose Mordred is buried elsewhere."

We pushed the lid back into place, grunting with effort. God, but it made a hideously loud grating sound.

"It's bad luck to disturb the tombs of ancient kings," I said. "This place is probably wound up in all sorts of protective charms. Merlin himself—"

My words ended in a yelp as I stumbled backward over an uneven paving stone. Richard caught me as the stone sank into the floor with a decisive click.

"Are you all right?" he asked.

I nodded, but my attention was fixed on the far wall of the tomb, which was slowly sliding open. Behind it, another chamber waited, this one filled with a soft, silvery light.

Richard gave a hoot of glee and rubbed his hands together. "Clever," he murmured. "You're a genius, Kitty!"

"I only fell down," I pointed out.

He took my hand again, and together we approached the new opening. The chamber beyond was larger than the first, its ceiling lost in shadows. In the center stood a figure in armor the green of new leaves. Each plate was etched with vines and flowers. The helmet's visor was closed.

"Is it a statue?" I whispered.

The knight's head turned toward us. One gauntleted hand grasped the hilt of the broadsword at its hip.

"Apparently not," Richard replied.

The knight drew its sword in one smooth motion. "Friend or foe?" it rasped. "Declare yourselves!"

25

FRIEND OR FOE?

"Friend!" Richard cried, raising both hands in a gesture of surrender.

The Green Knight stood motionless for a heartbeat, the point of its sword gleaming in the strange silvery light. I held my breath, hoping a simple reply to its query might be enough, but of course nothing about this night would prove simple.

"The word," rasped the knight. "Speak the word of safe passage or be cleaved in twain."

Richard shot me a worried glance. "Thoughts, Kitty?"

My mouth went dry. "I suppose it's a password. The one your parents would have taught you if they hadn't been exiled to Romania."

The Green Knight took a step forward, armor creaking like an ancient gate. "Speak the word or perish."

"Just a moment!" I called, grabbing Richard's sleeve and tugging him backward. "It's been ever so long since we last visited!"

Richard eyed the narrow space between the knight and

the door. "We can mull it over outside. I'll draw it away, Kitty."

He dashed left, as I went right. The Green Knight hesitated before following Richard. Its movements were stiff but purposeful, like a rusted clockwork toy.

"Meet me at the outer passage!" I shouted, skidding behind Mordred's stone bier, which was identical to Arthur's save for the absence of any device on the lid. Richard ducked a brutal slash of the knight's broadsword, which struck a shower of sparks from the wall.

We both sprinted for the opening we'd come through, but an ominous grinding sound filled the chamber. Stone scraped against stone as the wall slid shut, sealing us in with our implacable adversary.

"Oh, marvelous," I panted, backing away. "I warned you—"

"Not helping!" Richard ducked another ferocious swing, this one close enough that I heard the whistle of the blade through air.

He scrambled toward me and we crouched behind the bier again, breathing hard, as the knight lumbered around demanding the password.

"Any ideas?" I whispered. "It's *your* family who left this monstrous automaton!"

The knight's head turned toward the bier. We crawled backward, staying low.

"I'm sorry, Kitty. You're right, it is my fault—"

"No, I shouldn't have said that. Let's think. Maybe the name of an ancestor? A family motto?"

"*Virtus ex obscuro!*" Richard cried, to no discernible effect. "It means 'Strength from the unseen.'"

"Try again," I urged. "Maybe something connected to the fae court?"

"Shadows!" Richard shouted. "Silver! Moon!"

The knight slashed at the air. "Stand and face me, villains!"

"It's no use," I hissed. "There has to be another way out. I propose we find it."

The knight clanked around in a circle, and we split up once more. I ran my hands along the lid of the coffin, while Richard feinted left before cutting right, narrowly avoiding a downward cut. The blade struck stone, chipping off a fragment that skittered across the floor.

Think, think! What would the Ravencrofts use as a password? I rummaged through my mental catalog of village lore, the stories Nan had told me, the whispered rumours about the mysterious lord and lady of the manor.

The knight had Richard cornered now, advancing with deliberate steps. I cast about anything to distract it, but the chamber was bare. In desperation, I grabbed a loose chip of stone and hurled it at the knight's helmet. It connected with a dull clang, and the green figure turned toward me with what felt like annoyance.

"Excalibur!" I shouted.

The knight returned its attention to Richard, who skirted along the wall.

"Avalon!" I cried. "Camelot! Guinevere! Lancelot!"

Richard had run out of room to maneuver. The knight had him backed against the sealed entrance, sword raised for a killing blow.

"Nimue!" I shrieked, digging to the bottom of my limited store of Arthurian trivia. "Morgana! Gawain! Galahad!"

Richard ducked another downward slash and rolled across the floor. His coat was torn at the shoulder, and a thin line of blood trickled down his cheek. We retreated again, but the tomb was only so large. Our backs hit the far wall. The knight advanced, inexorable as the tide.

"Lady of the Lake!" Richard shouted, voice ragged. "Pendragon! For the love of God, what is it?"

The knight raised its sword, its armor limned against the light from Richard's dropped torch. This was it. We were going to die in this wretched tomb, and no one would know what had become of us until Montfort's bulldozers unearthed our bones.

Something in me broke. If these were our last moments, there were things that needed saying.

"Richard, I—"

The knight froze mid-swing. Then, with a series of clanks, it lowered the broadsword and slid the blade into its scabbard. Our tormentor gave a smart about-face, marched back to the center of the tomb, and resumed its original position, as still as if it had never moved at all.

Richard and I stared at each other, disheveled and panting. "What ... just ... happened?" he gasped.

I blinked, trying to make sense of it. "Your name," I said slowly. "That's the password. Your parents must have set it."

He shook his head. "No, it can't be. They never answered my letters, never tried to contact me—"

"Maybe they couldn't," I suggested gently. "Maybe they weren't allowed to. Or the letters were intercepted. It's not hard to imagine. But they chose a password that was precious to them. Something they could never forget. *You.*"

Richard frowned at the motionless knight. This didn't fit with the narrative he'd constructed about his parents—cold, disloyal, uncaring. I could see him struggling with the idea. But before either of us could speak, a low rumbling filled the chamber. The stone bier began to move, sliding sideways to reveal a staircase spiraling down into darkness.

"Thank God," I said, peering down into the gloom. "I didn't fancy rifling through Mordred's bones seeking the doorway."

Richard gave a shaken laugh. He retrieved his electric torch, which had miraculously survived the chase, and swept its beam to the gap. Rough-hewn steps curved out of sight, worn smooth in the middle from centuries of use.

"Ladies first?" he suggested.

"Oh no," I countered. "It's your magical legacy, after all. But first, let me see to that cut."

I dug out the first-aid kit Briar had insisted we bring and cleaned the slash, then stuck a plaster on it. Richard winced slightly but held still.

"What were you about to say?" he asked. "Just before the knight stopped trying to hack us to bits."

My cheeks warmed. "Oh, nothing important."

His gaze didn't waver. "Kitty."

I swallowed, aware of how close we were standing. "I was going to tell you that you're a stubborn, infuriating man. And that I'm proud of you."

A smile spread across his long, hawkish face. "Proud enough for another kiss?"

I patted his cheek. "Don't push your luck, Lord Ravencroft. We still have to face the Court of Silver Shadows with nothing but a half-baked plan and your dubious charm."

"Later," he agreed regretfully, stepping back. "But you owe me a kiss, Kitty Boot."

The stairs beckoned, a dark spiral leading down to who knew what faerie trickery. Richard took a deep breath and straightened his inside-out coat. Together, we started down, the Green Knight keeping its silent vigil behind us as the stone bier slid back into place with a final, ominous thud.

The stairway curved in a tight spiral, forcing us to

descend single file. Richard led, the beam of his torch dancing along the rough walls. I kept one hand on his shoulder, mainly for reassurance.

"How deep do you think it goes?" I whispered, my voice echoing in the close confines.

"Deep," Richard replied. "We must be well below the level of the Barrows by now."

The air grew colder as we descended, but not the biting cold of winter. This was the coolness of deep caves, of places the sun never touched.

The stairs wound down and down, an endless spiral that left me dizzy. Faint veins of silver threaded through the dark rock, growing more pronounced the deeper we descended. The atmosphere thickened, charged with something that made the fine hairs on my arms stand up. We were trespassers here, and whatever waited below was ancient and powerful beyond mortal comprehension.

When the staircase finally ended, Richard's torch flickered once and went out entirely, plunging us into darkness for a heart-stopping moment. Then a soft, silvery light bloomed, emanating from the walls themselves.

"Oh my," I breathed.

A gallery stretched before us, lined on both sides with tall mirrors in ornate silver frames. Each frame was different— some adorned with twining vines, others with crescent moons or runes that shifted when I looked at them directly. But it wasn't the frames that made my breath catch; it was what the mirrors showed.

Instead of our reflections, they displayed images that moved and changed as we approached. Not our present, but futures that might be.

"Don't look," Richard warned, but it was already too late.

I was drawn to the nearest mirror, where I saw Nyx's oak.

The single leaf, now brittle and brown, trembled in a snowy breeze. As I watched, it detached and spiraled down, down, down, landing in a drift of fallen leaves. Nyx sat beneath the bare branches, her skin cracked and grey, her eyes fixed on me with such fierce accusation that I took a step back. Then she faded, leaving nothing but a dead tree in a desolate clearing.

"It's the last leaf," I whispered, my throat raw. "She's gone."

Richard touched my shoulder. "It's not real, Kitty."

My eyes swam with unshed tears. "How can you be sure?"

Richard lowered his voice. "Because the fae are tricksters. And I refuse to believe we are too late."

I tore my gaze away, only to find myself staring into another mirror. This one showed Richard, but his features were sharper, his smile cold and cruel. He strode along the gallery, a cloak of midnight blue billowing behind him. His eyes were chips of black onyx, and when he flicked his fingers, sparks of dark energy danced across his palm.

Gilcarren scurried along at his heels, head bowed, shoulders hunched. The brownie kept glancing up at his master with barely concealed terror, flinching whenever Richard made a sudden movement.

"It's me," Richard said in a strangled voice.

"An illusion, remember?" I replied firmly, though my stomach knotted.

At that moment, a chorus of gloating whispers rose.

"The darkness is in your blood."

"Turn back before the magic consumes you and everyone you love."

"There is no escape from your legacy."

The voices slithered around us like poisonous smoke. I glanced at Richard and saw the horror as he stared at his reflection. The other Richard was still striding down the gallery, his image thrown back an infinite number of times by the endless mirrors.

"Don't listen," I said, grasping his hand. "This is a test, nothing more."

"But what if they're right?" he asked. "What if this is inevitable? My parents—"

"Are flawed humans who made a poor choice. But everyone in Little Groating stood by them, Richard. No one would talk to the press, not even when they offered loads of money for a story. Your family has been entwined with mine for generations. Without the Ravencrofts, we'd be just another ordinary village."

He continued to stare, transfixed, until I stepped in front of him, blocking his view and forcing him to look at me instead.

"The fact that you fear becoming this . . ." I waved a hand at the mirrors, "is precisely why you won't. Evil doesn't worry about being evil. It just is."

"The power—"

"Doesn't define you." I held his gaze, willing him to believe me, even as the whispers grew louder, more insistent.

"You will bring wrack and ruin . . . destroy all you touch . . ."

I raised my voice to drown them out. "They want you to turn back. Which means we must be on the right path."

Something shifted in Richard's eyes—doubt giving way to determination. He straightened, squeezing my hands in return.

"You're right," he said sheepishly. "This is exactly the sort of trickery I was supposed to be ready for." He glanced at the mirrors with newfound defiance. "Well, they'll have to try harder than that."

I took out the flask of anti-enchantment wine and we each had a bracing sip. The whispers faltered, then faded away. Richard gave me a crooked smile. "Thank you, Kitty."

"Don't thank me yet," I replied. "We still have to strike a new bargain that will help us defeat Montfort."

We continued down the gallery, keeping our eyes averted from the mirrors. I caught glimpses anyway—flashes of other possibilities, some beautiful, some terrible. Richard with grey at his temples, laughing in a sun-dappled garden. Myself, much older, leading a pair of dark-haired children through the Wild Wood. The two of us, standing back to back, surrounded by shadows with teeth.

When we reached the end of the gallery, we found ourselves facing a door of polished obsidian. As we approached, it swung open silently, revealing an elegant figure.

He was of medium height and slender, with unearthly, foxlike features that immediately marked him as fae. Half his hair was pale as frost, the other a cascade of ink-dark locks. His eyes were equally mismatched, one argent, the other a bruised violet that absorbed the light. He wore a tunic of shimmering cloth, like mail but softer, belted with blue silk, and high boots that came to his thighs.

"Richard Ravencroft," he said in a sly, mocking voice. "I am Halfglint, chamberlain to Lord and Lady Vael of the Court of Silver Shadows."

Richard inclined his head warily. "Thank you for welcoming us to their realm, Master Halfglint."

The faerie's mismatched eyes glittered. "Oh, it was not a welcome. Merely an introduction. Whether you are truly welcome remains to be seen."

I suppressed a shiver as Halfglint's lips curved in a smile that revealed pointed teeth. His gaze slid to me. For a brief moment, I thought a ripple of shock crossed his face, but it was there and gone so fast I couldn't be sure.

"We did not expect you to bring a companion," he said. "Particularly one so . . . " A theatrical sigh. "Mundane."

"Miss Boot is my trusted advisor," Richard said firmly. "I require her at my side."

Halfglint's eyebrows rose a fraction. "Indeed? How peculiar you mortals are." He gestured toward the door behind him. "Come, then. The Lord and Lady do not like to be kept waiting."

He led us through the obsidian door, which opened onto a short corridor lined with sconces that burned with silver flames. At the end stood double doors of pale wood inlaid with intricate patterns.

The chamberlain paused at the threshold, his mismatched eyes sweeping over us one final time. "Remember, Lord Ravencroft—in the Court of Silver Shadows, every word has weight, and every promise binds. Choose carefully what you offer, and what you accept."

With that warning, he swept through the doors. Richard and I exchanged a glance, drew deep breaths, and followed him into the Otherworld where the fae court awaited.

26

THE COURT OF
SILVER SHADOWS

Halfglint pushed open the tall arched doors, revealing a sight that stole my breath. Beyond the threshold stretched a midnight realm where stars crowded the sky, so bright and thick they cast a luminous glow upon the landscape below.

In the distance, perched atop a hill, stood a magnificent castle that bent the eye—towers twisting sideways, slender bridges with no visible support, all built of some pale, shimmering stone. Between us and this impossible palace stretched a dense forest.

I tilted my head back. Somehow, I'd expected to see the full moon here, too, but . . .

"She walks elsewhere tonight," Halfglint said. His mismatched eyes glittered with amusement at my confusion. "Luna visits our realm only when invited."

Richard's warm hand found mine in the darkness. "Is the court far?" he asked, nodding toward the castle.

Halfglint merely chuckled and led us into the forest. The

trees blocked the starlight and we followed the fae chamber-lain blindly until the wood opened into a vast glade. A feast was underway—long tables laden with honeycombs and berries in clotted cream and dozens of delicate dishes. Music floated through the air, a wild, skirling melody. The notes danced along my skin, urging my feet to move of their own accord.

Halfglint paused at the edge of the clearing. "The Court is at revelry. You will be presented to Lord and Lady Vael. Speak only when spoken to."

As we stepped into the glade, I tried not to stare. The fae were both more and less than I had expected—some tall and elegant with features of aching beauty, others sprouting antlers or the heads of beasts. Their clothing ranged from fine cloth of silver and gold to simple tunics of leaves and vines such as Nyx wore.

I scanned the revelers, searching for Mr. Deen. It had been more than two decades since he vanished. He'd worn a beard then, and had thick dark brows and curling brown hair, but of course he might look different now.

I saw no one even vaguely resembling Layla's father. Yet by unconscious habit, I found myself seeking another face. One that had haunted my dreams since I was a child. Might the fae prince Fenwick be here? My pulse quickened at the thought of seeing him again after all these years. Would he be grown as I was, or forever a boy?

"You seem to be looking for someone," Richard remarked softly.

"An old friend," I answered, swallowing my disappointment. "But I don't see him."

A few fae glanced our way, but most seemed disinterested in the presence of mortals at their feast. At the far end of the glade, elevated on a natural rise in the land, stood two thrones fashioned from intertwining branches of silver-barked trees. Upon them sat the rulers of the Court of Silver Shadows.

Lord Thalen Vael was a tall, spare figure with skin of burnished gold. A cloak of overlapping eagle feathers draped his shoulders, and shadows clung to his heels like devoted hounds. Around his neck hung a horn of gold and ivory. His face was neither young nor old, with deep-set eyes that contained the wisdom and cunning of centuries.

Beside him, Lady Seraphine Vael was pale as milk, her hair a cascade of white that poured down around her feet like a frozen waterfall. She wore a crown woven of bluebells that glittered with frost, and her gown shimmered between jet and silver, never quite settling on either. Her eyes were mirror-bright, reflecting everything but revealing nothing.

Halfglint led us to the foot of the thrones and bowed deeply. "My lord, my lady, I present Richard Ravencroft, heir to the Ravencroft legacy and petitioner to the Court."

Lord Vael's gaze fell on Richard. "Ravencroft," he said, his voice rich as honey, yet with the same crafty tone as Halfglint. "So you come to us at last."

Lady Vael said nothing, but her eyes—those terrible eyes—dissected Richard piece by piece.

"My lord and lady," Richard said, executing a bow. "I come to renew the ancient pact between my family and your Court."

A ripple of murmurs spread through the nearest fae, and the music faltered before resuming.

"You come to our realm as a supplicant," Lord Vael said, "yet you have shown nothing but contempt for our bargain." His gaze slid to me, then away, as if I were beneath notice.

"Do you know what becomes of mortals who break their word to us?" the fae king continued. "The blood turns black and sour in their veins. They go mad, and they die, and their names are erased from memory."

I felt Richard tense beside me.

"Here you stand," Lord Vael continued, "having broken your family's oath yet still drawing breath. Why do you suppose that is?"

Richard met his gaze. "I cannot say, Your Highness."

"It is because," Lady Vael interjected, "we are merciful. Or possibly just bored." A smile curved her white lips. "We shall grant you a trial, Richard Ravencroft, to determine whether your pact can be renewed, or whether your line ends with you."

Lord Vael raised a hand, and the music ceased. The dancers melted away, clearing a circle around us. "Call the witness," he commanded.

From the edge of the glade, a hunched figure in many coats approached. My heart sank as I recognised Gilcarren. He looked different here—more fae-like, with elongated ears and fingers that ended in delicate points. His eyes were large and frightened.

"Gilcarren of Ravencroft Hall," Lord Vael announced. "You have served since the time of the first bargain. Speak true of what you have witnessed."

"Yes, tell us of Richard Ravencroft's return to his ancestral home," Lady Vael commanded, her voice high and clear and cold as the hour before dawn. "Tell us of his words and deeds."

Gilcarren twisted his long fingers together. "When the young lord returned, he vowed sell Ravencroft Hall to the first buyer who offered coin."

The courtiers gave a low, angry murmur at this. Most faeries despised mortal currency nearly as much as iron.

Gilcarren paused, looking miserable. "The lord said—and I quote—'I want nothing to do with this damned place.'"

Richard winced.

"He denied his heritage again and again," Gilcarren continued, clearly reluctant. "He called the magic 'a curse' and 'a taint in the blood.' He said he never asked for this burden and didn't care to preserve anything his parents valued."

I glared at Gilcarren, but he refused to meet my eye.

"And the amulet?" Lord Vael prompted. "What of the moonstone?"

"He sought it only to take it away from the Hall," Gilcarren admitted. "He said, 'I don't want it, but it's unspeakably dangerous and I can't just . . .'"

"Just what?" Lady Vael demanded.

"Leave it behind," Richard said tightly. "I do not deny saying those things, Your Majesties, but—"

Lady Vael raised a pale hand and he cut off, looking furious.

"Is all that true, Ravencroft?" Lord Vael demanded.

Richard squared his shoulders. "It is, my lord. I said those things and more. I was wrong."

"You were more than wrong," Lady Vael said coldly. "You were contemptuous. Dismissive. Ungrateful for the gifts your ancestors received."

"I was afraid," Richard countered. "I was a child when I was taken from Ravencroft Hall. I grew up hearing only that my parents were traitors, that magic was dangerous, that I should deny my heritage and become someone else entirely. I was taught to hate and fear what I am."

"A tragic tale," Lady Vael said with a dismissive wave. "Yet it changes nothing."

"If I may," Richard pressed on, "I have the right to speak in my own defense."

Lord Vael nodded. "Speak, then."

Richard took a deep breath. "I was ten years old when I was torn from my home and given as ward to the Earl of Kilmarnock. I was sent to boarding schools where I was beaten if I mentioned magic, ridiculed for speaking of faeries, and taught that the Ravencroft name was synonymous with treachery and shame."

A flicker of sympathy crossed Lord Vael's face.

"I grew up determined to be the opposite of everything the Ravencroft name represented," Richard continued. "I buried myself in science and medicine, in things I could see and touch and prove. I convinced myself that my childhood memories of the Wild Wood, of the brownies, of magic itself were nothing but a child's fantasies."

He glanced at me, and I nodded encouragingly.

"When I inherited the Hall, I saw only the burden, not the gift. I was blind to the responsibility that came with my legacy." His voice strengthened as he turned to me. "It was this woman who showed me what I had forgotten. She reminded me of the magic that flows through the land, of the beauty and wonder of the Wild Wood, of the duty I have to protect it."

Richard turned to face the assembled courtiers. "I stand before you humbled. I ask not just for the renewal of the pact, but for your aid in returning the estate to its rightful master. A man named Ambrose Montfort has bought Ravencroft Hall through my ignorance and fear. He plans to destroy the Wild Wood, to capture and imprison the fae for mortal entertainment."

A murmur of outrage swept through the crowd.

"I need my magic restored," Richard finished. "Not for my

own sake, but for the sake of all who depend on the protection the Ravencrofts have provided for centuries."

A silence fell over the glade. Lord Vael leaned forward, his expression thoughtful. "You speak with passion, Ravencroft. Perhaps there is more of your ancestors in you than I first thought."

Hope flickered in Richard's eyes.

Lady Vael's laugh cut through the moment like a blade of ice. "How convenient that you discover your sense of duty precisely when you need our help," she said. "No, Ravencroft. I care nothing for your excuses. The original pact is void, broken by your willful rejection. The insult you have shown to our Court is unforgivable."

"My lady," Richard began, but again she silenced him with a raised hand.

"It was your duty to protect your legacy," she said coldly. "You failed. What happens now is no concern of ours."

Before I could stop myself, I stepped forward and dropped into the lowest curtsey I could manage.

"Your Majesty," I said, "if I may?"

Lady Vael's perfect eyebrows rose at my effrontery.

"I wish to speak for those who cannot be here," I said. "The dryad Nyx, whose tree is dying. The pond hag Nelly, whose waters will be drained. The brownies who have faithfully served Ravencroft Hall for generations." I raised my eyes to hers. "Many of your own people will suffer if Montfort succeeds."

"What happens in the mortal world is no concern of mine," she replied dismissively. "The fae of the Wild Wood have other refuges they can seek."

"But it's their home," I protested. "They've lived there for centuries—"

"As we have lived here," she cut me off. "All things change, mortal. Even faerie woods." She turned away, conversation closed.

Richard stepped forward, his face a mask of desperation. "Please," he said. "I would give anything to get my magic back, to protect the Hall and the Wild Wood."

I whipped my head around. "Anything" is not a word you use when bargaining with fae. I shot him a warning look, but it was too late.

Lady Vael turned back slowly, a terrible smile spreading across her face. Halfglint smirked, eyes gleaming with malicious delight.

"Anything?" Lady Vael repeated. "What an unexpected offer, Lord Ravencroft. I accept."

Richard paled. "What is your price?"

She pointed a finger at me. "That one. I want her to remain with me. She shall comb my hair and serve as my handmaiden."

Richard shook his head. "I'll give you gold, lands, my service—"

"You offered anything," Lady Vael reminded him. "And I have chosen. The mortal woman stays. She will dance with us. It is not such a terrible fate, is it?"

Richard opened his mouth to protest, but I gripped his arm. It had been a trap from the beginning. The mock trial, Gilcarren. We never stood a chance. There was only one way out now. Only one way to save the village, and the oak, and all of it.

"It's my choice," I said savagely, "not yours."

His eyes were wild. "You can't. I won't let you sacrifice yourself for my mistakes . . ."

I turned to Lady Vael, lifting my chin. "I accept your terms, Your Majesty. I will stay, in exchange for Richard's magic being restored."

The fae court studied me, some curious, others already bored of the whole affair. Lady Vael clapped her hands together, the sound ringing through the glade like a struck bell.

"It is decided," she declared. "Ravencroft's power shall be restored, and the mortal woman shall remain with us for the rest of her days."

27

A NEW PACT

F or the rest of her days.
The faerie queen's words echoed in my ears.

It hit home at that moment, stealing the breath from my lungs. I would never see my friends again. Never sit by the hearth with Barbarossa kneading my stocking feet, listening to one of Nan's tales as the fire popped and Mrs. Deen handed out hot chocolates.

I'd never wander through the apple orchard, the air fragrant with decaying windfalls, or have Sir Francis Drake call me a "mouse-dropping in the pepper" (my personal favourite Martin Luther insult).

But the village would be safe. Richard would have his magic back. Nyx's oak would live.

I met Lady Vael's triumphant gaze with what dignity I could muster. I won't lie—she terrified me. But I couldn't see any other way. It was almost funny; I'd been secretly hoping to stumble over a door to Faerie since I was a child.

Be careful what you wish for.

Richard's face filled with anguish. "No—"

"It's done," I said firmly.

Lord Vael beckoned. "Come forward, Richard Ravencroft. Kneel and receive what was lost."

Richard's pupils widened to a hard, glittering black. He approached the throne and stopped three paces away. The assembled courtiers went still, watching with new interest. He ignored them, his gaze locked with the faerie queen's.

"No," he said.

Lady Vael stared at him, expressionless. "You offered me anything my heart desired," she said with a dangerous, brittle edge.

"Anything in my power to grant," Richard corrected. "But this mortal woman" —he remembered not to reveal my name— "isn't my property to forfeit, nor some trinket to be exchanged for the favour of your court. If you insist on this folly, then I will take my offer elsewhere."

The court erupted into whispers—some aghast, some delighted at the prospect of fresh drama. Lord Vael's golden features darkened. "What do you mean, 'elsewhere'?"

"I mean," Richard said, "that an unbound wizard can serve any fae court of his or her choosing. If the Court of Silver Shadows is so petty as to demand an innocent life, I will ally myself with the Court of Gilded Dusk. I have already received an offer to become their mortal agent."

This was news to me, and, judging by the looks on the faces of the assembled fae, it was news to them as well. Even Lady Vael's mask slipped for a heartbeat. It was the king, though, who betrayed the greater alarm—his eyes darted to the queen, then to Halfglint, who seemed to shrink in on himself.

"You would not dare," Lady Vael hissed.

"Wouldn't I?" Richard's smile held no warmth. "King Aureth has already extended an invitation. I was reluctant to accept, given my family's long association with your Court, but if these are your final terms . . ."

I held my breath. Richard was bluffing—he had to be. But it was a masterful bluff, played with the confidence of a man who knew exactly which cards to reveal and which to hold back. While I slept, Richard had combed through ancient texts in the secret library, studying the faerie courts. Rivalries, alliances, ancient feuds. He had armed himself with knowledge, like any good wizard would.

And now he was using it to bluff his way out of an impossible situation. He had become, in this moment, every inch a slippery, double-dealing Ravencroft, and I adored him for it.

"You lie," Lady Vael said, but a flicker of uncertainty crossed her perfect features.

Richard gave a careless shrug. "Perhaps you've forgotten, but my family once swore fealty to the highest bidder. Your court outbid the others when the old bargains were struck, but loyalties can shift, my lady."

Lady Vael's eyes narrowed to silver slits. Lord Vael beckoned to Halfglint, who hurried to his side. The king bent to whisper something in the chamberlain's ear.

"Let the Court of Gilded Dusk have him if they wish," Halfglint declared lazily. "A wizard with no magic who has already shown his disdain for fae bargains will serve them precisely as well as they deserve."

There were titters of laughter, but Lady Vael was not amused. She tapped her long, pointed nails on the arm of the throne. "This mortal dares to renege on an offer made before my entire court. Perhaps he needs a reminder of the consequences of crossing the fae."

I held my breath, girding for the queen's wrath to descend upon us, but before Richard could respond, a new voice spoke up.

"Oh, mother, do stop glowering. You'll give yourself wrinkles."

A figure stepped forward from the ring of dancers—a faerie maiden slender as a birch sapling, with flowing silver-grey hair that drifted around her like cobwebs. Her dress was made of layered fabrics the colour of smoke, and she wore garlands of white flowers around her wrists and ankles.

"Daughter," Lady Vael said, her voice softening a fraction. "This does not concern you."

The princess glided forward, bare feet soundless on the thick grass. "A Ravencroft comes to renew his family's pact with our court, and you think that doesn't concern me?" She laughed. "But I find it fascinating!"

She circled Richard slowly, examining him from all angles. I felt a hot surge of jealousy as she reached out to touch his cheek with one finger.

"Of course he's trying to manipulate us," she said, withdrawing her hand. "He's a Ravencroft." She turned to her father. "They're clever, this bloodline. They know how to bend without breaking. How to navigate the currents of power. Isn't this precisely why the Ravencrofts have always intrigued us?"

Lord Vael nodded, a small smile playing at the corners of his mouth. "What are you suggesting, Maeryn?"

She moved to stand before her parents' thrones, her bearing regal despite her evident youth. "Deception can be a virtue in pursuit of lofty goals," she said. "The Ravencroft heir seeks to protect his home and legacy. There's beauty in such devotion, is there not?"

Lady Vael's expression remained frosty, but Lord Vael gave her a fond nod. "There is, daughter."

"Then allow me to propose a different price," Maeryn said, turning to face Richard. "One that honors both his heritage and his loyalty to his companion." Her gaze flicked to me, assessing and dismissive in a single glance.

The entire court leaned close, their whispers rustling like silk curtains in a breeze.

"I put forth," Maeryn continued, "that Richard Ravencroft must come to our court every year on the night of the Frost Moon to reaffirm the bargain. If he fails to appear, the contract will be considered null, and"—her gaze settled on me again—"the first bargain shall stand."

It was a better deal, certainly, but there was something in Maeryn's eyes when she looked at Richard that I didn't care for. Something possessive and spoiled, like a child who always wants the thing they can't have.

"The Frost Moon," Richard repeated. "That would be the full moon of November?"

"Indeed," Maeryn smiled, revealing sharp white teeth. "The night when the veil between our worlds grows thinnest. You will come to the barrow mound, bearing the moonstone amulet, and you will dance with me until the stars fade."

Lady Vael looked as if she might object, but Lord Vael laid a hand over hers. "If this is your desire, daughter, then we shall grant it," he said indulgently. His eyes, when they turned to Richard, held a warning. "Mark me, Ravencroft, this bargain is no less binding than any other. Should you fail to appear for any reason, your companion's fate is sealed."

Richard hesitated, and I knew he was weighing all the possible loopholes, all the ways this new bargain might be twisted against us. One dance a year seemed a small price to pay, but who knew what subtle enchantments might be woven into such a ritual? What if each dance bound him more tightly to the faerie realm? What if that was Maeryn's intent?

"Do the stars *ever* fade here?" Richard asked sensibly.

Mearyn laughed. "Yes, mortal. Just as they do in your own realm. This is not a place of eternal night." She pointed. "You see? The sky lightens."

It was true. The pale light of dawn was seeping into the glade.

"I still don't like it," I whispered to Richard. "There's something she's not saying."

"I know," he murmured back. "But it's better than losing you forever."

The fae watched us expectantly. Richard straightened. "I accept these generous terms. In exchange for the restoration of my magic, I will return on the night of the Frost Moon each year and dance with the Princess Maeryn until the stars fade."

Lord Vael nodded, satisfied. "So it shall be." He raised one hand, and a silver goblet materialised. "Drink to seal the bargain."

Richard hesitated, and I tensed. Everyone knew the dangers of consuming faerie food or drink.

"It will not bind you beyond the terms we have stated," Lord Vael assured him. "It is merely the catalyst that will reawaken your magic."

With all eyes fixed upon him, Richard took the goblet and raised it to his lips, drinking deeply. When he lowered it, a tremor ran through him, and he doubled over with a grunt of pain. I hurried to his side, but Lord Vael's raised hand stopped me.

"Do not interfere," he said, not unkindly. "The magic must find its own path back into his blood."

Richard's breathing grew ragged. He fell to his knees, fingers digging furrows in the earth. The moonstone amulet at his throat began to glow, brighter and brighter, until it seemed as if he wore a star against his skin. A wind rose, lifting his dark hair.

It howled through the clearing, whipping the branches of the trees and screaming in my ears. Then, as suddenly as it had begun, the wind stopped. Richard rose slowly to his feet. His eyes gleamed with an inner light that reflected the moonstone at his throat.

He held out a hand, palm turned upward, and whispered something. A small flame blossomed. "It worked," he said with wonder.

"Of course it worked," Maeryn snapped in an icy tone very much like her mother. "We are many things, but we are not oath-breakers." She moved closer and trailed a finger down his cheek once more. "I look forward to our next dance, Lord Ravencroft."

Maeryn threw me a sharp smile and walked away, lithe and graceful. The courtiers drifted back to their feast, their music, their eternal revels. Lady Vael swept off after her daughter without a backward glance, but Lord Vael paused to regard us both.

"You have won a reprieve," he said to Richard, his voice pitched low. "Use it wisely. And remember—my daughter waits for no mortal's convenience."

With that warning, he too withdrew, leaving us with Halfglint, who watched Richard's newborn flame with barely concealed envy. "If you are quite finished," the chamberlain said, his mismatched eyes glittering, "I shall escort you back to the mortal realm."

I let out a breath. "Yes, please," I said. *Before someone changes their mind.*

He led us away from the feast, down one of the sunken faerie roads that was not the path we'd taken to enter. When we reached the gallery of mirrors, I braced myself for more twisted phantoms designed to unsettle. But this time, the mirrors showed only our true reflections. I looked a sight, my shoulder-length brown hair rumpled, my green eyes a bit bloodshot.

Richard paused before one to study his own face. "I wonder," he said softly, "what my parents saw when they looked at themselves."

I took his hand and gave it a gentle squeeze. "You'll never know. But they would be proud of you. I am."

Halfglint cleared his throat. "The way will not remain open for long," he reminded us gruffly. "Daybreak approaches. Leave now or be trapped until the next Frost Moon."

He left us at the gallery. We hurried up the winding stair to Mordred's tomb, where the Green Knight kept his lonely vigil. Richard eyed him warily as we skirted past, but the guardian slept again. The outer door opened at a touch, and we stumbled out into the mortal world.

The sky was just beginning to lighten, streaks of pale gold breaking through the darkness in the east. The fields were swaddled in mist, the first larks singing from the hedgerows. After the unnatural starlight of the faerie realm, the plain beauty of an English morning brought tears to my eyes.

The barrow mound of King Arthur's tomb looked ordinary—just a grassy hill, one of many that dotted the landscape around Little Groating. As I watched, the sunlight struck it and the faint outline of the doorway vanished. If not for our inside-out clothes and the plaster on Richard's face, I might almost have believed the night's events were a vivid dream.

We made our way back to Ravencroft Hall in silence, too tired to crow about our victory (if that's what it truly was). As we crested the hill and the manor came into view, Richard stopped abruptly.

"Look," he said, pointing.

Lights blazed in every window of the Hall, golden and welcoming. Smoke curled from the chimneys, and a group waited on the front steps—Nettle, Gilcarren, and a dozen other brownies. Gone were the wretched rags; each wore a sturdy little coat. The instant they saw us, a rousing cheer went up.

"The master returns!" Nettle cried, capering in place. "Returned with his power, just as we knew he would!"

Delicious smells wafted from the open front door—eggs and toast, coffee and something sweet. My stomach rumbled, reminding me how long it had been since we'd eaten.

"I'm very sorry, milord," Gilcarren said in a rush, crushing his top hat in his hands. "I tried to hide, but the high fae dragged me from the Hall—"

"You are forgiven," Richard said wearily. "We shall not speak of it again."

The brownie bowed low. "Thank you, sir. Breakfast is prepared, and hot baths await you both."

Richard paused at the threshold. The entrance hall, which had been dirty and scuffed, now gleamed with fresh lemon polish. The flagstone floor shone, the suits of armor sparkled, and even the portraits along the wall looked content. He turned to me, wonder and exhaustion mingling.

"It's really happened, hasn't it? I'm a wizard." He touched the moonstone at his throat. "And all it cost was a nebulous debt to the most capricious beings in existence."

I laughed, the sound slightly hysterical. "Layla will

murder you. But we won't tell her until after breakfast. Welcome home, Lord Ravencroft."

He offered me his arm. "Shall we, Miss Boot?"

I curled my arm through his, and together we stepped through the door, the cheers of the brownies ringing in our ears like victory bells.

28

TWO LITTLE PIGS

"Here they come," I said, peering through the mullioned windows of the entrance hall.

Montfort's black Range Rover hurtled up the drive, narrowly missing a small brown hare that darted across the gravel. There wasn't even a flicker of brake lights.

"Right on time," Richard murmured, coming to stand beside me. "One must respect punctuality, even in villains."

In five minutes, at precisely noon on November the 15th, he was scheduled to surrender possession of the Hall to the Blight & Penhaligon Development Company.

We had slept most of the previous day, recovering from our journey to the Court of Silver Shadows. I'd woken in the Foxglove Suite to sunlight streaming through windows that had, overnight, been washed to a sparkling clarity by industrious brownies.

The Hall itself was transformed, no longer the neglected, musty pile that had greeted Richard upon his return, but a gleaming testament to what love and care could accomplish. The roof, which had been missing dozens of tiles and a good portion of its south-facing gutter, now sat whole and proud. The mildew stains on the upper landing were gone, the crumbling plaster on the staircase had been repaired.

Even the topiary beasts had been trimmed and shaped. Now I could make out what they were: a prancing hedgehog, two stalking lions, a water buffalo with curling horns, and one magnificent dragon.

Early that morning, Richard had driven to Southlea Cross to meet with his solicitors. He'd returned with a slim portfolio of documents and a quiet confidence that made my heart skip. Meanwhile, I'd made the trek into the village to update the Committee on our progress.

Everyone had wanted to come for the final confrontation, but I'd convinced them that Richard needed to do it on his own. (With me at his side, of course. I wouldn't miss it for the world.)

Three car doors slammed in succession outside. I studied Lord Ravencroft as he watched Montfort, Blight, and Penhaligon climb the steps to the front door. Gilcarren had returned Richard's clothes, and he cut a striking figure in one of his bespoke suits, dark hair neatly combed, jaw freshly shaven. But it was the change in his eyes that caught me most—a quiet power that hadn't been present before.

Montfort was the first through the door, all teeth and plastic charm. Penhaligon had the pinched, cadaverous face of a man who made his fortune crushing other people's dreams. Blight's watery blue eyes darted around the entrance hall, mentally calculating the cost of each stick of furniture and inch of paneling.

"Lord Ravencroft!" Montfort boomed, extending a hand that Richard took with cool courtesy. "Well, today's the day you're rid of this albatross, eh?" He chuckled at his own joke.

"And Miss Boot," Montfort added, turning his too-wide smile on me. "You look . . . er, charming as ever."

I was wearing leggings and a black hoodie, one of Layla's creations, that said *Fae Off* in purple glitter.

"Montfort," I said, not bothering to hide my scowl.

"Shall we begin the final walk-through?" Richard suggested.

"Lead the way," Penhaligon said, his gaze fixed on the grand staircase, mentally replacing it with an escalator no doubt.

Richard guided them through the main floor with the detached air of a museum docent. The transformation wrought by the brownies was remarkable—floors gleamed, wood paneling shone with the warm patina of beeswax, and not a cobweb dared show itself in any corner. If Blight and Penhaligon noticed the dramatic change from their previous visit, they gave no sign.

"The east wing would make an excellent location for the Kid Zone and ball pit," Blight mused as we passed through the portrait gallery. "Knock out these walls, install some plate glass so Mum and Dad can watch their tots at play . . ."

"The dining room could be a themed restaurant," Penhaligon added, barely glancing at the magnificent carved ceiling. "Medieval banquet style, serving those giant turkey legs the tourists love."

"And where would you put the roller-coaster?" Richard inquired dryly.

Blight gestured toward the Wild Wood. "We'll clear about forty acres out there. The EIA report suggests minimal impact on the local ecology."

"Minimal impact," I repeated. "On a thousand-year-old forest."

Penhaligon gave me a bleak smile. "Progress requires

change, Miss Boot. I'm sure the village will appreciate the economic boost from all the tourists."

"Speaking of the village," Richard said, "I understand you have plans for that as well?"

Montfort cleared his throat. "Phase Two will involve some redevelopment of the village center. Nothing drastic, just . . . enhancements. We'll clear out that dingy little bakery and bring in a Gregg's. Build a multi-level parking structure to accommodate the influx, of course."

"And you don't anticipate any resistance from Historic England?" Richard asked. "I understand they take a dim view of alterations to Grade I listed buildings."

A look passed between the three men—something smug and conspiratorial that made my skin crawl.

"We have friends in the right places," Montfort admitted. "Certain influential families who see the value in bringing the Ravencrofts down a peg or two. They've promised to smooth the way."

"Other wizard families, you mean?" I asked sharply.

Montfort's smile didn't reach his eyes. "I wouldn't know about that, Miss Boot. I merely cultivate a useful professional network. You might try it."

We reached the library—not the secret one, of course, but the regular library with its leather furniture and rows of mundane books. As Richard opened the door, I caught the faintest flutter of movement behind a lampshade. A tuft of blue hair, quickly withdrawn.

"Gentlemen," a familiar voice rasped from behind us. "Welcome to Ravencroft Hall."

We all turned to find Gilcarren standing in the doorway. He had abandoned his mismatched garments and wore proper livery, a long coat of black and silver, the Ravencroft colours. He bowed low, his pointed ears fluttering. "I am Gilcarren, head of household staff at the Hall."

The three men goggled. "You are a . . . brownie?" Montfort ventured.

"Indeed, sir." Gilcarren's face was a mask of servility, but I caught the malicious glint in his eye. "We are most eager to obey the master of Ravencroft Hall."

He used the singular, I noticed, but this went straight over the men's heads. Faeries don't lie, but what they say and what you hear are often two different things.

"Fascinating," Blight murmured, his earlier disdain replaced with keen interest. He turned to Richard. "Can they all manifest like this?"

"Most of the household brownies prefer to work at night," Richard replied. "Gilcarren is something of a special case."

"Work?" Montfort echoed. "You mean . . ."

"Yes, they clean and perform other duties—"

"Then we needn't pay for staff," Blight said in a tone that came close to pure joy. "No sick days, no time off, no safety codes or liability insurance . . ."

"And the children will love it!" Penhaligon declared, rubbing his skeletal hands together. "A real live brownie! We could have scheduled appearances, perhaps some kind of meet-and-greet . . ."

Gilcarren's smile stretched a fraction too wide. "Oh, we are all eager to meet the guests, sir."

With another fawning bow, he backed away and melted into the shadows. The three men chuckled amongst themselves, their earlier wariness replaced by greedy anticipation.

"Let's continue to the ballroom, shall we?" Richard suggested.

Blight immediately began discussing how they might

convert it into an indoor petting zoo, while Penhaligon suggested using the space for "immersive fairytale experiences." They were nearly at the library door when a faint rattling sound emanated from one of the desk drawers.

Penhaligon broke off mid-sentence. "What's that?" he asked, frowning.

"Mice, perhaps?" Montfort suggested, though he sounded uncertain.

"Or rats," Penhaligon said with distaste. "We'll need exterminators before we do any work. Best find out how bad it is now." He flicked a finger. "Ambrose, take a look."

The rattling grew louder. Montfort approached the desk cautiously and pulled open the drawer. For a heartbeat, nothing happened.

Then the air filled with whirring, iridescent wings and high-pitched battle cries. A dozen pixies erupted from the drawer, shooting straight for the three men like miniature missiles. The pixies dive-bombed their heads, yanking hair, tweaking noses, and screeching insults in their tiny voices.

"What in God's name—!" Blight yelped, swatting frantically.

Montfort snatched a newspaper from the desk and began whacking at the air, his face contorted. "Get off, you wretched creatures!"

One pixie, a bold female with dragonfly wings and a dress made of bluebell petals, hovered directly in front of his face and blew a raspberry before yanking viciously at his eyebrow.

I bit my lip to keep from laughing as the three men flailed about, all dignity forgotten. Richard caught my eye, his face a careful blank, but I could see the amusement dancing in his dark gaze.

Just as the men seemed to get the upper hand, driving the

pixies back with their frantic swatting, a new commotion began.

The leather sofa and armchairs shuddered, then rose slightly off the ground. For a moment, they teetered on invisible supports—and then, with a sound like cracking knuckles, they sprouted legs. Not human legs, but cloven hooves like those of goats or deer.

Then they began to dance.

The sofa executed a perfect gavotte across the Persian carpet. The armchairs performed a minuet around the men, who stood frozen in disbelief. The writing desk joined in, its drawers slamming open and shut like a gasping mouth.

"Run!" Blight shouted, and the three men bolted for the door.

Richard and I followed, no longer bothering to hide our laughter as the men fled down the corridor with the hoofed furniture galloping behind. They dashed into the billiards room; Richard and I slipped inside just before Montfort slammed the door and threw his weight against it, eyes wild and hairpiece askew over one eye.

"What the devil is happening?" Blight demanded.

"I fear the faeries don't like you very much," I replied sweetly.

Blight opened his mouth to retort, but a sharp click from the billiards table interrupted him. The balls, which had been neatly racked, began to vibrate. Then, with a sound like a champagne cork popping, they shot into the air.

The balls ricocheted around the room like cannon fire, smashing windows, punching holes in the plaster walls, and sending the men diving for cover. I ducked behind a sideboard with Richard, who was shaking with silent laughter.

"This is madness!" Blight shouted from where he crouched on all fours beneath the billiards table.

After a minute or two of complete chaos, the balls dropped onto the green baize with a synchronised thud. They rolled of their own accord, arranging themselves to form a single word: RUN!

The men scrambled to their feet and bolted from the room, careening into the entrance hall with Montfort close behind. He caught them by their coat tails, jerking them to a halt.

"Don't lose your nerve!" Montfort hissed. "It's just a prank, some kind of—"

His words died as Blight and Penhaligon began to change. Their expensive suits melted away. Their skin turned pink and sprouted bristly hair. Their faces elongated into snouts, their ears grew floppy, and they shrank—down, down, down until Montfort found himself clutching the collars of two plump, spotted piglets.

The pigs blinked up at him with disturbingly human eyes. Either Blight or Penhaligon—no way to tell which—gave an indignant squeal and tried to wriggle free.

"Change them back!" Montfort roared, rounding on Richard. "This instant!"

Richard shrugged. "It wasn't me. I'm afraid I have no control over the household spirits, Mr. Montfort."

Montfort's face twisted with fury. He released the pigs, which ran in panicked circles around his feet, and plunged a hand into his pocket. When he withdrew it, his palm was filled with something dark and glittery.

"I should have done this when I first arrived," he spat, and flung what looked like a handful of black sand across the floor of the entrance hall.

The effect was immediate. A wail rose as the invisible fae fled. The furniture, which had pranced merrily into the foyer, crashed to the floor. And the two piglets turned back into men.

Really, they were far better-looking as swine.

Montfort helped a bewildered Blight and Penhaligon to their feet, his face flushed with triumph. "Iron," he spat. "The faeries' weakness. We'll scatter iron filings across every floor. Install iron shutters on all the windows. These foul faeries will beg to serve. And they'll never leave!"

My heart sank. I turned to Richard, hoping our plan hadn't failed.

But his expression remained serene. He closed his eyes, and his lips began to move, forming silent words. The moonstone at his throat pulsed with bright silver light.

The air thickened. Power gathered like an electrical storm, raising the hairs on my arms. I retreated to the staircase and clung to the newel post as the three men rose into the air, feet kicking helplessly as they floated upward.

The massive crystal chandelier above the entrance hall extended its arms, reaching out with delicate chains that looped around the men's wrists and ankles, suspending them like Christmas ornaments twenty feet above the marble floor.

Richard opened his eyes. They gleamed with an inner light that wasn't entirely human. "I must have forgotten to mention the vengeful ghosts," he said. "An unfortunate oversight. Iron does nothing to dispel them, I'm afraid."

"Let us down!" Penhaligon shrieked, his face a worrisome shade of purple.

"We'll sue!" Blight brayed.

Richard sighed, the picture of regret. "I understand if you've changed your minds about purchasing Ravencroft Hall. In fact, I'm prepared to return your deposit in full—I have the papers right here." He patted the portfolio he'd been carrying under one arm. "Before you get in any deeper, as it were."

Blight and Penhaligon exchanged a furious glance. "Do it," Blight ordered Montfort. "This place is cursed. We're out."

"But what about the Merry Meadow Magickal Village?" Montfort protested. His voice climbed an octave. "The FaeRealm™ FunPark Family Lodge?"

"Is worthless if we're all dead," Penhaligon snapped. "Sign the bloody papers and get us out of here!"

Richard whispered under his breath and the three men floated down as gently as feathers in a breeze. Montfort's face was a study in barely contained rage, but without his investors' backing, he had no choice. He snatched the pen Richard offered and they signed the documents nullifying the contract of sale.

"This isn't over, Ravencroft," he hissed.

"Oh, I think it is," Richard replied, tucking the signed papers into his inside pocket. "Gilcarren will show you gentlemen out."

The brownie appeared as if conjured, grinning from ear to pointed ear. "This way, sirs," he said with mock deference.

The three men marched toward the door, Montfort's shoulders stiff with fury, Blight and Penhaligon casting anxious glances back at the chandelier. They practically ran to the Range Rover, slamming the doors and gunning the engine.

As the vehicle sped away, the topiary animals that lined the drive stirred. The lions roared, the water buffalo shook its horns, the dragon gave a mighty flap, and the hedgehog gave a sort of militant squeak. They bounded after the retreating car, chasing it all the way to the gargoyles.

I turned to Richard, laughter bubbling up. "That was magnificent! How did you master that spell so quickly?"

He grinned. "I imagine it will take years to learn all the magic contained in the secret library, but that one—" he nodded at the chandelier "—was a levitation spell from *A Child's Compendium of Curses*. I memorised it when I was seven."

Relief surged through me like champagne, fizzing in my veins. I grabbed his lapels and his arms went around my waist, pulling me close. I gazed into his warm dark eyes and everything else fell away—Montfort, the faeries, the Hall itself.

"Are they gone forever, milord?" Gilcarren rasped directly behind us, breaking the spell.

Richard sighed. His expression hardened as he gazed down the now-empty driveway. "If they return," he vowed, "I will do far worse."

Gilcarren nodded approval. "The house is yours again, my lord. Truly yours." The brownie shuffled away, humming a victory march.

"What now?" I asked, leaning against him.

He smiled, the last traces of vengeance fading from his eyes as he kissed me. "Now, Kitty, we begin to make it a home."

29

A FURY OF FAERIES

News of Richard's triumph at Ravencroft Hall spread through Little Groating like fairy mushrooms after a hard rain, and by mid-afternoon, our focus had shifted to the second villain in the drama—Silas Grimes.

"Time to pay the piper," Nan said, thumping her walking stick against the dirt lane as we hiked to Lothian Cottage with Layla and Briar. Grimes would no longer be a welcome tenant, not after what he'd done to the faeries of the Wild Wood.

"Where's Richard?" Briar asked.

"Meeting his solicitors in Southlea Cross," I replied. "He wanted to make sure the downpayment on the Hall was returned and the new papers nullifying the sale are settled."

Layla had been quiet since I broke the news that her father was not among the courtiers of Lord and Lady Vael. She'd taken it dry-eyed, with a stoic nod, but I knew how disappointed she felt.

Now I slowed to match her stride, linking our arms. "Are you alright, love?"

She cast me a side glance. "I'm fine. It's just . . . I always thought Dad must be with the high fae, and the Court of Silver Shadows claims the Wild Wood as part of its realm. If he's not with them . . ."

"Then we keep looking," I said firmly. "And now we have a wizard at the Hall again—a wizard *ally*. Richard will do everything he can to help. We'll start the search fresh. With magic this time!"

She nodded and wiped an eye. "It's just, I really miss him. Mum does, too. I want him to meet Briar. To get old sitting by the fire at the inn, where he's meant to be."

I found her hand and gave it a little squeeze. I thought of the Court of Silver Shadows, their endless revelry and the ice in the fae queen's eyes. Arush Deen was better off elsewhere —wherever that might be.

"We all miss him, Layla," I said. "But the Ravencroft name carries weight in the Otherworld. We *will* find your Dad."

She squeezed my hand back and smiled through her tears.

Lothian Cottage came into view at the northern edge of the village and we stopped short. A crowd had already gathered, some village youths and a contingent from Madame de Berry's boarding house. The latter clustered in front of the door, brandishing canes and walkers.

"Well," Briar said, "looks like the mob beat us to it."

Madame de Berry herself stood at the front, resplendent in a flowing silk caftan. A greying afro framed her light brown skin like a halo. She raised a hand in greeting.

"Kitty!" she called, her French accent thicker as it always was when she grew agitated. "Monsieur Grimes refuses to come out and face us!"

"He's in there?" I asked.

"Locked himself in about an hour ago," Miss Carlisle

reported, blinking at me through her thick spectacles. "The Davies boy spotted him slinking down the High Street. Word got around and we chased him back here."

"Now he hides," Madame de Berry added tartly, "like the *connard* he is."

Briar, who was fluent in dirty French, snorted and slapped a hand over her mouth.

"Don't worry, he's not going anywhere," I said, fishing the key from my pocket. "Not until he answers for what he's done."

"I'll go around back," Briar said, her laughter dying. "In case he tries to bolt through the garden."

The crowd murmured as she slipped around the side of the cottage, her red curls bouncing with each determined step. I approached the door. It was still warded by iron horseshoes, and an idea came into my mind.

"Mr. Grimes," I shouted. "Open up now!"

"Go away!" The voice was muffled but unmistakably him. "This is private property!"

"That's right," I replied, sliding the key into the lock, "and it belongs to my parents."

The door swung open, revealing a dimly lit interior. Grimes stood in the center of the sitting room, a suitcase at his feet. The pockets of his tweed coat bulged, and I thought of Montfort and his iron filings.

"I demand that you leave at once!" Grimes blustered. "I've paid my rent through the end of the month!"

"The lease is void when you conspire against the village," Nan said, advancing on him. "Not to mention kidnapping the Fair Folk!"

Grimes' beady eyes darted from face to face. "I don't know what you're talking about. I'm an artist. I was hired to document the local flora and fauna."

"With iron cages?" Layla stepped forward, her glasses flashing in the light from the window. "We found your records, Grimes. The letters from Montfort. The blueprints for the faerie menagerie."

His shoulders slumped. "It was a scientific endeavor! A zoological study! The faeries weren't harmed—"

"Oh, shut up," I snapped. "We saw them. They were suffering horribly."

A hollow thud, followed by splintering wood and the back door banging open, announced Briar's arrival. She was accompanied by several more villagers, including Sean Davies, who was big and strapping. Grimes spun in a circle, realizing he was surrounded. His face tightened with panic.

"I'll leave!" he cried shrilly. "You can escort me to the edge of town. You'll never see me again!"

"We *could*," I replied, "but that doesn't feel like justice." I shared a knowing look with Sean, who nodded. "Empty his pockets."

Grimes howled and wriggled, but Sean and his mates hauled him outside and made a thorough search. As I thought, his pockets were full of iron filings.

"Unhand me!" Grimes cried.

The men exchanged a look and backed away, but they'd already stripped him of his defensive charms. The air shifted, like the instant before a summer storm breaks.

"Do you feel that?" Layla whispered, rubbing her arms.

I nodded with satisfaction. "They're coming for him."

Grimes felt it too. His face, already pale, went slack. "What's happening?" he demanded, his voice rising to a squeak. "What have you done?"

"We haven't done anything," I said. "But I think the Fair Folk would like a word with you."

A high-pitched hum set my teeth on edge. Then, like a

swarm of angry wasps, they appeared—sprites and pookahs, dryads, will-o'-the-wisps and pixies. The villagers all drew back from Silas, even Layla, though her eyes shone with fascination.

"Mon dieu," Madame de Berry breathed, one hand at her throat.

The faeries descended on Grimes in a whirling tornado of wings and claws and teeth. He shrieked, throwing his arms up to protect his face, but they were relentless. They tugged his hair, clawed at his skin, bit his fingers, their tiny voices hurling a chorus of insults.

Grimes tried to run back into the cottage, but Sean and his mates blocked the doorway. With a final wail, he bolted for the Wild Wood. The faeries pursued, darting and diving around him like maddened hummingbirds, driving him onward. His screams grew fainter as he plunged deeper into the trees.

"Should we . . ." Layla began.

"No," Briar said calmly. "He had it coming."

For all her sunny nature and generous spirit, Briar Godwin was an implacable enemy if you crossed those she loved.

"Do you think they'll kill him?" I wondered, unable to look away from the spot where Grimes had vanished.

Nan slipped her arm through mine. "Probably not," she said. "The Folk have their own justice, but it's rarely fatal. Just instructive."

She chuckled. "When faeries are happy, they call it a 'frolic.' A frolic of faeries." She nodded towards the Wild Wood, where the last echoes of Grimes' shouts had faded. "But when they're angry, it's a 'fury.' Quite apt, I think."

One by one, the villagers began to drift away, their thirst for justice slaked. Madame de Berry patted my shoulder as she passed. "Come for tea tomorrow, cherie. We'll see what my cards have to say about all this."

I thought I heard one final, desperate cry from deep within the Wild Wood, but it might have been the wind. I decided I didn't really care either way.

AFTER THE VILE IRON CAGES WERE GONE—CARRIED OFF BY Sean and his mates, who vowed to melt them down in Sean's backyard forge—I found myself wandering back inside the cottage I'd grown up in.

Dust motes danced in the shafts of afternoon light. The air smelled faintly of turpentine and linseed oil—Grimes's painting supplies—but beneath that lingered the lavender sachets my mother used to make, the cold ashes in the hearth, and the indefinable something that makes any child-hood home instantly recognizable no matter how long you've been away.

Grimes's poorly executed landscapes littered the dining table, and dirty teacups formed a battalion on the windowsill. But I'd get rid of all that soon enough, and it didn't look like he'd done any real damage.

I climbed the narrow staircase, my hand trailing along the banister where I used to slide backwards downstairs. The third step still creaked, and I felt a comfort in that.

The door to my old bedroom was closed. I paused, hand on the knob, reluctant to face these particular ghosts. But it was only a room, after all. A bed and a chest and a small desk beneath the window.

Grimes had taken the master bedroom, leaving mine untouched. My bed was still covered with the patchwork quilt Nan had stitched. The curtains—faded cornflower blue —were drawn back to let in the sun. My collection of smooth river stones still lined the windowsill, and the water-colours my parents had painted hung in simple frames on the wall.

I crossed to them, wiping away dust with my fingertip. My mother had painted Nelly's Pond from a safe distance, capturing the way the light played across its dark surface at dusk. She'd always had a gift for water. My father preferred landscapes—his paintings showed the long meadow in early spring, dotted with crocuses and daffodils, and the old orchard with the ruined abbey in the background, apple trees heavy with pink blossoms.

They'd both been talented, though neither had pursued art professionally at first. It was just something they did together on Sunday afternoons, setting up their easels side by side.

A hard, sharp pang of longing hit me unexpectedly. I hadn't seen my parents in nearly three years. We exchanged letters, of course, and occasional phone calls on birthdays and Christmas. But it wasn't the same as having them here.

I wondered if they ever missed this cottage, this village, their daughter?

I trailed a hand along the worn quilt, gaze drifting to the wooden chest at the foot of the bed. On impulse, I knelt before it and lifted the heavy lid. The scent of cedar and mothballs wafted up, along with memories so vivid they nearly knocked me backward. Here were the treasures of my childhood: a collection of sea glass from a holiday in Corn-wall; a shoebox of letters with exotic postmarks from Nan before she moved back to the village; my first Polaroid camera, broken now, but once my most prized possession.

And there, beneath a pile of single mittens and old winter

scarves, was a splash of bright wool. I pulled out my red coat. The one I'd been wearing the day I met Fenwick.

I hadn't thought much of that coat in years, but holding it now, I could feel its velvet collar brushing my neck as I ventured into the Wild Wood, calling Mr. Deen's name. I'd been so foolish. If not for Fenwick . . .

I turned the coat over in my hands. One of the brass buttons was missing—torn off during my struggle in the briar patch. Fenwick had found me there, crying and trapped, my hands scratched and bleeding from the thorns.

Sometimes I wondered if I'd imagined him—a fairytale I'd told myself to make sense of a strange day. But the coat in my hands was real enough, and so was the missing button.

I smiled, bittersweet, and tucked the coat back into the chest. He'd planted a seed in my heart—an abiding love for this strange, magical corner of England. For that, I would be forever grateful.

But I knew then that I would never see Fenwick again. He was part of my childhood, and I was a grown woman now.

It was time to move on.

30

NYX

The Wild Wood always felt *awake*, but this morning it hummed with vibrant new life. I followed the path and hopped across muddy puddles, last night's rain still dripping from branches.

The air was ripe with the smell of wet earth and green things—not the damp decay of autumn but the sharp, nose-clearing scent of something coming back to itself after a long sleep. If I hadn't known better, I might have thought April had ousted November in a seasonal coup.

I heard the oak before I saw it. A symphony of joyful birdsong—wrens, starlings, robins, and a delegation of chattering blackbirds. Then I rounded the last bend and stopped, my heart beating wildly. The once-bare tree had thrown out a dense canopy of new leaves, fringed with dew and tipped with sunlight. Around the roots, bluebells and wood sorrel poked up—out of season and utterly unconcerned by it.

Halfway up the trunk, Nyx sat cross-legged on a limb, her skin dappled with shadow, her hair a wild tangle. She spotted me and grinned, teeth flashing in her bark-dark face.

"Kitty Boot," she called.

I rushed forward, my vow not to get all mushy forgotten. For a moment, my throat was too tight to speak. Nyx pretended not to notice.

"When the pact was renewed, I felt it," she said with a merry laugh. "Like rain after a drought, like sun after endless winter."

I stepped closer, laying my own hand on the bole. "I feared we might be too late."

Her eyes grew distant. "But you succeeded, didn't you? Tell me how."

I hesitated, mainly because I disliked thinking about the promise Richard had made. But Nyx deserved to know.

"We never could have done it without your help with the key," I said, "so I shall relate the full tale, if you like."

Her brown eyes gleamed. The fae loved stories.

I began with the tomb of Mordred and the challenge from the Green Knight. The way we'd scrambled to avoid being "cleaved in twain" and the eventual realization that Richard's own name was the password.

I told her about the gallery of mirrors, Halfglint and the moonlit glade, Lord and Lady Vael. Richard's bluff and the new bargain: that he would return every Frost Moon to dance with the fae princess Maeryn until the stars faded.

I only skipped the penalty if Richard failed to appear. We hadn't told anyone that part. What did it matter so long as we kept the peace between mortal and fae? But Nyx was old and sharp, and I should have known better.

She tilted her head, watching a nuthatch scamper upside-down along a branch. "You're leaving something out. That's too easy."

I made a noncommittal sound. Nyx waited.

"It's nothing," I said at last. "Just a technicality. If Richard doesn't hold up his end, the court can claim a forfeit. And the forfeit, in this case, is me. I'd have to serve as Lady Vael's handmaiden for the rest of my mortal life."

Nyx looked surprised. "That is a high price. You agreed to it?"

I nodded. "I'm willing to take the risk."

She considered this. "You're brave, Kitty. Foolish, but brave." She hopped lightly down from her perch. "Which reminds me, I have something for you."

She reached into a fold of her tunic and drew out a glossy brown acorn. "Plant this in a sunny place," she said, pressing it into my palm. "It will make a fine, strong child for my oak."

I stared at the acorn, going all mushy again. "But I didn't expect . . . I have nothing to give you in return!"

Nyx flashed her small, sharp smile. "You saved my beloved. That is the gift you gave me."

I thought of all the times I had come to this clearing seeking answers, or comfort, or just a place to sit and think. I thought of Nan, who believed that every act of kindness would someday be returned.

I closed my fingers around the acorn. "Thank you," I said thickly. "This is the finest gift I have ever received."

We sat in companionable silence for a while, watching the birds and the clouds. When it started to rain, I bid Nyx goodbye and left the clearing with the acorn snug in my pocket.

THE DANCING TOADSTOOL SMELLED OF FRESH BREAD, GARLIC, chimney smoke, and a whiff of Dr. Singer's Bay Rum Brilliantine Hair Tonic. I scraped the mud from my boots and stepped into the common room.

"You loathsome, accursed, atrocious monster," Sir Francis Drake screamed by way of greeting.

"It's nice to see you, too," I replied, stroking his head as he bobbed happily from his perch on the umbrella stand.

Richard sat in one of the window seats, feet propped on the ledge, arms folded behind his head. He wore his shirt sleeves rolled up to the elbows, a tartan scarf draped around his neck, and a smile that looked suspiciously like he was up to something.

He wasn't alone. Nan, resplendent in her velvet smoking jacket and an entire forearm's worth of silver bangles, was ensconced in her usual armchair. She'd commandeered the best spot by the hearth, where she could warm her knees and gossip at the same time. Dr. Singer was with her, propped up on cushions, his cane within easy reach.

"Kitty!" Nan barked. "You look like a drowned stoat."

It made my heart glad to see Dr. Singer sitting upright. His pneumonia had nearly gotten the better of him, but there was colour in his cheeks and a light in his eyes that I hadn't seen since summer.

"I hear you and Lord Ravencroft have been busy," he said.

"Only the usual," I said with a wink.

Nan cackled. "You two faced down a faerie court and lived to tell of it!"

Dr. Singer's laugh was dry but genuine. He reached across to pat my hand, then let his palm rest there.

"I visited Nyx," I told him. "Her oak is restored—full of leaves and life."

"Splendid news," Dr. Singer said. "I was just telling Richard he should consider writing a monograph on the medicinal properties of faerie-tended trees. Quite the gap in the literature there."

Nan snorted. "As if the Royal College of Physicians would publish such a thing."

"They might, if it came from a Ravencroft," Dr. Singer countered. "The name still carries weight in certain circles." He cleared his throat. "I have an announcement of my own," he added.

Richard removed his feet from the sill and sat up straighter.

"I am officially retiring," Dr. Singer said. "I'll stay on for the odd house call, but I plan to spend most of my time right here."

There was a pause. Then Nan said, "About bloody time. You're eighty-six. I thought you'd die with a stethoscope round your neck."

"I nearly did," Dr. Singer agreed.

Nan's smile faltered. "But who'll look after us? The next nearest GP is in Southlea Cross and she's already stretched thin."

"That's the clever bit," Dr. Singer said. "Lord Ravencroft here has agreed to act as the interim physician. His credentials are impeccable, and he's already been doing rounds in the village."

Richard looked at me, his gaze serious. "I'm not going anywhere," he said. "And it's the least I can do, after all you've put up with on my account."

Nan fixed him with a stern look. "Once you take the job, we'll never let you quit, you know."

"Then I'm delighted to serve as long as I'm needed," Richard replied, and I could tell he meant it.

There was a small, warm silence as this sunk in. Then, as if on cue, Mrs. Deen emerged from the kitchen with mugs of spiced wine. She passed them out and arranged herself on the sofa.

"A toast," she declared, raising her cup. "To new beginnings."

Nan and Dr. Singer lifted their cups. I hesitated a moment, then added, "And to old trees."

"To old trees," Nan agreed, her voice catching ever so slightly.

We clinked cups. The fire popped and spat, sending a shower of sparks up the chimney. Then Dr. Singer set down his cup and looked at Nan with an expression I'd never seen before—a mixture of hope, fear, and boyish giddiness.

"Rosemary," he said, "we've known each other for the better part of seventy years."

Nan's eyebrows shot up. "Jacob, what are you—"

"Please let me finish," he said gently. "I've loved you for at least sixty of those years, through your marriage to Harry, through my marriage to Eleanor, through all the decades when timing and circumstance kept us apart."

His voice grew steadier as he spoke. "But now, fate has given us this late chance, and I don't intend to waste another moment. Will you do me the honor of becoming my wife?"

Nan stared at him, unblinking, for a full ten seconds. Then she barked, "About time, you old goat," and reached over to squeeze his hand. "Yes. Yes, I will."

Mrs. Deen let out a whoop so loud that Barbarossa leapt from his spot before the hearth and streaked upstairs, tail bottle-brushed. Richard grinned and I felt a surge of happiness that threatened to overflow. Moments later, the commotion brought Layla and Briar charging in from next door.

"What happened?" Briar demanded, a rolling pin gripped in one floury hand. "Is Grimes back?"

Nan grinned at them. "Jacob has proposed, and I'm accepting. As long as he never makes me eat those dreadful lavender mothballs."

Briar beamed. "That's wonderful! We'll need to bake a cake."

"A huge one," Layla agreed. "With marzipan flowers. And edible glitter." She leaned in to Briar. "You owe me ten quid, darling."

Within minutes, the inn filled with neighbors drawn by the sound of celebration. Someone started to sing, and Madame de Berry poured out champagne at the bar. In the midst of the chaos, Richard took my hands in his. "Are you happy, Kitty?"

"More than I thought possible," I admitted.

"Good," he replied, and squeezed my hands tighter. "Because I plan on sticking around for quite a while, if you'll have me."

I thought of the acorn in my pocket, and the promise of new growth even in the darkest seasons. I thought of the Hall, and Nettle, and the way the Wild Wood had come alive again.

And I thought of myself, a little girl in a red coat, lost and found in the same day.

"I'll have you," I said. "But only if you promise not to wear that tartan scarf with a paisley tie ever again."

Richard laughed. I tugged him outside. The skies had cleared and we planted the acorn in a sunny meadow behind the garden, where the earth was black and rich with worms. When we returned to the inn, the fire was snapping in the grate, and the room was raucous with singing, and I settled in for another season of wild, improbable magic.

31

A CHILD'S COMPENDIUM
OF CURSES

At their ages, Nan and Jacob had no patience for a drawn-out engagement. They were married the following Saturday at the village church amid the first snowfall of the year.

Richard was pressed into service as best man, since Dr. Singer had outlasted his brothers and most of his cousins. I walked Nan down the aisle. It felt right given that she'd walked me through every catastrophe and triumph of my life.

The whole village turned out—even Mrs. Deen, who hadn't darkened the church door since the vicar's dog bit her in 2006. She arrived in a fancy hat and gorgeous mint green sari with gold embroidery. Briar, Layla, and I wore matching slinky grey sheathe dresses that Madame de Berry somehow procured from Paris at the last moment (there had always been rumours she was part fae, which she tacitly encouraged).

After a brief but touching service, the newlyweds paraded down the aisle to a standing ovation. Richard had insisted on hosting the reception afterwards at Ravencroft Hall, and no one cared to argue with the lord of the manor when he was in a generous mood. Nettle, Gilcarren, and the rest of the brownies worked round the clock to get the place in splendid shape for the party.

Guests arrived in waves, gaping at the huge Christmas wreaths, garlands of holly and mistletoe, and strings of twinkly white lights. Women wore hats and gloves, children their church suits, and slouching young men had borrowed their fathers' second-best jackets. Everyone milled about the ballroom, drinking punch. Sir Francis Drake flitted excitedly above their heads, pausing occasionally to shriek, "Bottoms up! Don't mind the bitter taste, it's only gin!"

The single absence was Silas Grimes. A few people claimed that they'd seen him lurking near the edge of the Wild Wood, stark naked, but he ran off as soon he saw them.

Richard moved through the crowd introducing himself as the village's new doctor. The elderly ladies from Madame de Berry's boarding house doted on him, and he danced with them all.

After the wedding brunch—a kingly feast followed by an enormous cake shaped like a sailing schooner that Briar had spent days constructing—I found myself watching the revels from the edge of the ballroom. Nan and Dr. Singer were making the rounds, accepting hugs and congratulations, but I could tell Nan was getting tired. She'd never admit it, but the events of the past few weeks had drained even her inexhaustible reserves.

Well, there were plenty of quiet nooks for the two of them to canoodle in once they decided to take a rest. I slipped upstairs and found Briar in the nursery reading to a group of toddlers, including Madame de Berry's twin grandsons and the vicar's hyperactive daughter.

The story was about a bear who wanted to be a bee, and Briar gave every character a distinct and silly voice. When she finished, the children clapped and promptly began to ransack the toy chest, leaving her to collapse on the rug in mock exhaustion.

"I didn't know you were good with kids," I said.

"I bribed them with chocolate." Briar stared at the ceiling, red hair fanned out around her head. "If they get any more sugar, they'll be building nests in the rafters."

I grinned and sat cross-legged on the carpet beside her. "You're a natural."

She shrugged. "I like kids. They're honest about what they want. Usually cake, and to know whether faeries like cake."

"They do," I said absently.

"Don't I know it," she replied, rolling over to reach for a stack of books she'd scavenged from the nursery shelves. She lay on her stomach and flipped through the titles. "We'd better not let them get their sticky little hands on this one," she remarked. "It's a spellbook."

"A real one?"

Briar handed me a volume with a red cover and a title in gold leaf: *A Child's Compendium of Curses*. I flipped it open to the table of contents, half expecting to find instructions for turning a sibling into a toad or making your parents forget bedtime.

I was not disappointed.

"Hexes for Beginners. Chapter One: Unpleasant Itches," I read aloud. "Chapter Two: Banishing Unwanted Fae." There was even a section called "How to Escape from Any Cellar, Cupboard, or Nanny's Lap."

Briar cackled. "We ought to hide that one before the kids learn to teleport."

I thumbed through the pages, remembering that Richard

had used a levitation spell from this very book to dangle Montfort and his cronies from the chandelier. But it wasn't the contents that troubled me when I examined the cover again. It was the author's name: Ardys Fenwick.

"*What . . .?*" I muttered.

The memory hit me with sudden force. I was seven again, stumbling through the Wild Wood, my red coat snagged on brambles and evil laughter echoing in my ears. Then he appeared—a boy not much older than me, with black hair and black eyes and a smile that was both mischievous and kind. He said his name was Fenwick.

But he had lied, hadn't he?

I stared unseeing at the book cover. It had been Richard all along. He must have known who I was, must have recognised me, and never said a word.

I closed the book and pressed it to my chest. I'd assumed that the faeries deferred to my rescuer because he was one of them. But they'd feared him because he was a Ravencroft.

Perhaps it was petty, but I felt bitterly deceived. I imagined Richard enjoying a joke at my expense. Laughing about it afterward, maybe even telling Gilcarren.

In hindsight, it seemed obvious. Ravencroft Hall bordered the Wild Wood, and Richard would have been the right age back then, ten to my seven. Yet the possibility that he was Fenwick had quite literally never crossed my mind. I'd believed so completely in my fae prince there was no room for doubt.

I set the book aside and picked up an old Beatrix Potter, but the words swam on the page. Briar eyed me with concern. "You okay, Kitty?"

"Fine," I lied.

She didn't push, which made me want to hug her and also to scream. Instead, she started organizing the children into a game. Late afternoon sun slanted through the nursery windows, illuminating the bright yellow of the rocking horse's bridle. Below us, the music from the ballroom started up again, and I heard Nan's boisterous laugh float up the staircase.

Maybe Richard hadn't meant to hurt me. Maybe it was just the ordinary trickery of children.

But I would not forgive him easily. Not this time.

I LEFT THE NURSERY WITH THE TRUTH BURNING INSIDE ME LIKE a live coal. Twenty years of cherishing a memory that never really existed. Twenty years of wandering the faerie roads, calling Fenwick's name. What a perfect fool I'd been.

With the wedding guests dancing to old swing records Layla was spinning on a gramophone, and the house brownies keeping the tables groaning with food and drink, I found my quarry near the punch bowl chatting with Mrs. Deen about where he could buy trout to stock Nelly's Pond.

"Sorry to interrupt," I said sweetly. "I thought Richard might like a sample of my walking tour before it gets dark." My smile widened as I turned to him. "Since you've never properly experienced it."

He eyed me askance as if he suspected something. A tiny furrow appeared between his dark brows. "I'm always happy to spend time with you, Kitty."

Mrs. Deen beamed at us both. "Go, enjoy your walk."

We bundled up in coats and mufflers and gloves. I led him across the snowy lawn, past the joyfully romping topiary beasts, and toward the Wild Wood. Redwing blackbirds trilled from the marsh by Nelly's Pond, a tranquil scene at odds with the storm brewing inside me.

Richard kept glancing over. "Have I done something wrong?" he finally asked.

I shot silent daggers at him and pressed on. The woods closed around us, familiar and strange at once, for as we traveled one of the sunken faerie roads, we left winter behind and entered the realm of summer again. Streams gurgled, bees hummed in the meadows, and warm sunbeams broke through the green canopy above our heads.

I watched Richard from the corner of my eye. He looked awed but not exactly surprised, and I understood why.

He knew these woods even better than I did.

When we reached the spot—a tangle of blackberry brambles beneath an ancient yew—I rounded on him, brandishing the spellbook I'd hidden under my jacket.

"So, *Fenwick*," I said, "what do you have to say for yourself?"

Richard froze. A succession of emotions crossed his face. "Wait," he said faintly. "It was *you*? All those years ago?"

"Yes," I replied, watching for signs of mockery. "The little girl in the red coat. The one who got lost in the Wild Wood looking for Mr. Deen. The one you rescued and spent the day with."

His eyes widened. "We ate watercress sandwiches. My God, *you're* Rosemary!"

"You pretended to be a fae prince!" I snapped, unwilling to cede ground.

"I never said I was," he retorted. "You assumed it."

"And you didn't correct me! Why didn't you tell me your real name?"

"The way you told me yours?" he shot back.

He did have a point there. I'd been taught never to tell a faerie my real name, so I'd borrowed Nan's for the day.

"But . . . but you spoke their language!" I cried. "When you saved me. You said something to the dark fae. A threat . . ."

"I was just starting to learn the Faerie tongue. It was part of my education." He raked a hand through his hair. "Well, there's more than one language, but Gilcarren focused on the local dialect. He was my tutor . . ." Richard trailed off. "Why exactly are you so angry, Kitty?"

I clamped my lips shut. It was too embarrassing.

"Oh, I see." Richard's eyes narrowed. "Would you prefer I was fae?" he demanded. "Is a mortal not good enough for you?"

"No," I retorted, my cheeks hot. "I obviously prefer a mortal!"

This was true. Our brush with the Court of Silver Shadows had tempered my romantic illusions about fae royalty.

Richard's gaze darkened in a way that made my pulse quicken, but when he spoke, his voice was gentle. "I never forgot you. After that day, I ordered Gilcarren to ask about a village girl named Rosemary. Of course, there was none."

I stared at him, my anger wavering. "You looked for me?"

Richard nodded. "I was alone at the Hall most days. My parents were always busy with magic, politics—I was never allowed to know. But I was desperate for a friend." He paused to unbutton his coat. "Christ, we overdressed, didn't we? Look, that day with you was . . . well, you'll think me pathetic, but it was the happiest I'd had in years."

I felt like an even bigger fool now. "Why didn't you tell me who you really were?"

"Why do you think? I feared that if you knew I was the son of the dark wizards of the Hall, you'd run away." He sighed. "So I made up a name and went along with your assumption. Just to get you to stay for a while."

"Oh," I managed. "I see."

"I had every intention of finding you again," Richard continued. "But a fortnight later, my parents were arrested and I was sent away to Scotland." He reached into his pocket and took something out. A brass button lay in his palm, tarnished with age.

"This popped off your coat," he said, "when you were struggling in the bramble. I kept it all my years at boarding school as a reminder that people could be kind. I thought I'd lost it, but I found it at the bottom of an old trunk when I was packing to come back to Ravencroft Hall."

My heart was beating so hard I thought it might burst from my chest. I stared at the button, remembering how my parents had scolded me for the escapade. When I looked up, Richard was studying me with heat in his eyes.

"Your hair was lighter then," he said. "And you were a scrawny little thing with a missing tooth and freckles all over your nose."

"And now?" I asked.

"You're certainly not scrawny," he replied, his voice going husky.

I swallowed. "So when you said there was a girl you liked very much . . ."

"That was you." Richard closed the distance between us in three steps. His hands framed my face. "I love you, Kitty Boot," he whispered. "I always have, ever since that day. I just didn't know it was you I was looking for."

My eyes grew blurry. I touched his face, tracing the rough stubble of his jaw. "I love you, too," I said. "Even when you're insufferable."

"Especially then," he murmured with a grin, and kissed me.

It wasn't like our previous kisses—tentative, questioning. His arms pulling me hard against him as if he never intended to let me go. I clung to his broad shoulders, the spellbook dropping forgotten to the pine needles. The Wild Wood sighed around us, branches bending to create a private world.

Twenty years ago, I'd fallen for a boy who showed me the secret magic of the forest. Now I'd fallen for the man he'd become, who'd taught me that the most powerful magic of all was the kind we conjured together.

Richard pulled back slightly, his forehead resting against mine. "I wish I'd never left. I wish we'd known each other growing up—"

"Hush," I said, and pulled him down for another kiss.

There would be time for that later. But in this moment, surrounded by the improbable hum of bees in December, I felt complete. Not just at finding my Fenwick at last, but in knowing that our small corner of the world was safe.

And when you save one part of Faerie, when you *believe*, you help to save it all.

So the next time you go into the woods, try to be quiet and keep your eyes open, especially when you walk among the very old trees. For you never know where the path will lead—and whom you might meet along the way.

AFTERWORD

Dear Reader,

First, thank you for your support, it means the world to me. As an independent author, I could never make a go of it without you, whether it's leaving a quick review, telling a friend about my books, or just reading and enjoying!

I hope you'll join me for the next book in the series, *A Riddle of Wizards*, which follows Kitty, Richard, and the gang in a new adventure, as the worlds of mortal and faerie continue to grow beyond the boundaries of Little Groating and Ravencroft Hall. Coming 2026!

Join my newsletter for news, sales, and adorable cat pictures.

Warmest, Kat